# FIGHTING DIRTY

ICE KINGS, #5

STACEY LYNN

**Fighting Dirty**

Ice Kings, #5

**Stacey Lynn**



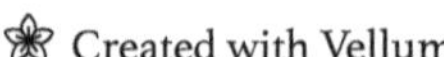 Created with Vellum

## 1

### JILLIAN

"Have I mentioned how much I hate that lying, cheating, scumbag?"

Across the table from me, my best friend Becca shoves a donut hole into her mouth. White powder puffs from her mouth as she speaks.

"Because I do."

"Once or twice." In reality, it's been closer to a thousand times in the last nine months.

Running my finger over the gold filigree of the invitation sitting on my counter, a thousand thoughts pummel me. Most of them having to do with my own humiliation.

In hindsight, I'm glad I'm not marrying Roman Holmes next week, but inviting me to his wedding? It's a slap in the face, which is why I have avoided opening the stupid envelope for so long. It's sat on the corner of my kitchen counter, mocking me for the last month, but now I've run out of time to avoid the reality barreling down on me.

The taste in my throat sours, ruining my appetite for what's left of my Saturday morning donuts and mimosa brunch, a long-standing tradition Becca and I instituted right before finals week our junior year of college.

I shove away the donuts. Damn Roman. He not only cheated on me and destroyed my trust in men, but he's also now ruining my love of donuts. I might hate him for this more.

"You're right. He's a scumbag." I grab the envelope addressed to me and written in Julianna's perfectly scripted calligraphy. I'm sure she started taking lessons as soon as he slid a three-carat diamond on her finger. It's not like she has much else to do with her time.

"This is all sorts of twisted and nasty," Becca hums around another donut.

I skewer her with a glare. "Can you not *eat* right now? What am I going to do?"

"Set Julianna's wedding dress on fire as she walks down the aisle?"

"Tempting." I'm surprised that's what she offers up. It's one of the tamer scenarios we've discussed since I heard of their engagement.

"You don't have to go. Screw them. And your parents for even thinking you'd go along with this bullshit."

I have no idea why she's surprised. Ever since I caught Julianna and Roman in the act of sucking each other's faces off when I showed up at his office unannounced, my parents have championed their wedding—my ex-fiancé to my now ex-best friend.

I'd gone to have my monthly lunch with my dad and stopped by Roman's office on the way out. He's heir to Stearns & Holmes Shipping, a corporation my grandfather and his built together. My father and Roman's are co-presidents of Stearns & Holmes Shipping, which handles ninety-five percent of container shipping from the Eastern

Seaboard. Not exactly glamorous, but the Holmes and Stearns families have been connected since before South Carolina was a state. All the oldest sons are groomed to take the helm as soon as they finish their graduate studies, and Roman is no different. I'm pretty sure my parents loved our relationship for so long. Since they weren't blessed with sons, us getting married would allow the two families to finally join together as one.

Although, no one ever asked me what I wanted.

However, up until that fateful day in his office, I'd thought Roman and I were going to forge our own path. He was going to put in his time at the family business gaining experience and then he was going to move to where I am in Charlotte, where we could live our own lives outside the purview of everyone else's expectations.

Little did I know Roman was playing me the entire time. That became incredibly clear the day I stopped by his office, only to find Julianna practically bent over his desk, their mouths fused together. They barely noticed my presence, or the *plunk* of my diamond ring smacking Roman in the back of the head.

And now they're the ones getting married.

Our families are so closely intertwined there's no way I can't show up. Everyone in the upper echelon of Charleston will be there. My absence will be noted even more than my presence.

There's also no way I can go.

Roman's betrayal was just the tip of the iceberg. It was my parents' full support of their relationship afterward. But mostly, it was Julianna, my friend I'd had since we were in the same preschool and went through everything together that hurt the worst.

I fled back to Charlotte, North Carolina, to Becca, who

let me cry in her arms for days. Then I picked myself up, threw myself into work at the marketing firm where I work, and swore off men forever.

With a heavy sigh, I reach for a donut.

Screw Roman and Julianna.

They might have taken a lot from me and kicked my pride straight to the curb of our centuries-old and generational family home in the historical district of Charleston, but like hell they're going to steal my love of donuts.

"Seriously, Becca." I look at her, blinking away the burn in my eyes. That stupid invitation has made me face everything I've spent nine months avoiding. "What do I do? I didn't even RSVP to this ridiculous farce, but my mom's email last week said she expects to see me there." With a roll of my eyes, I take on my mother's tone and squish up my face. *"Family supports family, Jillian.'* Please. Because they supported me?"

To say I've always been the black sheep of my family is a severe understatement. My father would probably have an aneurysm if he saw me sitting in my own kitchen, cut-off sweat shorts, unwashed hair flying all over the place from the knot at the top of my head, no makeup, a T-shirt that says DRINKS WELL WITH OTHERS in gold glitter. If he saw me stuffing my face with fat-inducing, cheap donuts from the corner gas station, he'd probably have a heart attack. My mother would no doubt comment on how the carbs are bad for my hips.

She takes a sip of her mimosa and arches one perfectly microbladed brunette brow. "You have three options, as far as I can see."

I take a minuscule bite of the chocolate cream-filled donut before me, savoring the sugary sweet taste before I reach the cream center. "Those are?"

"One, ignore them because screw them all. I can't believe your parents have approved of this so quickly and completely ignored you. Although that would give your parents a hernia and you'd never hear the end of it. Two, you show up, cause a scene and like the first option, you let Roman and Julianna have the satisfaction of knowing you're still pissed about this." She points her finger at me. "And you know Roman would get some sort of sick thrill over it."

My lip curls at the thought. Roman getting any kind of thrill from me makes my stomach roll.

"And my third?"

"Get yourself a hot date, show up to the wedding with your head held high, and act like you don't give a crap about any of them."

"And who should my hot date be, exactly? Just swipe right on the apps you made me download and press my luck?"

To say I've had cold feet in getting involved with anyone new is an understatement. Plus, I've been crazy busy. Also, there's the whole concept of meeting men online, getting to know each other via text and not even our voices that holds little appeal.

Besides, there's only one guy I'm interested in, in that way. Unfortunately, he's made it clear where my place is in his life.

The dreaded friend zone.

Becca finishes her mimosa and reaches for the pitcher containing more. With a wicked grin that makes me regret I asked, she replies, "Call Klaus."

Speak of the devil.

## 2

## KLAUS

The barbell I'm holding slams to the ground, shaking the bar from the hundreds of pounds of weight I've deadlifted. Sweat makes my tank cling to my chest.

Shoving my hands to my hips, breathless, I glare at my trainer across from me. "We done now?"

Crank Matthews rolls his black eyes and grins, showing off one gold tooth at the side. "You're a pussy."

"Screw you."

I know damn well that lift was my personal best. I've been working on my strength all off-season and I'm improving. Not quite the best yet, but I'll get there even if I die trying.

"Nice lift, man." Sebastian Hendrix, friend and fellow teammate for the Carolina Ice Kings hockey team, holds out his gloved fist. We don't usually workout together and he's rarely at the team's facility this early.

I bump his fist. "Thanks. Don't usually see you here."

"Gigi's having designers come today to help her redo our

living areas. Since that's her domain and she's changed her mind thirty times already I figure it's safer if I'm here."

"Giving up the ghost?"

"Yeah." He scratches the back of his neck. His hair, usually resting at his shoulders in typical hockey player waves, has been cut, and the beard he sports all season is absent. "Think it was starting to bug Gigi. She insists she doesn't want to move. Just wants to make it ours."

Sebastian's ex-wife Madison lived with him in that home and liked everything stark white and impersonal. She left him eight months ago although the bastard held on to that information for a while before letting the team know. During that time, he started having a fling with the bartender where we like to hang out. Now, Gigi is pregnant with his kid and living with him.

I was traded to the Ice Kings from St. Louis when he and Madison were already having problems so I've never seen the guy actually look happy until the last few months happened.

"Not a bad idea. How's she feeling?"

"Good. I guess the second trimester is when they get an energy burst so she's busy at the bar, planning her takeover."

I don't know anything about pregnancies or trimesters so I grab weights and slide them onto the bar at the squat rack. "So you're here avoiding your woman because you don't want to talk about what... new couch colors?"

He huffs and wipes his gloved hand over his forehead before lying down on the weight bench. "Something like that. Mostly I just want Gigi to feel like she has free control to do whatever she wants. But God, yeah... I'd really like to get rid of that white couch."

I grunt through my set, where we both barely speak until

I slam the bar back to its hooks and Sebastian and I are both headed toward the showers.

"How's Jillian? Seen her lately?"

"Not since the hospital event last week. But I will tonight."

"Nice." He drawls out the word earning an immediate punch to his solar plexus.

"We're friends. That's it," I mutter, and unfortunately at that too. If I had my shot with Jillian Stearns, I'd jump so fast at the opportunity I'd probably scare the shit out of her.

She's made it clear since we met at the first signing I did with the team where she runs marketing on all of our promo gear that she isn't interested. At first, I chalked it up to her being in love with Roman but even once their relationship blew up and ended last year, she's never looked at me differently. I've been hoping she would give me some sign there could be something more in it for us.

Outside giving me shit for my hockey skills, getting together to watch soccer—something we're both fans of—and occasional early morning runs on the Sundays when I'm in town or in the off-season when I need to get my distance conditioning in, I've never once gotten any indication from her she'd be receptive to all the moves I want to make on her.

It's hard enough not to take her and shove my tongue down her throat every time she laughs that ridiculously loud and throaty laugh of hers. She's independent, and totally unimpressed with any professional athlete since she works with us all the time. If anything, it's a checkmark in my con column, although I've never had the guts to ask.

That could screw up our friendship. I might want to know what she tastes and feels like in her most intimate places, but I'm not about to ruin what we already have if she doesn't feel the same.

I think of my grandma's Lutefisk dish, something as a Swedish immigrant I'm supposed to love but absolutely despise, to get rid of the hard-on growing in my shorts.

Jillian.

Yeah. I like her. A whole hell of a lot.

"So what are you two doing tonight then?" Sebastian asks once we're in the showers. They're separated by walls giving us privacy but at his question, my dick says hello at the reminder we get to see Jillian in a few hours.

Damn him—both my dick and Sebastian. I'd just gotten the not-so-little guy under control.

But when it comes to Jillian, my southern head has a mind of his own.

"Dinner somewhere. She said she has something to talk to me about."

"Like ending this stupid friends-only thing you two have going?"

"We *are* just friends."

"Yeah. Okay."

He's given me shit about this since well before Jillian was single and available. That happened last November, nine months ago and since then, she's shown absolutely no interest in me otherwise. Nothing has changed between us outside the one night she cried in my arms after she found Roman and Juliana together.

Jillian's friend, Becca, called me on day three of her crying jag, letting me know what happened. I went straight to her house where I held her for hours, plied her with her favorite wine, wishing I hadn't had to get on a plane for ten days immediately after. All I'd wanted to do was stay with her. Or alternatively, drive down to Charleston and beat the shit out of Roman.

But still, even as I think of all that, I remember how she'd sounded when she called me yesterday, seeing if we could hang out tonight.

Almost... nervous?

When it comes to me, what in the hell would Jillian have to be nervous about?

I'm a sure thing, no matter what she needs or wants from me.

How about *I cook dinner instead? Don't really feel like going out.*

Jillian offering to cook for me? Sign me up.

There's a space on her kitchen counter with a massive pile of cookbooks and recipes she's printed from online food bloggers due to her incessant need to try new things. Despite the fact that she's a vegetarian and I'm a heavy meat eater, I love her cooking. The woman can whip up a meal that belongs in five-star restaurants.

**I can be there in thirty. What can I bring?**

I need a quick shower and a change of clothes after another workout in my own home gym, this time a run on the treadmill and another hour on the Peloton. With pre-season coming up in only a couple of weeks, I can't miss a workout and have taken to doubling up doing most of my cardio at home.

*Do you really need to ask?*

**Red wine it is,** I text back.

When it comes to Jillian, the answer is always wine. Bad day? Here's some wine. Celebrating? Here's some wine.

Need a night to chill out and rewatch six episodes of *Vampire Diaries* or *Supernatural*? Here's some wine.

I finish with a quick, **See you soon, Jilly-Bean,** already knowing the reaction she'll have when she sees it.

Cheeks pinked. An eye roll that could reach the heavens. She claims she hates it when I call her that.

I adore seeing her blush too much to stop.

All this means is that as I strip out of my clothes, chucking my sweaty shorts and boxers toward the hamper, but not quite in, and step into the shower, turning it on full blast, I'm thinking of Jillian.

And her cheeks. Her pouty lips and full smile. I'm a pretty damn good gentleman when it comes to women, and I respect the hell out of my friendship with her. I can even temper my sexual attraction when I'm around her so I don't make an ass out of myself or make her feel uncomfortable. I should be ashamed that I jerk off in the shower to thoughts of one of my closest friends I've made since moving to Charlotte three years ago.

But I don't. I don't feel any of that.

I only feel the blinding white-hot release slam through my spine and into my fist as I groan out my climax with Jillian's name on my lips.

Like clockwork, thirty minutes later, I pull up to her quaint bungalow ten minutes from my own house. Armed with two bottles of wine after a quick stop at Total Wine & More, I don't bother knocking before entering. We always unlock our doors when we know the other one is coming over. Knowing Jillian as well as I do, though, I'm betting she only did it a minute or so ago for me. She's smart about her home security.

"Wine delivery is here!" I call out over the country music playing full blast. She's always bopping around to what she calls bro-country. It makes my ears bleed, but it also makes her shake her ass and tits while she dances to it, so I've wisely kept my mouth shut over my disdain for the country twang.

"Good! I need it!"

I slide out of my leather thong sandals, kick them to the rug next to the entry door, and drop my keys and wallet on the table right next to her couch before heading back to the kitchen.

"Montepulciano or Chianti?" It took me a few times of buying American wine before Jillian confessed she only likes old-world varieties.

The first time I brought her something she specifically said she likes, she'd looked at me with a dumbfounded expression, like she couldn't believe I remembered.

I thought I'd shown my hand then. Then I realized it's because her ex is a bigger douche than I first thought, and he'd never paid close attention to her.

Which is fucking ridiculous. Jillian's the easiest person to make happy.

Make her laugh. Keep her in Italian wine. Watch soccer with her and never... never fuck with her Saturday brunches with Becca. That's it.

"Chianti will go great with dinner."

I glance at the spread of vegetables all over her island countertop in all manner of being cleaned, sliced, chopped, and julienned.

"What are we having?"

She scoops a handful of veggies into a bowl and grabs more. "I'm trying this new Moroccan-inspired roasted vegetable and couscous. Most of it's from my garden."

"Awesome." She has twelve raised garden beds out back and spends at least an hour a day keeping everything watered and weed-free. This past March I bought her an organic weed killer as a joke. Worst gift I ever gave someone, but I can still see her blinding smile and happiness, just because I thought of her and got her something useful.

Yeah. Her ex is a complete dick, although I mostly blame her family. From everything Jillian's said, they don't pay much attention to her, which is a damn shame. I think she's incredible. What twenty-seven-year-old intelligent, beautiful woman grows up not being appreciated or having her own interests noticed?

I pull out her electric wine bottle opener and begin opening the wine. "What has you stressed?"

She does heavy chopping when she's unhappy. Says using the knife calms her. A bit freaky, but as long as it's vegetables, I'm guessing it's a healthy way to release stress. Not that I can judge, I pummel a punching bag when I'm pissed. Same thing, I suppose.

"Nothing. I'm not stressed."

My gaze narrows on her. She's not looking at me. She's *always* smiling at me.

I let her lie go. A glass or two of wine at dinner and she'll open up. After I open the bottle, I slide a glass in front of her and take a stool across from her.

There's a dance to the way Jillian cooks, and I learned long ago not to bother asking to help. She slices and dices with frenzied speeds. On the stove behind her, water boils, assumedly for the couscous.

I'm not a great cook outside being a master at the grill. Some nights, Jillian cooks at my house, a vegetarian dish for her with sides we can both eat while I grill steak or chicken outside. It's perfectly friendly... yet intimate.

I adjust myself on the stool when she's not looking.

Tonight's not the first time I sit across from her, getting

turned-on by her concentration. It is one of the rare times we don't speak while she cooks.

She takes a small sip of the wine and makes a humming sound that sounds like sex.

"Hard day?"

"Not really. We're prepping to sign a couple new football players which might have me traveling to Wisconsin this fall, but otherwise, it's all the same pre-season prep work."

"Tell me about it." With training camp and a new season barreling down on me, this month of prep before everything begins is always the most grueling.

"Hard workouts?" She glances at me with a small grin which quickly fades.

"Two-a-day. They're kicking my ass."

Something's going on. She might *sound* normal, but there's a tenseness in her shoulders and a tightness around her lips I don't like. And the way she's not acting like her happy-go-lucky self? There's no point in waiting until she has a glass or two in. "Want to stop destroying that zucchini and tell me what's really going on?"

She drops the knife and sighs. "You know me too well."

"I apologize. I'll start being a self-involved dick and treat you like crap. How does that sound?"

She curls her lip and grabs her wine. "Speaking of Roman—"

"I wasn't." I don't ever speak of him.

She shakes her head and tugs at the knotted mess of hair on top of her head. "It's their wedding on the eighteenth."

"Finally opened the invitation?"

"Becca made me on Saturday."

"And did you light it on fire and call your parents and tell them never to speak to you again like I suggested?"

"No." She sighs, chewing on her bottom lip. I have never,

not since the first three seconds we met three years ago, seen her give me any indication she has the ability to be nervous. About anything. "We came up with a plan to get them all off my back."

"Sounds good. What is it?"

"That I take a date with me. I just need to find someone."

Well, fuck.

Sign. Me. Up.

## 3

## JILLIAN

"I'll do it."

"What?" I mean, that was Becca's plan, but I still hadn't decided if I was going to ask Klaus.

He'll have to pretend to be my boyfriend. Someone who loves me enough to prove I've totally moved on from Roman and Julianna. I'm not sure my mental health can handle spending a weekend with Klaus pretending we're dating and then coming back home after and going back to being friends.

"Sure. Why wouldn't I do it?"

"Are you sure?" I take a small sip. Too much wine will go straight to my head. My appetite still hasn't returned since Saturday, mostly because I've been dreading this moment. "Because it's not just a date, I mean, it is, but we'd have to act in love and all that stuff."

Klaus laughs and pushes off his stool. "I do understand the general idea of being a boyfriend and what that entails."

A warm, calloused, and gorgeous hand covers mine, forcing both my hand and the avocado oil glass bottle to the counter.

"Look at me."

When I do, he steals my breath. I've been able to hide my reaction to him for years. First I pushed it aside because I was stupidly in love with Roman, and then we were friends.

Are friends.

Right. Friends shouldn't feel this way or have their body heat just because they're in close, touching proximity to each other.

Someone should tell that to my vagina.

"What about Bailey?" Bailey's his on-again, off-again cheerleader girlfriend with the local NBA team. She's also a pre-med student and sweet as hell. It's difficult to hate her even when I tried. And before Bailey, there was Barbie and Brianna and Bianca. Klaus has such a fascination with women whose names start with the letter B I hesitated to ever introduce him to Becca. Fortunately, Becca's immune to his charm.

"I haven't seen Bailey in months."

"What?" I ask again. "I thought..."

"We weren't serious. And she wanted something I couldn't give her."

"What's that?"

"Commitment. My heart." His steel-blue eyes are perfectly framed with long, golden-brown lashes that blink slowly. "I didn't feel that way about her, so we ended things, firmly, months ago, and I don't want to talk about her anymore. I'd love to take you to the wedding. In fact, I *want* to take you."

A tiny little bubble of hope lifts my voice. "Really? You'll pretend with me?"

His eyes bounce from mine, to my nose, to my lips before meeting my gaze. I swear that steely blue deepens into another emotion before he smiles. "Sure. I'll pretend with you."

A flutter of warmth skips across my shoulder, to my neck, down my spine.

Pretend to be in love with Klaus Newman?

I can totally pull that off.

But can I do it while hiding the fact I think I'm already halfway in love with the guy?

I guess we'll see how good of an actress I am.

"Good. Thank you."

"No thanks required." He kisses my cheek, something innocuous. We do it all the time. This time, I swear he lingers. Then he whispers, "I've been waiting for a chance to show Roman how big of a dipshit I think he is anyway."

"Right," I whisper.

The bubble of hope pops like a balloon.

He's doing this to shove it to Roman.

Of course he is. It's not only futile because Roman won't care, it's unnecessary. The only part of me still hurting over our failed relationship is my bruised ego. It's certainly not my heart. I'm pretty sure after the years I spent with Roman, I never really gave that to him.

"I need to finish dinner."

"I need a drink."

"Your favorite vodka is in the freezer."

"You're so good to me, Jilly-Bean."

I scrunch up my face, earning a deep, happy chuckle from Klaus as he pulls back and heads toward my refrigerator. I allow myself one quick moment to check out his backside as he walks away from me before refocusing on dinner.

~

"If I match your salary, will you quit your job and become my personal chef?"

"Asked and answered, Klaus."

He wipes his napkin over his mouth, his plate quickly emptied.

I'm not even sure how we started hanging out, but I know the first night it was after a signing at the mall. I'd spent hours prepping posters and hockey pucks and miniature sticks for the four guys on the Ice Kings team my company represents. He'd sat there, making me laugh, teasing me about running out of breath and somehow, through the lines of children and adults queued up through South Park Mall in order to meet their favorite players, he'd suggested we go running together sometime.

So we met up a couple weeks later to my surprise when he texted. We ran six miles before grabbing lunch. Eventually, our runs became longer, our friendship grew closer and then we were alternating after-run meals at either my house or his. Then it grew to soccer games. Dinners out. And over the last several months, when he needs a plus-one for a community fundraiser even like at the hospital last week, I'm his go-to girl.

But it doesn't mean anything more than that. Since Roman cheated on me, left me and decided to marry my best friend, nothing between Klaus and I has changed... even though in the last six months especially, it's difficult not to realize how attracted to the guy I am.

There's no way I'm screwing up our friendship and the good thing we have going because of hormones, though. After my embarrassing breakup, Klaus has been there every step of the way reminding me there are good guys in the world, but never once has he offered himself as one of them.

This meal isn't the first time, or the third or twentieth he's asked me to become his chef.

"Yeah, but this is really good." He gives me an adorable grin that makes my stomach flutter.

"I'm not going to work for you."

"What if I double your salary?"

"Oh. In that case..." Pretending to think it over, I tap my finger to my chin.

"Jilly-Bean..."

I point at him. "Only if you never call me that name again."

He gives his head one quick shake, thick sandy brown hair swishing with the movement. "No dice. Offer rescinded."

He drinks his vodka tonic while I laugh. "What? You won't promise not to call me some ridiculous nickname in exchange for never having to cook again?"

He despises cooking almost as much as he hates cleaning or folding laundry. Klaus's list of basic life skills he doesn't like doing is long and extensive. Hence why he has a weekly cleaning lady and pays for a laundering service. All he has to do is throw his dirty clothes in a bag and leave them on his front patio. Two or three days later, everything is back, folded perfectly like magic.

"No. Your deal is too heavy for me to comply."

"Why?"

He stops mid-drink and lowers his glass. With a look I can only describe as scalding, he simply says, "Because I like the way it makes you blush and smile."

I sit across from him, blinking stupidly, as he stands and takes his dishes to the counter.

With the ease of a guy who's been here many times

before, he rinses his plate and loads it in the dishwasher, one of the few menial tasks he actually does.

I stare at the place he vacated.

*What is going on with him tonight?* Because he's acting different.

So much more different.

Dare I think... flirty?

"Oh come on!" Next to me, Klaus shouts at the television where we're watching Charlotte's MLS team going head to head with Minnesota. It's Charlotte's inaugural season and as lifelong soccer lovers—we're all in cheering for the home team.

Charlotte's losing, but that isn't why I'm practically moping in the corner of my couch, sipping my third glass of wine of the evening.

After the initial *sure I'll pretend to be your fake boyfriend for a weekend to stick it to your ex* conversation, Klaus went right back to normal, complimenting my cooking and helping me clean up. We talked about where I'm traveling to for more promotional signings for players my company represents, and we tried to figure out if we can schedule any long runs together. That becomes more difficult once he starts traveling during the season.

We only have a few more chances, one being the weekend of the wedding. And I haven't yet brought up our sleeping arrangements.

This shouldn't be that hard. In the years where we became almost instant best friends, we've passed out on each other's couches—thank you wine and vodka—or guest bedrooms. Yet... this one... it's the clincher.

Possibly.

Maybe not.

And kind of... *hopefully* not?

As I'm thinking all of this, sipping my wine, Klaus spears me with a look. Does he have to look so damn good *all of the time*? It's madness!

His face should be outlawed, from the square jaw and harsh cheekbones, and sexy, curled hair that isn't too long and sheered on the sides, the man is practically edible. Like strawberries dipped in dark chocolate.

He calls his hair cut a fade cut. I call it a *let me run my fingers through your hair and shove my mouth to yours* kind of cut.

Not out loud. I'm not completely inept.

"Are you going to tell me what you're thinking and what's worrying you or are you going to sit there, curled in a ball, glaring at the game all night?"

"I'm not glaring at the game." I leave out the mention of being curled in a ball. I'm totally curled in a ball, feet to my ass on the cushion, knees up, one arm wrapped around my shins. Also, even though Charlotte is a new team, they have loads of talent which means they shouldn't be losing by two. An excellent reason to glare, thankyouverymuch.

"Uh-huh. Have I mentioned lately that I'm also the Pope?"

I snort, and the wine I just sipped burns my nose. "Damn it."

I set my glass down on the side table and pinch the bridge of my nose. Damn it. This hurts.

The humiliation of the entire night. My neediness in even needing a fake boyfriend. Let's not delve into the fact that my ex-fiancé is marrying my oldest and now most hated friend, for crying out loud.

If there was a wanted poster for most humiliated human, that spotlight would be shining right on me.

"Hey."

Two warm hands press against my knees and I drop my head. God. Seriously. I'm going to have a mental breakdown in front of Klaus. Unfortunately, it's impossible to burrow my forehead into my knee caps because Klaus's hand moves to my cheek, his thumb beneath my chin and with a warm pressure that slides down my throat straight to my nipples, he lifts my head.

Not that I fight it much. His hands are divine. Gifts from God. Both on the ice, and I imagine—oh yeah, I've *imagined* —off the ice as well.

"You are totally freaking out tonight."

"Am not," says the twenty-seven-year-old who still acts like she's four.

"Are too," says the twenty-eight-year-old who can match me in any argument.

"Klaus."

"Jilly-Bean."

It's the name that does it. The stupid, ridiculous, and immature nickname makes me crack a grin.

This will be fine.

It's a weekend, and it's Klaus. He knows me almost as well as Becca does.

What can go so horribly wrong?

"What are you freaking out about? Tell me, or I'll be forced to bring in the big guns."

To prove his threat, his hand spreads, and damn... they're big hands. Thick fingers. Long also. Can we judge a man on the size of his hands? Or is that just his shoe size? Because I'm judging... and hoping.

"Don't."

"I'll do it."

"Swear to God, you touch my knee and I'll kick you in the balls."

"Then you'll have to kiss them and make them better."

He says it with a smile, a wicked one, one I've never seen on his *let's be friends and friends only* face before.

I gasp at the heat in his cornflower blues. Stormy. They've darkened.

Mine have as well because I can practically feel his breath skate across my skin as his hand lowers to my knee.

"Don't—"

"Tell me—"

He touches my knee. Pressure begins to squeeze just above it.

It's my worst nightmare come to life. Times two.

So it's no surprise to me when I blurt out, "If you come to the wedding with me you have to stay at my parents' house, because they won't let me get a hotel room and since we're in love and dating, they won't let you have a guest room which means you'll have to sleep with me, as in, sleep in the same bed kind of sleep with me."

I inhale a deep breath and press my lips together.

And kill me.

Kill. Me. Now.

"What?" he asks, and that storm in his eyes has muted. "You might have to repeat that."

"I don't think I want to." Curling my hand around his, I try to remove it from the tender spot above my knee. My skin feels like it's burning. My thigh from Klaus's touch. My face from my humiliation. "I think you heard me just fine."

"Maybe." His hand at my knee tightens.

With a firm yank, he shifts and pulls my leg more. I

squeal, kicking my leg up at him but Klaus has leaned off the couch, out of my reach, until I'm splayed on the couch.

He falls on top of me, one knee shoved between my legs and the back of the couch and his other at my side, foot braced to the floor. He's hovering over me, and that storm brewing in his eyes?

It magnifies.

"Klaus—"

My question stalls in my throat. His hand at my knee loosens, and he brushes my knee and then the outside of my thigh as his gaze stays frozen to mine.

It's possible I've entered an alternate dimension—one where Klaus looks at me like he wants to kiss me.

"Do you snore?"

"What?"

His dark, tan lips kick up at a corner. "Do you snore?"

"No." I scoff. "Of course not."

"Talk in your sleep? Have night terrors where I'll have to worry about my balls getting kicked?"

"No!" Is he crazy? What is he even talking about?

"Then what's the problem?"

My current problem is the fact he's on top of me. Close enough where I catch the alluring scent of his woodsy cologne. It's my favorite of his and I realize I'm arching toward him, drawing in a shuddering breath.

Collapsing back to the couch, I blow out a breath. If only that breath could expel my attraction to him. He's being ridiculously silly, with all of these touches and looks and the way his rock-hard body hovers over me. One foot is firmly planted on the floor, one hand at the back of my couch. His knee pressed to my hip and his other hand on the cushion by my head.

He's amused, based on the tilt of his head and that cock-sure grin of his.

"Klaus. Sleep in the same bed."

"I heard you. We can do that."

"No. We can't."

"As long as you don't kick or snore or steal covers, we totally can. Scoot over."

I have nowhere to go. If I roll, I end up on my cream, tufted rug. Not that it's uncomfortable. But this whole conversation is.

"You're losing your mind."

His grin is infectious. My own threatens to break free.

"I'm not." He rolls me to my side. I curl a hand around the couch cushion so I don't face plant on the floor while he shoves his body behind me. His chest, so warm and exceptionally muscled, is now pressed to my back. His hand falls over my hips to my stomach.

And his cheek presses against my temple.

He feels so damn good. Or at least he would, if it was possible for me to relax into it. As it is, my knuckles ache from gripping the couch cushion and my chest has turned to a chunk of cement.

I can't breathe with him like this! All pressed up against me and legs tangled together.

This does not feel friendly.

It feels like heaven.

"Relax. See, we can sleep. We can snuggle just fine, too."

His breath skitters along my cheek to my ear. It does crazy things to the tops of my thighs where a heat is starting to throb. I'm powerless to prevent my physical reaction to him.

"We'll probably have to hold hands, I would imagine." The hand at my stomach leaves, finds mine clutching the couch. Slowly, he pries my fingers from their position and entwines mine with his.

I might pass out. What is he doing?

"You also have to breathe." He chuckles, that low, sexy rumble.

I squeeze my eyes closed. He's right. Breathing is good for me. "Maybe I didn't think this through."

"Hmm. I think we're doing okay."

He's so nonchalant about this. I want to turn to him, see his face. See if he's as unaffected by this as he sounds, but I don't. I'm a coward.

What would I do if he's actually not?

"And kiss once or twice to really sell it. What do you think?"

"Klaus—"

"What? Is it my breath?"

No. It's the racing of my heart and the pulse of heat at the crease of my thighs.

Undeterred, he continues. "We should probably practice."

Before I can protest, or throw myself at him—whichever —he's shifting his body until once again he's *over* me. Gracious. The feel of him behind me was bad enough.

This? Gaping up at him like a fish out of water, too scared to ask what he's doing...

Well—this is madness.

He's lost his mind. Maybe my Moroccan food poisoned him. Made him go insane.

"I don't think—"

"Kiss me, Jilly-Bean."

"But it's not—"

*Necessary.*

I don't get to finish.

Klaus's perfect, full and *warm* lips—*oh, they are so warm*—are pressed to mine, shutting up my protestations and igniting a fire inside me.

He doesn't stop at our lips pressed together, oh no, Klaus teases, tantalizes. He uses his tongue and as soon as I get that taste of him on my lips, my mouth opens. He doesn't hesitate to slide inside, and oh dear sweet heavens, this is the best kiss I've ever had and the dumbest thing I've ever done.

My hands, on their own volition, slide up Klaus's rock-hard, trembling body and find his hair.

Oh yes. I've wanted this for *months*.

What is happening right now?

Who cares! Klaus is kissing me and we're practically making out on my couch. I am milking this for every beautiful, fantasy-inducing moment this is going to create.

"Oh." I make a sound against his mouth, roll my hips, and just when I think things are getting even hotter, he's gone.

Vanished.

My eyes fly open and there's Klaus, still on the couch, no longer touching me. He swipes his bottom lip with his thumb and just like that, the taste of me is gone from him.

His chest heaves like he's just finished a practice involving way too many laps around the rink and his cheeks are flushed.

"Yeah. I think we can sell it," he says and shoves off the couch. Are my ears deceiving me or does he seem completely unaffected?

I still feel like the ground is shaking.

How absolutely mortifying.

"I should probably get home though. Early workouts again tomorrow. You good?"

Holding out his hand, I ignore the tremble in my palm as I slide it into his.

"Jillian."

"Yeah?"

"You okay?"

I blink. Of course I'm not okay! My throat is scratchy, my breath still ragged. My gosh, it's going to take *hours*. Days. Possibly weeks to forget this and it was a kiss. "Yeah. I'm good."

I swear I see a hint of some emotion, some indication he has some reaction to kissing me, but then he blinks and it's gone. He pulls me to my feet and drags me to the door.

There, he slides his wallet and phone into his pocket and slips into his leather sandals.

His hair hides his eyes, but I take in the deepened color on his cheekbones. The slightly swollen look of his glistening lips... from that kiss.

"Lock up behind me, right?"

"Of course. And um... thanks. I think."

"No worries." He brushes his lips at my forehead. "We've got this. Talk soon, okay?"

"'Night."

My knees stay steady until he's down the narrow walkway to the street and climbing into his truck. I close the door, wait until he pulls away, and then collapse against my front door.

What in the world happened tonight?

4

———

## KLAUS

I didn't think this plan through. Not for one single second.

Do I regret kissing Jillian?

No way in hell. That was the best damn kiss I'd ever had, and it wasn't because she knows how to kiss. It's because of the way her body felt pressed to mine, how easy it was to lose myself in it. How one small shift of my hips would have shown her how entirely into it I was.

And I almost did. Until that needy, *hungry* sound left her mouth. Her gasp was a bucket of ice water on me, immediately dumping me back into the present.

This is Jillian.

My friend.

I have no idea if she feels the same way about me, despite it being obvious how much she liked it, too. The first time I have her, I'm not going to go from a kiss to screwing her on her sofa. Days later and on my way to pick her up for the weekend, I'm getting hard all over again. The mere memory of how good she felt curled in my arms, tense as a two-by-four, is something I won't only never forget.

It's something I will fight hard to make sure happens again, as soon as possible, for much longer—and definitely without clothing on.

I'm ready for the weekend of a lifetime so I can stop hiding my feelings for Jillian from her. I'm ready to be able to touch her and kiss her as much as I want. Bonus, since I *have* to, she can't push me away.

If she only gives me the weekend to show her how much I care about her and want her, then I've got my work cut out for me. In addition, there's another urge I have to show Roman exactly what he's missing out on, exactly what he stupidly threw away. That means I'm going to need to kiss Jillian a hell of a lot more and get her to the point where she can kiss me back without tensing and freezing first.

Yeah. I've got my work cut out for me.

I pull up to her house, completely unsurprised Becca's car is parked in Jillian's driveway. Jillian probably has at least three pages of typed notes for Becca to follow to take care of her gardens while we're gone even if it's only for two-and-a-half days. Why we have to be here on Thursday, the night before the rehearsal dinner is beyond me, but as far as I'm concerned, I'm more than ready to spend a weekend with Jillian curled up in my arms in her childhood bed.

The very thought of it forces me to make a quick adjustment as I climb out of my Ferrari. It's flashy as hell, but I love the damn thing.

More, I know it'll piss Roman off. Jillian used to talk all the time about how obsessed Roman was with making money, always wanting more, always wanting to prove to his father and grandfather he was better and smarter than them.

It'll piss him the hell off to know Jillian's with someone

who makes millions more in a year than he'll see in a decade.

Sauntering up to Jillian's, I prepare myself to see her. Every time I get that first glimpse of her, it's a shock to my system. It's a wonder I'm able to hang out with her at all some days without having a constant hard-on. Being in the closed quarters in my car for so long will be pure torture.

Her door opens as I hit the front step and Becca is there, giving me a knowing grin and wink.

She's on my side and figured out a long time ago how much I like Jillian despite me insisting she didn't see a damn thing.

"Hey there, handsome. Ready to steal away our princess to the ball?"

"Not a princess!" Jillian's shout comes from her kitchen and I enter as Becca steps back, giving me space.

"Jesus. Does she think we're going on a month-long vacation?"

Not that I'd complain about that. Becca laughs. In front of me are two suitcases along with a garment bag. I have all my shit shoved in a small weekend bag.

"Sometimes I wonder how well you know our girl," Becca teases as Jillian appears in the doorway to her kitchen.

"I heard that." Her hand is propped on her hip, jutted out. Her dress is short, showing off how long and tan her legs are, toned from all her running. The heels she's wearing look like spikes they're so high and I lose all my words.

That familiar jolt of heat shoots straight to my chest, my dick, and my brain at the same time threatening to short-circuit my insides.

My hands curl into fists, resisting the urge to pull her into my arms and slam my mouth to hers.

Her dress is blue, with a tiny collar wrapped tight around her throat. Small buttons go down the length of it and her yellow belt pulls in at her waist, showing off her hips, her tits.

"You look incredible," I say without thinking, without remorse.

She's always beautiful.

I'll fantasize about her wearing nothing else but those shoes and a smile and her curled, chocolaty brown hair that falls past her shoulders. She doesn't look ready to see a family she doesn't particularly like, she looks ready to seduce the hell out of me.

And I. Am. Willing.

"Thank you." A pale hue heats her cheeks and she wobbles, giving me the only indication she's affected by me.

"You kids should get on the road," Becca says and when I glance at her, that knowing smirk of hers is lighting her face. "It's going to take you a half-hour to Tetris all of these bags into your trunk."

Right. Pack the car. Charleston. Pretend to be in love with Jillian.

Piece of fucking cake.

"On it," I say and grab the first two bags. "Shit, Jilly-Bean. Did you throw cement blocks in here?"

"Figured you could use the extra workout."

"Thanks for thinking of me."

"Always." She grins and brushes her hair off her shoulder.

"Smartass," I mumble and head out to my trunk. Once there, I realize Becca wasn't entirely wrong. My trunk space is practically non-existent, so I toss my weekend bag into the back seat of my Portofino. I'm able to get her largest bag in the back and by the time I'm done shoving it in, Becca and Jillian are both heading outside, the rest of her bags in tow.

"Those will have to go in the back seat," I say, stopping them from coming to the back of the car.

"I can repack," Jillian says. "I didn't realize…"

"That you were going to be gone for seventy-two hours and not seventy-two days?"

She sticks her tongue out at me. "Well, there's a dinner and tea and the rehearsal and the wedding and then the reception plus my running clothes and swimsuit and—"

"Say no more." Thinking of her in a swimsuit right now will throw me over the edge.

I grab the suitcases, toss them in the back, and lay her garment bag over the top of everything. "This should do it."

Grabbing my key fob from my pocket, I turn on the car and raise the convertible top. Jillian hates the top down anyway. She says the noise makes her ears hurt and the wind tangles her hair.

"I thought you'd bring your truck," she admits, and she sounds almost wounded. "I should repack."

"Hey. It's fine." I wrap my hands around her forearms to stop her from reaching for the car door, pushing through the electric jolt that sears my flesh every time I touch her. "Nothing to be worried about, and besides, the Ferrari will piss off Roman."

"Right." Her face twists into something sour and she steps back, brushing her arms where I've just touched. "Can't forget this is all about sticking it to Roman."

Before I can ask what that's all about, she turns to Becca and gives her a quick hug. "Don't kill my vegetables."

"Three days, honey. It's three days."

Jillian frowns. Her nerves are turning her into a mess

and it's so unlike her, it's just one more reason to punch Roman in the face if I have a chance.

She's still so screwed up over what he did to her, some days I wonder if she'll ever be able to leave him behind. Which is why I've played this friend game for so long. I figured at some point, she'd *see* me. See that there are men out there who won't treat her like a sidepiece when she should be treated like the queen she is.

*Three days. I have three days to show her exactly how incredible she is and how much of a loser Roman is.*

I can do it.

I didn't make it to the NHL by giving up when shit gets hard.

~

SOME GUYS HAVE ALL the luck.

That's a song, right? I'm sure it is. Or at least the lyrics to one.

It's also true in life. Some guys, and women, are lucky. Find a penny, and tails never fails for them and the rest of their day is sunshine and smiles.

And me?

I can't say that's the case. There's been a lot of sacrifice. A lot of work. Hours in the gym and more on the ice and private coaches and personal trainers. There's been missing out on all manner of experiences a typical childhood has. High school activities, summers spent working and making friends. I missed almost all of that kind of stuff due to training camps and tryouts and the like.

Not that I'm complaining. I'm grateful for every sacrifice, and hell... I chose it, hoping it'd get me to where I am now— playing second line right winger for a professional hockey team. It's everything I've wanted since I can remember. Doesn't mean I didn't miss out on some stuff though.

But today?

Oh yeah.

I'm feeling pretty damn lucky.

I have the world's most beautiful woman sitting next to me in a car that drives like it's hovering above the steaming asphalt.

And if that kiss is anything to go by that we shared a week ago, she wants me at least as much as I want her.

I won't risk ruining the weekend or our friendship by throwing all my cards down on the table too quickly. She'll learn soon enough.

I want to stick it to all of them this weekend. Roman for cheating on her. Julianna for taking her friend's guy right out from underneath her. Her parents, for going with the flow.

So this car I'm arriving in is as much to stick it to him, shove my wealth down his rich throat until he chokes on it.

Because Roman will never have what I have... which, at the very top of the list, is some freaking respect for Jillian.

No, for now, I'll continue to let Jillian believe we're still just friends, even if I want to reach my hand across the seat, slide it along her dress, lifting it until her sex is bared so I can see what kind of panties she's wearing beneath her modest, but still sexy as sin dress.

Lace. Hopefully. And please, let it be a thong I can tear with my teeth someday.

"You're quiet," she says, as we zip down the interstate. "Everything okay?"

The lingering image of a lacy thong evaporates, and I grip the wheel tighter. "I'm good. It's me who should be asking that, isn't it?"

"I'm fine." She rests her head on the headrest and turns to me, sweeping hair behind her ear. "Well no. I don't want to do this at all. I haven't even seen Roman since last Christmas and that was barely a month after we broke up."

When her parents demanded she return home so their families could celebrate together. I'd met her back in Charlotte after that fiasco with a bottle of tequila and a handful of limes. She cried for hours.

"He lost out on the best thing that could have happened to him, Jilly-Bean. It's a good thing you're over that asshole. Trust me, I'll make sure you enjoy yourself this weekend despite the madness."

She's silent for so long I peel my eyes off the road and glance at her. Her lips are parted, eyes soft, staring at nothing out the window.

"You are, right?"

"I am what?"

"Roman. You have moved on, right? You don't miss him?"

She scoffs like I'm an idiot, giving me an incredulous look. "No way. Not in the least."

"Good. Then I hope you get a picture of his expression when he sees your dad taking this thing for a test drive."

An unbidden laugh falls from her.

"Thanks Klaus. You're really good to me."

"It's not a problem. I'd do anything for a friend."

"Right."

She turns toward the window, but I swear I see something sad in her eyes before she closes them.

I'm left wishing I could somehow manage to kick my own ass while stuck in this cramped space for the next three hours.

5
___________

## JILLIAN

"*Anything for a friend.*"

Four simple, innocuous words that put together reverberate through my mind like jumping beans for hours.

I'm being absolutely ridiculous and yet after that conversation before we were outside Charlotte city limits, I closed my eyes and feigned sleep until I actually did fall asleep.

Klaus is my friend.

Reminder message: activated.

I wake as he slows through the stop and start traffic of the historic Charleston area and ache to stretch my legs. His car is incredibly smooth with buttery soft leather, but the legroom is less than desirable.

A knot curdles in my stomach as we turn down my street. Cars line the narrow streets, framed with draping willow trees and oak trees that have survived wars dating back to before the dawn of when our country was founded. Growing up in one of the oldest cities in the south has always sent a flush of pride through my veins, but today, my hands are curled into fists and my heart thrums to an unnatural beat.

We pull close to the pencil-thin narrow drive of my parents' house, and my hand slaps down on the door.

"Stop."

"What?" Klaus stomps on the brake, jolting the car. He's blocking the road, uncaring, focus solely on me. I feel his gaze burning the back of my head while I take in the sight in front of me.

Obviously I knew I'd have to see Roman. It *is* his wedding I'm attending. But to be here now? I can't even get settled and say hello to my parents before I'm forced to deal with him?

"Roman's here."

I'd recognize his silver Mercedes anywhere.

"Shit." With the precision I've learned only a vehicle like this has, Klaus does the exact opposite of what I've demanded. The car flies into the drive, narrowly missing the low-hanging branches of old willow trees covered with Spanish moss and pulls to a stop inches from Roman's Mercedes.

It stops on a dime, right as I grip a handle in fear of bumping the silver car in front of us with its blacked-out windows.

"Listen to me," he says.

I can barely hear Klaus over the roaring fury rushing through my ears, but I force myself to focus on him. Klaus has a way of helping me feel centered when everything else around me is going mad.

*Why in the hell is Roman even here?*

"What?"

He grins. Quirks a thick brow over his left eye, simultaneously lifting the corner of his lip on the right side. "All you have to do is pretend you like me and I'll do the rest."

"I do like you." Because, *duh.*

"Then you have nothing to be worried about this weekend."

"Right." The word falls from my mouth in slow motion but saying it, almost like a promise, calms me. "We've got this."

"I won't let any of them hurt you. I don't give a shit who they are."

With that, he presses the button and turns the car off. "Should we get our bags?"

"I'm sure they've hired a butler for the weekend or something else equally ridiculous. Leave them. We can take care of them later."

I pass Roman's car, *barely* resisting the urge to slam the heel of my sandal into one of his taillights and meet Klaus at the front. He takes my hand and links our fingers.

"So, who else is here?"

I scan the cars lining their private drive. Other than Roman's car there are a few I don't recognize, probably workers or last minute caterers or staff or whatever. And then I find the one at the front. It's a child's game of what doesn't belong, and my grandma's early 2000 Buick stands out like a sore thumb.

A grin bursts forth and I laugh.

The one person in my family I adore to pieces. "Nana is here."

"Nana? I get to meet her?"

Crazy and quirky, I'm pretty sure my mother despises every single thing about my grandmother and the simple way she grew up. As soon as she married my father, she renounced her poor upbringing, barely allowing visiting my grandmother's home because she didn't want to be reminded of the small house, not much larger than my own, she grew up in.

I'm pretty sure Nana *loves* the times she gets to visit my parents. She never lets my mother forget for a moment where she came from.

It makes my mother's blood boil.

It makes me howl in laughter—privately of course.

Klaus has heard all of this woman's crazy stories, but hasn't met her since she doesn't travel well.

"Come on." I grab his hand, and for the first time in weeks, I'm excited to step back into my childhood home. "You're going to love her."

I'm almost bubbly with excitement, anticipating her antics. After Roman and I broke up, she called me, asked how I was doing and when I cried, she said, "Chin up, darlin', you'll find better. That boy got a stick shoved up so far where the sun don't shine it's amazing his eyes haven't turned brown yet."

On a day when I'd felt devastated, she made me laugh.

And she's going to *adore* Klaus.

"Nana. This is the woman who puked up green beer on St. Patrick's Day in your toilet and walked topless through Mardi Gras, right?"

"Yup." I swear she tells at least one of these stories every time we see her just to make my mother's face turn a beautiful eggplant shade. Best part, she was sixty when she did the topless strut.

I'm careful of my steps over the uneven, cobblestone drive, but there's now a bounce in it.

With Klaus *and* Nana on my side this weekend, I'll be lucky to be within choking distance to Roman or Julianna. They'll provide the buffer I'll need so I don't return home on

Sunday with a mugshot and a night spent in Charleston County Jail.

We're almost to the gleaming white, and surely recently power-washed steps that lead to the pale yellow Antebellum home I used to love, when Klaus tugs on my hand. He stops abruptly, yanking me backward and somehow, pulling me to him at the same time.

"One more thing before we go in there," he mutters. He takes our interlocked hands and curls his arm around his back, pressing me close to him. My head is tilted back, and I swear... that look in his eyes.

My heart leaps. For the last few minutes I've been able to forget my intense attraction to him, but it's here now, a living, bubbling thing beneath the surface.

"What?"

"This."

He kisses me without warning. Firm, warm lips press to mine, and he does not keep this kiss in any way friendly. Oh no.

Not Klaus. He wasn't joking earlier.

If he's working hard to sell that we're in love, this kiss is a winner. Except we're alone. So what he's doing it for?

*Who freaking cares?!*

I kiss him back, curling my other hand over his shoulder and rolling to my toes so I'm closer. We're almost superglued to each other, so close I can feel the patter of his heart beneath his light gray polo shirt.

He opens his mouth, and the tip of his tongue grazes mine sending sparks straight to the rocks beneath my sandals.

Oh dear sweet heaven and Jesus.

A throat clears and I freeze.

Worse, I know who that sound belongs to.

"Jillian."

Klaus's eyes open, looking down at me. I slide my hands to his hips to push him away but he moves slower, lingering on my lips, ending the kiss as if we don't have an audience of one ex-fiancé behind me.

"You must be Roman." He lifts his head minutely, his lips at my ears as he introduces himself to Roman for the first time. In one svelte move, Klaus brings me to his side so my arms have to wrap around his body.

"I am." Roman steps toward us, holding out a hand for Klaus to shake. He does it reluctantly, and I'm pretty sure he squeezes too hard when I catch a small flinch in Roman's tight expression. "Jillian. How are you?"

"Wonderful." I squeeze Klaus harder and plaster on the fakest smile I've ever tried to wear. "And you?"

Roman, for all he's lousy and miserable, definitely got the lion's share of looks. Handsome and refined in the most richest way possible, he doesn't hold a candle to many.

Fortunately, that heat spreading through me from kissing Klaus diminishes his shine.

He slides his hands to his hips and gives a lackadaisical shrug. "Can't complain. You look well."

As he says it, his gaze scans my body, lingering on legs I wish were fully covered. Klaus lets a loose rumble flow from his chest and adjusts me so I'm standing more behind him than next to him.

I ignore his comment and oily look. "What are you doing here?"

"I live here now."

"What?"

He points his thumb toward the carriage house, a two-bedroom apartment above what used to be the guest quarter's garage. It's connected to my own home through a covered breezeway, making it easy for servants years ago to come and go while escaping the weather. At one point when I was a child, my nanny lived there. "Moved in a few weeks so Julianna can get settled in our new home. She didn't want us living together before the big day."

As he mentions Julianna, his voice flatlines.

I take a perverse thrill that there might be something wrong and quickly kick it to the curb, along with my anger.

My parents allowed him to move in?

So many questions pummel me. The first being, why didn't he move in with his own parents? Their house is plenty large enough even if they lack a guest house for him.

"Okay." I grit my teeth to keep away my arguments. Klaus's hand at my side tightens like a warning. "We should go in. Say hello to Mom and Dad."

"Careful." He smirks. "Your mom's in full party planning for the post-rehearsal dinner party. But I'm glad you came."

*What?*

Behind Klaus's back, my fingernails dig into the backs of his palm. If he feels my ire, he doesn't show it.

I slap on what I hope is my best acting voice and press closer to Klaus's body. "Why wouldn't I? It's my best friend's wedding."

At the mention of Julianna, his smile flattens and he rocks on his heels.

I step forward, forcing him to move backward or fall down the marble steps, not that that'd be the worst thing to happen.

One horrific greeting down, too many more to go.

6

___________

## KLAUS

Goddamn, this woman is *strong*. I shouldn't be surprised with how she works with her garden or chops her vegetables and I know Jillian goes to the gym, but as soon as we cross the threshold into her home—which is insanely old and beautiful and polished and glamorous—I wiggle my crushed fingers in her grip.

"If you don't want me to start the season on the IR list due to a broken hand, you're going to have to loosen up some, darling," I whisper it close to her ear, smiling, because no way am I letting anyone in this home see this might all be a ruse.

But I'm starting to think I might have the wrong idea about Jillian and our friendship-only status.

There's no fucking way she can kiss me like she just did, whimper into my mouth at the first taste of my tongue, and not have at least *some* feelings for me outside a friend.

Which means I'm already winning one battle. And Roman? The man I saw peering through the sheer curtains as she ducked her head and carefully stepped up the drive? He's nothing more than a bug I'll squash the moment I have a chance. Especially since I didn't miss the lustful way he leered at her.

Asshole.

So yeah... I kissed her to remind Roman he'll never have her again, even if he wants it, but I'm almost glad he interrupted us.

I don't want to meet Jillian's parents while I'm mauling her in the gladiola shrubs outside, and I was about five seconds away from not caring.

"Oh shit."

She instantly releases my hand and apologizes, massaging my hand while cringing at the moon-shaped divots she's created.

"It's fine. I was joking. Sort of. You're hella strong, honey."

The honey is for who might be overhearing us. I definitely prefer Jilly-Bean.

"Honey?" she mouths, blue eyes sparkling and not a hint of worry in sight.

Let's hope it's the kiss that took that away.

"I doubt your mom would approve of Jilly-Bean."

"No. Probably not. Speaking of, we should find them."

As if we've summoned them, Claire and Stetson Stearns make their appearance at the top of the curved and elaborate wood staircase, Claire's heels clicking on the wood, giving them away before they announce themselves.

And if Stetson Stearns isn't the name for a guy who should be wielding a cowboy hat and leather lasso on the Texas range, I don't know what is. Too bad the guy at the top of the stairs is dressed in a full black suit, probably not going to work, but unable to dress down in anything else, especially when there's family visiting and points of his wealth to make.

"Jillian," her mom says, face tight, smile pressed together. "How lovely for you to finally be able to make it home."

At my side, I reach for Jillian's hand. Screw the pain. If she needs to make me bleed to be able to handle this weekend, I'll get stitched up later.

"And with a visitor." The disdain in her father's voice travels from twenty-two perfectly polished stairs away. Her father despises me.

I've met him once, when they came up to Charlotte to see Jillian. I'd happened to drive her home after a promo event because her Camry's alternator took a quick trip to the alternator graveyard. I arranged the tow truck and insisted on getting her home so she didn't have to lug the unsigned gear home in an Uber.

Her parents were at her house for a weekend visit, unbeknownst to Jillian, when we pulled up.

She introduced me, her father sniffed and curled his lip, replying, "Oh yes. You're one of those athletes." It sounded like he meant *"Oh yes, you're one of those drug dealers who peddle your heroin to innocent little children at elementary school playgrounds."*

He's marginally nicer than her mother.

How Jillian even came out of this family halfway normal is a testament to the strength of her own character and morals, and possibly her nana.

"Father, you remember Klaus Newman, right? You've met him once."

"I remember."

"Mr. Stearns, nice to see you again. Your home is as lovely as Jillian described."

"Did she now?" Disdain and doubt rings loud and clear in his voice.

I try not to drink too much in pre-season while I'm working on getting in tip-top shape. This weekend and any moment spent with this man might set me back weeks of hard work.

They descend their five-foot-wide staircase as elegantly as I imagine my native homeland king and queen do. Her mother releases the banister as if she's recently had her fingernails painted and the polish is still wet.

I have to hand it to the Stearns. They are some damn good-looking people. Her mother, trim and lithe and at least five-seven, is almost my height in her four-inch heels. Her well-highlighted blonde hair doesn't show a single gray hair, and although I know she's inching close to sixty, she could easily pass for forty. Other than her eyes, the same sparkling blue of Jillian's, they have nothing in common—from looks to personality, thank goodness.

Stetson, on the other hand? From his dark coloring and sharp features, Jillian is him in feminine form with softened edges.

I'm pretty sure that's why her mother hates her. From what I've gleaned, Claire Stearns believes everyone should be exactly like her and anyone who isn't—is nothing.

Reaching us, Claire gives Jillian an appraising look, the similar blue eyes colder than Jillian's but no less intelligent. Her pink painted lips lift into a curt smile as she must find whatever Jillian is wearing acceptable.

"Did you have a safe trip?" she asks, pressing Jillian into a hug akin to something stranger-like and air-kissing her daughter's cheeks.

"Yes, Mother. It wasn't long at all. You look well."

"Of course," Claire murmurs, brushing down the wrap dress that flows at her hips.

I notice she doesn't say the same to Jillian before she

glances at me and nods. "Klaus. Welcome. I hope you enjoy your weekend. I wasn't aware Jillian was seeing anyone, or bringing a date."

"Oh?" Jillian asks. She leans into me in a show of affection. "My response must have gotten lost in the mail. I swear I mailed it in weeks ago."

"Hm. No bother. We'll simply let Melinda know and redo your bedroom appropriately."

"We don't mean to make extra work. We're happy to look into Hotel Bennett."

As I say this, Jillian grins up at me. I figured we should have a back-up plan in place so I looked into nearby hotels.

"Nonsense." Claire flips her hand in the air. "Of course you'll stay here. Everyone will expect it."

"It could be easier. They have a workout room which I need for pre-training. I'd hate to wake anyone up on such an important weekend."

Thankfully, I'm not talking out of my ass. Hotel Bennett might be old and quaint, but they're one of the closest hotels —within walking distance—and they have the best workout room of any hotel around. Plus a pool where I can swim laps if it's too hot to run.

"It's not a bother. And I insist you staying here. We should have everything you need and if we don't, Roman moved in his exercise equipment."

Jillian's spine goes ramrod straight and those nails of hers dig into my hand again.

"You're still playing the sports, then?" Stetson asks with his nose so high in the air it's a wonder he can even see us. He still hasn't even bothered to greet his daughter.

"Yes, sir." *Dick.*

Stetson huffs and then clasps his hands together in a gentle manner, eyeing me. Pretty sure he might be planning my death. "Well, we all must do what we must sometimes."

"If you two would like to get settled after your trip, I'll have someone grab your bags. Mother is in the solarium resting if you'd like to see her. Melinda and Patrice have been busy preparing afternoon tea and hors d'oeuvres if you're feeling peckish."

"Peckish. I am very peckish," Jillian responds.

"Yes, well, had I known you'd gained so much weight, I would have altered the menu. Really, Jillian, your hips cannot handle the amount of carbs you must take in."

With that, Claire leaves on a whirl, elegantly gliding out of the entry area. Stetson follows without so much as a goodbye, or hell, a hug hello for his only child. Jillian practically lunges out of my arm, so I pull her tight to my chest, lifting her off her feet.

"Calm down, honey," I mutter. Once they're gone, I set her back down. "Good God, your parents are more nightmarish than you've ever described."

"And just think," Jillian says, exhaling a shaky breath. "I only told you the nicer things."

Well, hell.

"So. Nana?"

## 7

## JILLIAN

It's sometimes unbelievable to me I could grow up in such a gorgeous spectacle of old-world Charleston. Blocks from Battery Park and the ocean, I grew up feeling the saltwater breeze licking my skin and experiencing the most gorgeous of sunrises. Our neighborhood has some of the most colorful homes filled with many of the richest histories in the southern states of my country. Yet despite the glamour and pride I love about my heritage, I feel sick to my stomach as I ascend the staircases I used to get scolded for sliding down.

There is so much ugliness within these walls.

So much pretentiousness the hallway and staircases to the third floor practically reek with it.

I'm still fuming up the staircase, almost taking them double-time due to my mother's parting remark.

"Carbs," I practically spit. "Like she knows what I freaking eat or how many carbs I take in, and weight gain. Psssh. I've been this weight since I went to college."

"I'm not quite positive, but talking to yourself might be a symptom of mental collapse."

"Shut up," I grumble. Although Klaus might be right.

Spending the weekend here might send me straight to a mental hospital for as crazy as it's sure to make me.

"You know she only says those things to get a rise out of you, right? I'm betting your mother wants you to *want* to be like her, so any helpful advice she can give, means it swings in her favor you'll ask her for help."

My steps stall halfway up the much less grand staircase to the third floor. "What?"

Klaus shrugs, and I swear he almost blushes. "That's my theory anyway, when I'm at least attempting to think the best of her, but from everything you've said about your mom, I also think I'm right."

"Of course you think that."

His confidence isn't lacking in any area. Ever.

"Do you think I'm wrong?"

I stopped trying years ago to figure out why my mother is so critical of me, but I consider what he's saying. I threw fits over food, insisted on trousers or jeans unless I was forced into a dress for special occasions. Even then I usually spent so much time climbing the willow trees, they were guaranteed to be ripped or wrinkled by the time photo opportunities came along.

I brought a garter snake to my cotillion in seventh grade so I didn't have to practice the waltz.

I've never been what my mother wanted, even before I realized who she wanted me to be. Had I been more compliant, would her criticism sting so much or would I take it as the helpful advice she might intend it to be?

He might have a point.

"Whatever," I grumble, and head down the hall toward the solarium. I don't have the mental bandwidth to spend a lifetime of frustration this weekend.

Klaus falls into step next to me, our hands brushing as our arms sway, we're so close. His cologne is mild but spicy, and I'm pretty sure the taste of him still lingers on my tongue from that kiss outside.

In front of Roman.

A smirk twists my lips and I bump into him. "Thanks for putting Roman in his place when we first got here. Forgot to thank you for that."

"You never have to thank me for kissing you. I quite enjoyed it myself."

My jaw unhinges, straight to the navy blue with white fleur-de-lis carpeted floor runner.

Klaus, like he hasn't knocked me straight to my ass for at least the third time today, twists the doorknob and opens it, walking straight into the glass-enclosed sunroom. I follow, instantly pelted with the warmth from the summer sun.

"Shh," he whispers, and I swear there's a sparkling gleam in his eyes. He *likes* making me speechless.

Hmm.

I spy Nana immediately.

She's sitting in a floral chair, wearing her standard bright-color muumuu—this one covered in what looks like hibiscus flowers—almost making her camouflaged with the chair.

Her feet are kicked up on an ottoman, toenails painted a bright, fire-engine red.

*"It's the color of victory, dear child, and all women should paint themselves victorious."*

She'd told me that once when I wore a red Christmas dress and yanked and pulled on the uncomfortable thing all day. That'd shut me up and made me straighten my shoulders.

*I could be victorious.*

Her graying hair, properly pressed and curled is as silvery as it's been since that day so many years ago. I swear she hasn't changed.

"Maybe we should let her sleep," Klaus whispers, his lips brushing against my ear.

"Don't be silly." I don't bother lowering my voice. I know Nana's games. "She's not sleeping. Are you, Nana?"

She rolls her head in our direction and cracks open one eye. "'Bout time you got here. If I had to sit in this room any longer pretending to be asleep I was worried your mama was gonna have me hauled outta here in a hearse."

Next to me, Klaus chokes on his laughter, earning her attention.

"And well, hello... who do we have here?"

More spry than any woman should be at seventy-eight, Nana hops to her feet. "Aren't you just the most handsome man I've seen all week long."

*All week.* This woman is a trip. She's sweet as peach pie with a side of sass, straight down into the marrow of her bones and pistol-whip smart. I still have the hardest time believing my own mom grew up with Nana. On the other hand, I always heard my grandpa was a bear of a man. He took off when Mama was too little to remember him, and Nana's never mentioned his name since without spitting to the ground at her feet.

Maybe my mom takes after him?

Hm. More to ponder when I have a minute. Which isn't now, because Nana has moved so quickly her wrinkled and age-spotted hands are firmly pressed to Klaus's cheeks.

"You are just the handsomest man. And you came with our beautiful Jillian?"

As she talks to him, squishing his face up, she shakes his head back and forth. Klaus's blue eyes are at risk of popping out of his head and he gives me what can only be a *HELP!* look.

I stand back, rolling my lips together.

"Thank you," he mutters, but it comes out sounding like, "Shan—uu."

I cover my mouth to hide my laughter. Klaus's eyes narrow on me and I shrug.

And here we go. Because if we can't sell this to Nana, no one will buy it.

"Nana. Can you please stop accosting my boyfriend? You'll scare him straight into the ocean."

She's barely acknowledged me, but at my words, her hands fall from Klaus's cheek and she goes straight to giving him a huge hug, almost lifting him off his feet. For a small woman, and knocking on eighty soon, she's surprisingly strong.

"Well, thank you heaven for all that's good in the world for bringing this strapping young man into my favorite granddaughter's life. Praise the Lord!"

"Nana, this is Klaus. Klaus this is my nana. Also, I'm your only granddaughter."

I humph. I still haven't gotten one of her famous hugs. Nice to know where I stand in her eyes.

Klaus hugs her back, although it looks might he's more trying to pry her off him in the nicest way possible. "It's lovely to meet you, Nana. I've heard so much about you."

She glares at me. "You didn't tell him about St. Patrick's Day, did you?"

"I'll tell him now if you don't stop grabbing his backside and give me my hug."

Her hands lift off his black dress pants although her bottom lip presses out in a pout.

I'm lying. I've already told Klaus all about the day she

drank so much green beer she ended up throwing up in my toilet. Green puke.

Nasty.

She lost her dentures that day as well. Pretty sure they fell out the third time we flushed.

"Don't worry," Klaus teases, smirking at her in that lethal way of his. "I won't tell anyone about the dentures."

She gasps, "Why you!" She swats at his chest and pauses. Pressing her palm there. "My. Well... you are just... there isn't a lick of fat on you, is there."

"No, ma'am." He covers her hand with his and pulls it off. Her frail fingers cling to the fabric of his shirt longer than necessary.

"Nana," I warn. "My hello?"

She grins up at Klaus. "Klaus, is that your name, young man?"

"Yes, ma'am."

"You're not going to put her heart through the meat grinder like that dumbass Roman did, are you?"

"Don't even own a meat grinder." He draws an X over his heart, once again bringing Nana's gaze to his pecs. "And no way. Jilly-Bean's way too special to hurt."

I swear she flushes. "Jilly-Bean," she mutters more to herself and then finally, *finally* comes to me. "He calls you Jilly-Bean," she says, and she pulls me in for one of her famous hugs.

She smells sweet, like she always does—gardenias and fruity wine. Her hug feels so darn good, moisture gathers in my eyes. "Yeah, Nana. He calls me Jilly-Bean."

"I like him."

"I like him too, but you can't fool me. You just like the way he looks."

"Well, you can't lie to me and say it's not one of his best features."

Behind her, Klaus is watching us, amusement shining all over him. He crosses his arms over his chest and flashes me a cocksure grin.

"Yes well, I definitely like him more when he's not speaking," I say, sticking my tongue out at him.

He wiggles his brows, gaze dropping to my tongue, my mouth. I suck it back in and clamp my lips together. "Seriously, Nana. I'm so glad you're here."

"Wouldn't miss the chance to see you for anything in the world, and besides, we might not always like our family, but they're the only ones we got so we gotta take care of 'em as best we can. Ain't that right?"

She pulls back and presses her warm palm to my cheek.

"I suppose." I don't really mean it. Far as I'm concerned, my family can take a long walk right off Battery Park. The waves shouldn't pound them *that hard* back into the rocky wall that keeps Charleston from falling into the ocean.

"Now, now. Looks to me like you're not hurting all that much anymore, are you?"

"Not hurting. Still embarrassing, though."

"I think the only one who will be embarrassed this weekend is Julianna. Mark my words. That girl doesn't know what's coming."

"What do you mean?"

"Time will tell." She pats my hand and then loops her arm through mine. Nana's always been vibrant. She's full of personality and sass and has an attitude much larger than her petite frame. Next to me and Klaus, she looks dwarfed, but that doesn't stop her from commanding the room. "So, let's go for a walk. You can help get me to my room so I can prepare for your mother's *tea time*."

She snorts. She actually snorts, earning a massive smile from Klaus and an eye roll to the glass ceiling from me.

"And on the way, Klaus, you can tell me all about yourself. Imagine my surprise, Jillian showing up with someone like you. Funny how she never mentioned she was dating anyone, but I sure have heard a lot about you."

"Is that right?" He swoops to her other side, taking her other arm and effectively kicking me to the rear so we can walk through the door.

With a glimmer in his eyes, he continues. "Perhaps you and I have much to discuss then..." He trails off, and I flinch. I've never called her anything but Nana. And no one calls her Iris.

"Nana," she supplies. "Everyone calls me, Nana."

"All right, then, Nana. You tell me everything Jillian's said about me, and I'll tell you everything about me and why I like your granddaughter so much. Deal?"

"Oh yes. That's the best deal I've heard all week."

8

## JILLIAN

We escort Nana to her room where I sit like a bystander as Nana and Klaus talk about everything from hockey to the first time we met to how we became friends and then turned it into more. Strangely enough, I become the third-wheel, barely given a moment to speak, but a frequent focus of their smiles and winks—from Klaus, anyway.

Klaus sells our lovely relationship so well—speaking of how it was only a few weeks ago when we realized that the friendship we've clung to was so much more and now we're madly in love—I almost believe him myself.

Probably because I want to believe him.

When Nana can no longer hide her yawns, she kicks us out so she can rest before our tea time. All of her vibrant conversation with Klaus must have worn her out. Or maybe it was the fake napping she did earlier.

"Come on. I'll show you where my room is."

I take Klaus down the hallway, past the solarium we originally came from.

"Your nana is a trip and a half," he says, bumping into my shoulder. "I like her."

"She's hilarious. Just wait until she gets a drink or two in her. That's when Mom usually gets mad at her."

We reach my bedroom door and zings of nerves trickle from my fingertips to my arm. Klaus and I have crashed at each other's places plenty over the years, but this is my childhood home. Where I grew up. Where I thought at one point, I'd be the one marrying Roman. Pretty sure behind photos of me on my corkboard above my desk are paper hearts with our initials scribbled inside of them.

I've never had an issue with Klaus in my house or my space. I love him there.

But this feels so much more intimate that it takes his hand squeezing mine to grab my attention. "Are we going to go in or just stare at the door? Not that I don't like the wood-work, but..."

He lingers on that, brows arching in question.

"It is a nice door, isn't it?" I lean back and cross my arms, bringing my fingertip to my chin and tapping it. I stare at the door like it's the world's most magnificent art painting and hum.

"Smartass."

He goes first, opening the door and I close my eyes, picturing the cream duvet with the black iron bed. The old-world style dresser and desk that was passed down through generations.

"This is... not at all what I imagined."

Inside, I cringe. It can't be that bad to him. I remember the room being done modernly but calmly as well. Opening my eyes, I follow him into my room and my jaw almost hits the new, dark wood floor. Where did my peach rug go?

"What the hell?"

I lean back out down the hall and check I'm in the right room. Nothing, absolutely nothing inside my old room is what it used to be. It's only been a year since I've been back to visit but everything has changed.

In the place of my old queen bed is a new king-size mattress framed with a massive, dark wood four-poster bed. The walls are a light, gray-blue, reminding me of a beach-themed condo I stayed at once, and the linens on the bed are so stark white they almost blind me. Above the bed is a painting that looks like it could have come from the shores of Hilton Head Island. Other than the artwork, the room is a clean slate.

Klaus turns me, face twisted with an adorably confused look. He's the only thing I recognize in my bedroom. "You grew up in a hotel room?"

That's exactly what this room looks like.

"No," I huff, but it's exactly what it looks like. I spin in a slow circle, taking in our luggage that's been placed to the side of the closet door. I assume my garment bag is already hanging because it's nowhere to be seen. "I suppose it makes sense for them to redo it at some point, but this is…"

"Cold."

"Impersonal."

"Barren and void of any personality. Like your mom."

I snicker. He has her pegged perfectly. "At least this way you don't have to see my embarrassing artwork or pictures of me at high school dances. I should thank my parents for sparing me that humiliation."

"I bet you were adorable."

Puppies and kittens are adorable. *Awesome.* I head toward one of my suitcases. The two large ones stacked next to Klaus's small bag makes me shake my head. It's *possible* nerves got the best of me while I was packing earlier.

"I'm going to use the restroom." While I dig through the bag to find my makeup kit, Klaus plops down on the bed.

He's so tall, with his body splayed out, he takes up all the room. Visions of me trying to find room on the bed with him pop into my head like popcorn kernels, short-circuiting everything I've been trying to forget since last week.

Like the way he felt so damn good on top of me. The way I'd been two seconds from gripping his shirt and tearing it over his head. Now, on my bed in my room that feels nothing like *mine*, his shirt has ridden up above his waistband, leaving a hint of tanned skin.

I've seen him half-naked lots of times. On our long runs together, he frequently removes his shirt and tucks it into the waistband of his shorts. Sure, the first time he did it, I tripped over a perfectly flat road, scratching my palms and digging myself into an embarrassed hole. But like always when I act ridiculous around Klaus, he took it in his easygoing stride.

He moves on the bed, and his arms that were flung out to his sides slide behind his head, so he's propping up his head, hands linked beneath the back of his head, elbows out.

That grin on his face tells me he saw me salivate over that stretch of exposed skin. The move he's done now only makes it worse.

"I thought you were going to use the restroom."

"Right."

I duck into the bathroom and shut the door behind me. I'm already breathless, and when I glance at my reflection, I look a complete, turned-on and lustful mess. My eyes are glazed and my pupils almost takeover the blue of my irises. And my chest? My heart is beating so fast I'm afraid it might leap from my rib cage and land on the floor.

I settle my hand there, trying to calm my breathing, but it's no use.

How *in* the hell am I going to return home after this week and have things between Klaus and I go back to *normal*?

His stealth kisses that come from nowhere and take over all manner of rational thought might ruin me forever.

And yet, isn't that what I've always wanted? To be ruined by Klaus? To have him see me?

How many times have I wanted him to wake up one day, look at me, and see with sudden clarity everything we've been missing out on?

If only the fairy tale Klaus wove for Nana's benefit and for anyone else who asks isn't something I truly dream of happening.

Is it actually possible I can turn this weekend of feigning love into a reality?

Am I willing to risk everything we already have to end up realizing he's only acting for my sake?

I retie the thin belt at my waist. I should change for this ridiculous farce of tea time, like we're from the British royalty instead of ancestors of soldiers who fought for America's freedom from tyranny. I've tried explaining the hypocrisy of this to my mom many times since learning of our ancestor's part in not only the American Revolution, but the Civil War, to no avail.

She wants to pretend she grew up wealthy? There's really no harm in letting her. It all just seems more pomp than circumstance to me and something I've always despised.

Possibly another reason why Roman prefers Julianna.

She *lives* for pomp and flash and pageants and waving her dainty hand on a floral float or from a yacht. Whichever.

As long as she gets the precious attention she desires, she's happy as a clam.

There's a quiet knock on the door, and I hesitate until Klaus calls my name.

"What is it?" I open the door and once again find myself gaping at him. He's already changed into a pair of slick gray slacks and a white shirt. He has a thin, gold chain at his throat with Sweden's flag that nestles right at the divot at the base of his throat. It's a homing beacon for the softest part of his skin.

"Do you need to use the restroom?"

"What's wrong?"

"Nothing." I'm lying. He sees it.

"Liar, you've been in here not making a single sound and you always bang around in the bathroom. Besides the fact you fled in here so fast you almost smacked your head against the doorway."

"Nothing's wrong, Klaus. This is all just... overwhelming." I flip my hand in the air and let it fall to the side.

"Something got you wrapped up tighter than my hockey sticks before a game in the five minutes you've been in here and that's fucking ridiculous."

"Wow. Thanks."

He rolls his eyes. "It's ridiculous because you have nothing to get riled up about. Julianna is a cardboard cutout imitation of every socialite you've said you don't want anything to do with, and Roman is the slimeball who threw away a good thing. He tossed aside a beautiful woman with a heart of gold for someone who will say *yes sir,* for the rest of his life. You're better than them, and you're *more* than either of them could ever imagine to become."

Ohh. Well then...

"Thank you," I murmur. "That's nice of you."

His hand presses to my neck, tilting my face up to meet his gaze. His hand is warm and my pulse does a heated hop, skip, and a jump when he brushes his thumb at my tender flesh. "It's absolutely the truth. Even if I wasn't here, you'd have *nothing* to be embarrassed about. They do. Anyone who supports them does, but even then... who cares? Roman would have made you miserable and you should have seen it years ago. Isn't that what you told me once?"

I hate it when he's right.

I also hate he smells so good and that he's so tall and muscular and so damn *wise*. "Yeah. I did. And I know that, but now that I'm here..."

"Now that you're here, you get to show them all you're *over* it. That their betrayal meant nothing to you because *they* mean nothing to you."

"You make it sound so simple."

"It will be. All you have to do is follow my lead."

"And what lead is—"

*that.*

I'm unable to finish my thought because Klaus's lips press to mine. He slides his mouth over mine, tongue along my bottom lip, and I open for his unspoken request.

He kisses away my words, my thoughts, and all my common sense until my heart is racing.

And yes. It's unfair he's so *perfect* at everything, including kissing.

Can't the man have a flaw? At least one?

"Take your time getting put back together, but don't do it for them. Do it for you, and only if you want to. For me, I don't think you've ever looked better, even with your flushed cheeks and your slightly smudged lipstick and swollen lips. Let them see how little they bother you, how easily you've replaced him with someone better."

"And cockier."

"And richer."

Oh yes. Roman will *hate* knowing that.

Laughing, I say, "That'll really feel like a punch in the balls to Roman."

"Then let's go get our fists ready." He holds out his hand. "Ready?"

On second thought... who cares about looking nicely pressed for my mother and family?

I, too, prefer myself a little mussed and wrinkled. Let them see me imperfect, Klaus on my arm, and imagine how I got that way.

"Ready."

9

___________

## KLAUS

I'd spend all afternoon talking Jillian down from leaping over the proverbial ledge, but fortunately for me, kissing her seems to work better than words. She's pliant and relaxed as we head down the stairs toward her family's formal dining room, even though her palm is clammy against mine.

So far, the only person I've met and can stand is Nana, but she's not here yet. I'm not the least bit surprised to see women dressed in formal servant wear, finishing setting the table while Claire and Stetson speak quietly across the table, ignoring their help.

"Where's Nana?"

"She'll be here," Jillian says. "She likes to arrive one minute late because it irritates my mom."

"Of course she would." Seems to me, Nana does a lot for the sole purpose of getting under her daughter's skin. If she wasn't so amusing, I'd say she's in the wrong. Hell if I can't wait to see them in the same room together.

"Jillian." Her mother calls her name, sitting back in her chair at the end of the table. Other than beckoning her daughter like she's a puppy, she makes no move to welcome either of us. "Please. Come sit. Melinda and Patrice are running behind, but everything should be ready soon."

I scan the table and smirk when I see name cards set elegantly on top of white china and most likely, genuine silver plates beneath.

"Are you kidding me?" Jillian says, yanking on my hand. Fingernails dig into the back of mine, but I don't flinch this time. I'm getting used to Jillian's physical abuse.

"What?"

She points to one of the cards, but her ire is firmly set on her mother. "You've invited Roman and Julianna?"

"Of course, dear. They're our guests. It'd be rude not to." She pats the corners of her mouth with a napkin and resettles it in her lap. "Besides, she's your best friend, and Roman is practically family."

"Yeah, she was my best friend until she started sucking face with my fiancé."

My hand tightens around hers. It's a warning, but I'm too late. I've seen this look on Jillian's face before. Usually during a soccer match that's tied with minutes left in the game and the team she wants to lose gets the ball.

But there's also pain in her voice as she speaks and when I pull her more firmly to my side, her arm is starting to tremble.

"Really, Jillian. I believe it's time to put the past in the past, isn't it?"

Pain slices into the back of my hand and I glare at her mom. Is she truly that oblivious to the pain she causes her daughter, or does she enjoy it?

"Jillian, please. Sit. Enjoy your tea. You too, Klaus."

I slide my gaze toward her father and see his jaw firmly set even while he's focused on his wife.

Hm. Perhaps he has a heart behind the stone exterior he prefers to show to the world.

"Come on." I lean down and kiss the top of Jillian's head. "It'll be okay. Just a tea and dinner."

She shakes her head and says nothing, so I bend my head more until my lips brush over her ear. "We were going to kick him in the balls with how much richer I am, right? Can't do that if we can't show it off a little bit."

She shivers as I speak and sighs. "Fine. But this is bullshit."

"I agree. The whole weekend is, though, right?"

"Yeah," she mumbles and glances at me. "Everything is one big lie this weekend, isn't it?"

She pulls her hand out of mine and heads toward the other side of the table where our names are written in calligraphy. Tossing her name card to the side, she moves down one chair closer to her father, which means I'll be sitting directly across from Roman instead of her.

At the small rebellion, her mother sighs.

Once we take our seats, I kiss her cheek. "Proud of you."

She's stiff as a board. For the first time since I've started kissing her, it's like kissing an ice block instead of Jillian and I pull away, frowning.

Her words before she sat down reverberate in my head. *"The whole weekend is one big lie, isn't it."*

The hell it is.

WHEN MOVEMENT from the doorway grabs my attention, I lazily drape my arm over the back of Jillian's chair.

Roman and Julianna enter and the first thing that strikes me is how similar she is in looks to Jillian. While Claire might have been talking business-wise with how Roman is practically family, Julianna and Jillian could be sisters with their similarities in looks, long dark hair, and height. But that's where their similarities end. Where Jillian's eyes shine brightly, ready for the next adventure, Julianna's light brown eyes appear dull, almost lifeless.

Her hand is draped over Roman's forearm as he guides her into the room, dressed like a man who needs to shove his money down other people's throats. He changed into a suit for shit's sake to have tea and later, a dinner, with people he's known his entire life. Even Jillian's father is dressed like he's ready for a golf game.

"Sorry we're late," Roman says, even though he's still five minutes early.

"No worries, dear," Claire says. She stands as they make their way toward us which is followed slowly by Stetson.

I glance at Jillian, waiting for our cue to stand and greet them, but she's turned into a statue, one on the cusp of turning green at that.

"Hey." I poke her thigh to grab her attention. "We can still leave and say fuck it if you need to."

"Don't be ridiculous," she grits out. Tossing her napkin onto her plate, she shoves back her chair and stands. I follow her movements, staying close to her while she doesn't make the effort to move around the table to say hello, she does extend her hand toward both Julianna and Roman.

"Jillian. You're looking lovely. It's been a while."

"Yes. I vaguely remember." She nods toward her ex-best friend and glances at Roman. "Nice to see you. Again."

"Always a pleasure, Jillian."

His eyes do that softening thing again, like earlier, where he's practically undressing her with his eyes. While still holding onto Julianna's arm.

It's disgraceful. I pay more attention to the fiancée than him, watching her expression, but if she notices, she doesn't act like it.

"Klaus Newman." I hold out my hand to Julianna. Before taking my hand, she glances at Roman. At his nod, she holds out her hand daintily. If she expects me to kiss her knuckles like a gentleman, she's far from thinking clearly, but her smile seems genuine.

"Lovely to meet you, Klaus. We're so happy you both could be here this weekend to celebrate us."

Probably so she can rub her good fortune in Jillian's face.

"Thanks for having us." I shake her limp fingers before letting go and settle my hand at Jillian's back. She's vibrating with emotion and if we weren't surrounded by her family, I'd kiss her until she relaxed. Probably not allowed, given the proper manners of the situation. Fortunately, I'm saved from having to do anything when, as soon as Roman and Julianna take their seats, Nana arrives.

"Let's get this dumb tea outta the way! I got soap operas to get caught up on. And whoo-eee, that Netflix in my room is something else." She scans the room with the flare of a woman who doesn't give a damn. "Y'all can watch every episode of almost every show ever without commercials. I might not ever leave!"

Claire's face pales.

Jillian snorts.

And I fall in love with Nana.

AFTERNOON TEA with the Stearns is filled with long, awkward pauses, gentle clinks of teacups on saucers, and munching on cucumber sandwiches. I could eat the entire platter and still not be filled. The men speak of their business and deals they have in the works, effectively ignoring me, which doesn't bother me one damn bit. Claire peppers Julianna with questions about her wedding. The more Julianna speaks, the more exhausted she seems. She's probably the first soon-to-be-married woman I've ever met who doesn't gush about details.

Jillian watches all of it with the same tight jaw. A similar eagle-eye precision look is on Nana's face. She hasn't said anything except what's necessary in order to thank the help and to ask for the cream to be passed. Once the tea is done and our ridiculously small plates are whisked away, drinks are poured, champagne and wine for the women. I say my first words of the afternoon to request a bourbon from Melinda.

Other than that, I've zoned out until out of the blue, Jillian says, "Oh, I've met Klaus's parents."

What in the hell have I missed? As I sip my whiskey trying to figure that out, a chilling pulse shoots straight to me from the glare in Roman's beady eyes.

"You have?" Her mother sips from a glass of champagne, perfectly done brow slowly rising up her forehead that has not a hint of a wrinkle.

Botox. My guess. No wonder how she doesn't look a day over forty.

"I wasn't aware you two were that close. They're not from here, correct?"

I'm not entirely sure if it's a knock at me not being from the south or that I'm Swedish, but I'll play this game. This is the most I've been invested all afternoon.

I take Jillian's hand in mine, a move that irks Roman based on the twitch in his cheek. I've noticed him pay attention to Jillian every time I've touched her, which basically means I haven't let her go yet. If it pisses him off, even better.

"Yes ma'am. My parents have loved Jillian ever since they met her in Buffalo years ago."

"You were in Buffalo?" Roman barks the question, making Jillian jump. His features have hardened, another reason why I want to punch him. I'm not quite sure if he's pissed he's stuck with the dumber and dafter best friend, or if he doesn't like to share his tossed aside toys but either way, I've about had enough of him.

Jillian, ever the graceful woman but no shrinking waif, grips her Prosecco tightly in her hand. Her lips thin as she replies, "As I'm sure you remember, I travel frequently for my career. We have clients in Buffalo, so I've been there several times."

"And you just happened to meet his parents?" His gaze darts between us, almost menacing. His tone condescending. For a supposedly smart guy, he needs to learn how to hide his thoughts better. It's flashing across his face he believes Jillian cheated first. Shmuck. Jillian never would have done that to him, and at that time, we were barely friends. We hadn't even started running together. More friendly acquaintances than anything else.

I open my mouth to put him in his place, but Jillian beats me to it. She places her hand on my thigh. It might be meant as a calming gesture, but all it does is heat me further.

For the love of God. We've touched more in the last four hours than in the last twelve months. My body is practically salivating with the need to have her.

Again, Roman notices, dropping his gaze to the edge of the table before glaring back at her.

"We were at an event and yes, they came. Since Klaus

told them we were friends, they insisted on taking us out for dinner, as well as the two other local players there."

"How sweet," Roman says. "Isn't it, Julianna?"

"I don't know." She sighs as if the mere thought of boarding a plane makes her need to take a nap. "Traveling for work seems like it'd be exhausting."

"Of course it would be." As if we're in some ridiculous competition, he places his hand on her leg. "That's why you'll stay close to home so you can take care of me."

"Won't that be lovely?" Her entire face perks up. "I can't wait until I can take care of you and our home and family."

"Actually, having a career—" Jillian starts to say, her entire voice vibrating with irritation but she's cut off.

"Tell us more about your family, Klaus." I could kiss Nana for the opening she's given me. And thank God it's Nana who interrupts. There are knives within Jillian's reach.

I've already seen what she can massacre when stressed.

Next to me, Jillian hides her smirk behind her glass of Prosecco. Bold, beautiful blue eyes shine on me. "Yes, Klaus. Tell them."

Taking the bait as easily as I was sure they would, Stetson asks, "Yes, what does your father do?"

"He's a neonatal cardiothoracic surgeon at Buffalo's Children Hospital." I take a sip of my drink.

"Oh?" I can't imagine Stetson Stearns is at a loss for words very often. At my side, Jillian squeezes my thigh. It's possible she's as delighted as he's speechless.

"Yes, sir. He does good work."

"Neonatal... that's an interesting specialty."

"My father has always said he enjoys saving the most vulnerable."

"Hmm. Of course."

"Well, that and he says since their bodies are the smallest, they're the most challenging to work on. He enjoys the intensity of that most of all."

"Ahh." Stetson tips his drink in my direction. "Now, that sounds like a man I'd like."

Because a competitive man is, but a compassionate one isn't? I forgo the dig I could easily take.

For the first time since I've met him, he actually looks pleased. Even more than when he was talking business with Roman. While I don't give two shits about what Stetson thinks of me, pissing Roman off is fun as hell.

"And your mother?" Claire asks, altogether sounding completely uninterested in anything relating to me or my mom. Are they this obvious with trying to find distasteful things about others? "She must stay busy with your father working in such a demanding profession."

"Yes, ma'am." I glance at Jillian. She's almost bursting with glee but it's not just that. She knows my parents. Despite the bomb I'm about to drop, she knows how different they are than her own.

But sometimes, you just have to enjoy shoving someone's wealth down their throat a little bit.

"My mother's a biomedical engineering professor at Buffalo U. She's actually the head of the department there and her promotion is what brought us to the States from Canada when I was younger..."

"Oh." Claire's perfectly painted lips form an O and her brows dip together. Everyone at the table seems a bit disappointed at this news.

I definitely notice how they don't seem pleased their daughter is with someone who comes from such wealth and prestige. Probably because it's in opposition to me—at least the prestige part, and that's only a matter of who you're asking.

And if you care. Which I don't.

"So what do your parents think of your hockey thing?"

This guy. I'm almost surprised the question comes from Roman instead of Stetson. He's enjoyed treating me like I'm nothing more than a dumb jock ever since we first met.

"My father respects a man capable of thinking for themselves. He also has high admiration for anyone who's willing to work hard for their goals, sacrifice and fight for what they want."

With that, I lean back and casually drape my arm over the back of Jillian's chair. It's highly inappropriate given her family and their need for proper manners.

Thankfully, she leans in.

*Eat that, Roman.* I smirk at him and watch as his eyes turn to fiery steel aimed straight at me. Yeah, he's pissed at me. Good.

"And they're very kind people," Jillian says. It's almost a dig at her parents when she smiles at Nana, completely ignoring the sour looks on her parents' faces, before smiling up at me. "They're so gracious. Please tell them I say hello next time you and your mom speak."

"Of course, honey," I murmur, and then lean down and brush my lips to her ear where her family can't see. "Is Roman green yet?"

Her hand on my thigh gives me a quick pinch. "Does putrid have a color? You might be overselling this, sweetie."

I'm not selling anything. I'm just being me and showing Jillian how much I like her. But if she wants to keep her head in the sand, that's fine. I enjoy this game... this fight. It's been a long time I've had to fight for anything worthwhile off the ice.

10

---

**KLAUS**

"Is that... is that a Portofino?"

The interest in Stetson's tone is clear as day. Since conversation during drinks moved on from my family, I caught Stetson giving me surreptitious looks, almost like he has no idea what to do with me now.

I can feel Roman's glare directed at my hand settled low on Jillian's back, my fingertips brushing her underwear line beneath her thin, silky dress.

Anytime I can stick it to Roman, I'm all in, but I'm surprised to hear Stetson knows what kind of car I'm driving.

Roman is taking Julianna home, so I offered to walk outside with them and move it so they could get out easier.

I hadn't anticipated the excitement in Stetson's voice. Next to me, Jillian grins down at her toes peeking out from her sandals.

"Yes, sir. It sure is. Do you like Ferraris?"

"Like them? I've been wanting one for quite some time. Just can't convince Claire to let me sell my Jag for one. How does she ride?"

"Beautifully. Perhaps before dinner, we can take her for a spin." I pull Jillian closer and kiss her temple. "Do you mind?"

"No, not at all. I plan on taking a nap, anyway."

"What do you say then?" I pull my keys out of my pocket and hand them over. "You can move it for Roman and I'll meet you out front after I get Jillian settled?"

Might as well play the gentleman card.

I didn't exactly think I'd get Mr. Stearns on my side over a short weekend, but I can say I didn't feel like an ice block was between us after he assumed my parents' wealth. Which is still smaller than his own.

Minuscule compared to mine.

Regardless, there was a thaw in the distance he previously set.

Now?

Well, now, I think the man is actually smiling at me.

Although it could be the afternoon sun making him squint, too.

Whichever.

"Sure. Of course. Sounds like a great idea." he says, and even more surprisingly, holds out his hand and turns to his daughter. "As always, Jillian, it's nice to have you home. We'll see you in a few hours?"

"Thanks, Dad. It's good to be back."

"Hmm." His tone is doubtful. For being a rather arrogant ass, I actually think he likes his daughter. At a minimum, he's neutral toward her, which is a far improvement over Claire's seemingly utter contempt.

"Be back in a few," I tell him and guide Jillian inside.

Roman and Julianna are on the front porch, fuming. We leave them without a good-bye. I'm over their twisted relationship and Roman's possessive instinct around Jillian. The next time he glances at her breasts, he's liable to end up with my fist in his face.

"You don't have to walk me up."

"I know. Come on, Jilly-Bean."

The tea wasn't easy for her, even if she finally settled in. Before I take off with her dad, I want to make sure she's doing okay.

I escort her to her room, and as we cross the threshold, the stress from the day falls from her shoulders.

"Your dad is an interesting man."

"Sometimes I think he cares. Other days, he can't be bothered since he can't talk sales numbers and metal suppliers with me."

"Your mom, on the other hand, is worse than you described."

"You get used to it." She yawns, covering her mouth and shaking her head. "Man. It was only an afternoon tea and I'm already exhausted."

"Perhaps it was the Prosecco," I tease.

"Perhaps." She shifts her head in my direction and opens her eyes. She does look sleepy. Worn out. "You know what I was thinking, sitting across from Roman, and watching how he and Julianna interact?"

I know what I was thinking and none of it was good. Still, she once loved this man.

"What?"

"I have no idea what I ever saw in him. And I was with him for more than six years. How can that be?"

I chuckle.

"What?"

"Only that was what I was thinking, too."

"Was I like that with him? So..."

"Differential?"

"I was going to say wimpy, but we can go with that."

"Mousy?"

"Biddable."

"No."

She shuffles to the bed, undoing her belt I eye with piqued interest. She won't undress here, not with me in the room, but as she sits on the bed and begins to unbuckle her shoe, I imagine her slowly stripping off the rest.

She gives me a look full of doubt and I go to her, sitting next to her to throw my arm around her. "Hey, Roman's a jerk. That you didn't see it doesn't mean you acted differently. And no, I don't remember you ever being any of those things. You're too strong."

"Doesn't say much about my ability to make good choices, though, does it?"

"Having your boyfriend lie to you and cheat on you doesn't negate your intelligence, Jillian. Stop being so hard on yourself. That's all on him. Unless you wish it was you sitting next to him tonight?"

I can see the appeal. Her mother's approval and fawning all over her. The comfort of a man... who I still don't believe is a great one. But everyone wants to be loved and accepted by their family.

"No. I think for the first time, I was glad I wasn't next to him. Seriously... she asked him about which sandwich he prefers she have."

I snort. "I almost gave her three of each when he suggested she have two."

"What kind of woman would want that?"

She's working something out in her mind and I'm unsure of what it is, how far I can push. "Why do you think Julianna's marrying Roman?"

"Probably because she gets the thrill of taking something of mine. She always did the same as kids. Toys, money... she stole everything from me. I'd forgotten that, before."

"And just think, she's the one now stuck with the man she stole from you."

"Good riddance, I guess, then."

"Exactly. Come on." I stand and tug down the covers of the bed. One we'll be sharing later. If I don't get out of here soon, I'm going to push this farther than either of us intends for it to happen. "Get in bed and sleep. Things will be better later."

"Always so sure of yourself," she grumbles.

I eye her, keeping the covers lifted.

"Fine." She kicks off her other sandal and shuffles into the bed, curling on her side toward me.

"Sleep well." I kiss her temple. Lingering there and not hiding it.

"Klaus?"

"Yeah, honey."

She yawns again, lashes slowly fluttering closed. "You're my favorite."

Her lips part almost instantly and she's out. It's not a surprise. Jillian can collapse into sleep in the middle of a heavy metal concert if she's tired enough.

I drop the covers and step back.

If I don't get out of here, I'll be climbing in behind her and she won't be asleep for as long as she needs.

"Later," I promise with a whisper and head toward the door with her sleepy words bouncing in my brain. *You're my favorite.*

If only I knew for sure what that means.

At the doorway, I give her one more quick glance and take in my favorite part of the room.

The bed.

One glorious and elegant king-sized bed.

For us to share.

Definitely later.

I RETURN to the front of the house and climb into my car with Stetson, fighting a hard-on the entire time. What he planned on being a leisurely jaunt around Charleston ends up with us flying up and down the interstate. Every time he glances at me, I sense him ready to interrogate me about my intentions with his daughter.

Thank God he doesn't glance down. He'd see my damn intentions for Jillian is pressed right against my dress pants.

Fortunately, he says little, but his looks say he doesn't know what to make of me, what to say to me, when I'm not involved in a Fortune 100 company.

By the time Stetson thanks me for the drive and tosses me the keys, I'm still hard, irritated, and restless.

And I'm a damn perv because all I can think of is climbing into bed next to Jillian, slipping my hand to her waist and kissing her until she wakes up, realizes what the hell I'm doing and where I'm leading us right before she shoves me away. I'm a glutton for punishment, only I abso-lutely no longer care. I've been falling in love with Jillian since the first moment I met her and if she can be in the same room with Roman and know without a doubt she's totally over him, then I'm getting us to where I want to be.

I open the bedroom door slowly, inhaling the scent of her flowery perfume that's already filled the room.

Jillian is sleeping with the most peaceful look I've seen on her all week. Chestnut hair spread out all over her pillow like a dark halo. The most beautiful dark angel. My pulse kicks up at the sight of her.

Screw it. I'm a man on a mission, after all. Ripping off my shirt first, I also ditch my socks and dress pants and slide into the bed behind her, keeping my lower half covered as if the cotton fabric on my boxer briefs is an irremovable barrier.

But this is just about wanting to test the waters, not taking everything I want at the potential first sign of the word *go*.

As soon as my hand settles on her hips, a gentle puff of breath comes from her lips, whispering my name.

In her sleep? If she's dreaming of me...

I pull her gently to my body, aligning the soft curves of her body with mine and warmth immediately invades me. This. This is what I've wanted for years and now I'm touching Jillian, listening to the soft hum of her breathing.

I should stop this. I should definitely stop this. But touching her without it leading to more? It's a feat far greater than any man outside of one having supernatural powers can resist.

She's too beautiful. Too soft in all the right spots and toned in all the perfect ones. She smells like sunshine and happiness, and I imagine she tastes like the most delectable treat.

I'm about to pull away, to end this all, when Jillian's head turns on the pillow and her eyes flutter open. "Klaus."

We're so close, stupid of me for even thinking of acting on this, especially when she's sleepy, but before I can move, she does, leans up and whispers my name again with her mouth brushing over mine.

And holy crap. Jillian is kissing *me*.

Braced with one hand, arm bent up on my elbow, my

other hand slides across her body to her neck where my hand tangles in her hair at the back of her head.

Lifting my mouth from hers, I gaze into her eyes, lashes fluttering slowly, sleep haze fading from her blue eyes that become clear as a cloudless sky.

And before I can think, she kisses me again, pressing her mouth to mine with the confidence of a woman who knows what she wants and is taking it.

It's so damn sexy. I not only immediately comply, I am all in, going with this new burst of pleasure she's spiking down my spine.

"Jillian."

"No words," she whispers against my mouth. Her hands go to my shoulders and she tugs, pulling me toward her as she rolls to her back.

Oh, hell yes. *Game on.*

I want to sink my weight on top of her, roll my hips against her welcoming center and feel her hardened nipples against my chest.

Screw the dinner.

And her family.

All we need is *this*. Us.

She arches up, her back bowing off the bed while she seeks more kisses. It takes effort, so much effort my biceps are trembling from the cost of my restraint. Ever since that day on her couch, when I took my shot with her, letting her believe this was all a game to me, I've wanted this moment... or perhaps a moment very similar but with far less clothing.

As it is, my dick is hard, pushing against my briefs, trying to get free.

This should definitely stop.

Unfortunately, or fortunately, depending on the angel or devil on my shoulder I'm currently in the mood to listen to

—the devil, always—Jillian seems to have the same struggle as me because her fingers are curled around my shoulders, fighting against my pull to stay away and bring me closer.

And God. The sounds she's making.

*Needy.*

*Wanting.*

My resolve crumbles like a dandelion and the softest breeze.

Dropping to one arm, I run my hand down the length of her side, playing with the satin fabric of her dress beneath her breast. Testing. Teasing.

She arches into me and mewls down my throat. I swallow her needy little whimper like candy to jerk off to later.

"Tell me to stop," I murmur, pulling back just enough to see her closed eyes, lashes fanning against the top of her cheeks. She blinks once, hazy, glassy eyes with dilated pupils.

"Do you want me to?"

"You should."

"I know. I just... I can't find it in me to use the words."

"Shit." I drop my forehead to hers and groan, settling my weight close to her, and as soon as my erection finds the warm center of her legs both of us groan. She gasps, rubs against me.

"Jillian—"

"Don't."

Who am I to deny a woman's request, especially when that woman is Jillian, the woman I've been in love with for far too long and only imagined having like this.

Squeezing my eyes closed, I revel in the feel of her soft, warm hand sliding from my shoulder to my neck and then my chin. She tugs me down until our lips are brushing against each other's and then she pushes off the bed, her lips hitting mine.

Screw it. I'll deal with the fallout of this later.

Without wasting time, I take her mouth, running my hand to her breast. A handful and perfect, her pebbled nipple is easy to find and when I brush my thumb over it, her hips jolt against me and her grip on my shoulder tightens.

I play with her, tease her, feel her, hating the fabric between us but not pushing to do anything to take it further, giving her time to stop this, but she doesn't. My need to know what she feels like and how wet she is takes over. I bunch her dress in my hand, shoving it up until she's bared from the waist down, hot pink silky underwear on display.

"You're soaked," I murmur. I can already feel her heat, but seeing the evidence of her arousal is gripping.

I've wanted this for so damn long.

"My dress," she says, shifting, trying to find the buttons at her collarbone.

"Clothes on. Let me take care of you."

"But—"

"No." I allow her to see my seriousness. As much as I want to make love to her, to show her I care about her way more than a friend, that won't happen now. Not until we're in agreement. Not until I can think straight with the full use of my brain and not the blood coursing to my dick.

I'll please her, but I won't take advantage of her.

Leaning back, I push up the rest of her dress, run my hands up her thighs to the waistband of her panties. They're so damn soft, and surprisingly, not a thong. But they're sexy and I imagine if I were to flip her over, they'd cup her ass perfectly, giving me the perfect shot of her sexy backside.

"This is for you." I keep my eyes on her as I peel them

down her legs, running my hands in their wake and grinning at the goose bumps I leave behind. She shivers, biting that bottom lip of hers.

And when they're gone, flung to the side, I slide my hands back up her thighs and bend down so I can kiss her legs, that soft spot at the back of her knee, up until I can smell her arousal, her desire for me. And it's so damn heady, so damn incredible, it kills me to avoid it, to move back up her body until I'm kissing her again while my fingers find her clit.

"Oh God," she moans.

Her hips buck against my hand and God... her desperation is such a huge turn-on I'm afraid of coming in my pants like I haven't done since I was on the junior hockey team.

I gather her wetness that's dripped from her, slide it around her clit, manipulating that bundle of nerves until she's being driven wild, clasping my hair, my shoulders. She clings to every part of me she can while I taste her throat, trail my lips down her olive skin to the spot behind her ear.

"Damn it. Klaus—"

"Yeah."

"I'm close."

I can tell and I haven't even been inside her yet. But now I need to. To feel her walls clamp around me even if it's not the part of me I want feeling her.

"Patience," I murmur, sucking on that skin again.

Her shampoo, flowers, and freshness invade my senses along with the smell of her sex. Her sounds drive me over the edge straight to wild and then I press one finger inside of her.

I earn another tortured groan from her, peel back enough to watch how the features on her face have tightened.

"You're so fucking tight and wet."

"It's been a while," she huffs, trying to make a joke.

I shut her up by adding another finger. I have no desire to joke about her sex life.

As soon as I'm inside, I begin fucking her with my fingers, pressing my thumb to her swollen clit. I watch her as she pants, as her breathing becomes ragged, memorize the feel of her legs trembling right as she opens her eyes, her mouth falls open and the most beautiful sound of a woman orgasming fills the room, my ears, my memory banks forever.

"Shit," she pants, her body spasming beneath mine. I lean down and kiss her, take her mouth like I'm taking the rest of her while she rides the waves of her ecstasy until she's spent, hands clinging to me.

She rips away her mouth, gasping, and kissing my cheek. "Is there anything you're *not* good at?" she asks, and she sounds so upset by the idea I don't have flaws—which I do, many of them—that I bury my head in the crook of her neck and laugh.

"That's what you want to say to me right now?"

"Well... thank you for the stress reliever, seems a bit selfish."

Stress reliever.

Right.

Because all she thinks is that I'd do this so she doesn't think about her family.

Sinking into a bathtub of ice after a hard practice couldn't kill my erection faster than her words.

"Anything you need, Jilly-Bean."

I slide my fingers out of her and pull down her dress. Once she's covered, I roll off her, slide in behind her and wrap my arms around her.

## 11

## JILLIAN

*What in the hell just happened?!*

I'm stuck between listless limbs unable to work after that incredible orgasm and heart-pounding fear over what we've just done.

And did I honestly *thank* him for being a stress reliever?

If it wouldn't make it so obvious I'm a totally freaking basket case and on the very edge of freaking out, I'd slap my forehead. As it is, Klaus curls me to him, my cheek to his shoulder and runs his hands through his hair. His heart is racing.

His body is steaming.

There are so many *more* things I want to do with him and to him and for him, my mind is speed racing through dozens of scenarios I've imagined over the years.

But this? *Now?*

His lips press the top of my head. "I can hear you thinking. Stop. Everything will be fine."

"Hmm-mmm." Of course it will be, because we're friends. And guys can make their friends come so hard they see stars and hear angels sing and be back to normal less than thirty seconds later.

"I'm going to go shower. I assume you need a few minutes to worry in private?"

He's chuckling as he says it. It's a shame I like him so much. Especially since I'm going to have to kill him. That might be drastic. Perhaps I'll simply maim him in his muscular thighs on broad display beneath his gray boxer briefs as he heads to the bathroom.

"Hey Jilly-Bean?"

I yank my gaze off his thighs, to the still visible bulge straight to Klaus's sexy as hell smirk and gleaming blue eyes. "While you're lying there, freaking out and wondering what all this means, just know that was the best twenty minutes of my life."

He ducks inside the bathroom.

Good thing, too, because I've already reached for my phone. I whip it from my hand, but Klaus is too fast. My phone slams into the wood door as it closes, landing on the floor with an unsatisfying *thunk*. From behind the closed door, Klaus's laughter echoes.

I fall back into the bed, the scent of what we've done and the reminder of it so vivid, a tremulous smile breaks out.

*This was the best twenty minutes of his life?*

*Mine too. Holy moly, I'm going to feel him for days.*

I stretch my limbs before I climb out of the bed and head toward my closet. The parental dinner always means heeled sandals and dresses.

"Thank you, Melinda." My closet is lined with all the contents from my garment bag, dresses on display, perfectly spaced, and I'm assuming, steamed and pressed and wrinkle-free. I flip through them once, then twice before I realize my hands are still trembling.

From what Klaus did? From the fear?

And holy crap. What did I say to him right before I fell asleep? *You're my favorite.*

Oh no.

I ball my hands into fists and flex them to get the sensation to go away. It's useless.

With one orgasm from Klaus, I'm twisted into a neurotic mess. It's the last thing I need this weekend when I'm thirty-six hours away from watching Roman and Julianna tie the knot in the church I was supposed to marry him in.

It's enough to mess with my mind on its own. I don't need *whatever this is* with Klaus making me dizzier.

By the time he comes out of the bathroom, dressed in only a white towel wrapped and tucked around his hips, I'm resolved.

Until I see that towel. The muscles in front and in back as he heads toward his own suitcase. And dear sweet baby Jesus in a manger. Should a man's ass look so good in a towel?

How does he manage to be so perfect?

I grip the cool metal hanger in my hand. I can do this. I can let Klaus know whatever just happened won't happen again and when we get back to Charlotte we'll figure everything out.

But then he stands, pair of black boxer briefs in his fist, that V-muscle of his hips on full, dripping wet display above that towel. I not only swallow my words, every brain cell of mine goes with them.

"Ugh," I choke out. *Work, mouth! Speak! Think!*

Klaus's lips lift at the edges, giving me that swoon-worthy smile. "You're not done freaking out."

It's a statement, not a question. I'd slap him if he wasn't so far away... or if I wasn't more afraid of getting too close to him. One little flick of my thumb and finger at that knotted towel and I'll be dropping to my knees and thanking him for all the stress he's relieved me from and created at the same time.

"Not really."

"Did you like that?"

"Um... is my back yard full of vegetables?" What a ridiculous question! Of course I liked it. What red-blooded woman wouldn't want the things he can use his hands for?

"So that's it."

"It's not that simple."

"You're right." His hands go to his waist, drawing my attention to that flimsy little tucked in towel corner. I press on, lifting my gaze, snagging on the V-muscle. Those glorious abs, all the way to his throat, where he swallows slowly. I swear he's doing this on purpose. How dare the man have the decency to swallow at a time like this! I'm already trembling and my hands might as well be dipped in mud for as clammy as they are.

He's *too* much. Too perfect. Too sexy. Too... grinning at me with a delightful smile I want to slide my tongue across.

"I feel like I should be offended for the way you just molested me with your eyes. Or get paid."

"Please." I huff. Useless. My cheeks are on fire and my hair is sticking to the back of my neck. I need a shower. A cold one to ice down all these rioting sensations. "You're all right."

"I think you're the most beautiful woman I've ever seen. And I haven't even taken your clothes off yet."

My hands clench around my dress. I'm pretty sure he's moving closer. Or maybe the room is spinning. What is happening!? All my earlier, well-reasoned arguments have fled out the window, skipped over the privacy wall, and dove straight into the ocean.

"Klaus—"

"Give me this weekend."

"What?" I blink. That's not what I was expecting, although at this point, I have no idea what will come out of his mouth.

He *is* moving closer. Sauntering slowly, almost as if he's afraid of scaring me. He's right! My gaze darts to the bed, to the door, to my room. If I move quick, I might be able to hop, skip, and jump my way to freedom and sanity.

"I don't want us to pretend to be in love this weekend." He swallows. That damn apple bob of his in his throat. It's so tantalizing. I lick my lips. "I want us to live it."

"You want us—"

"Yes."

He's here. Inches from me, eighty-two percent naked with water droplets still tumbling down his chest, between his pecs, curling around and down the center of his abs... right to that towel.

Oh... to be a water droplet right now.

"Tell me you didn't like what I did to you and you don't want more and we can go down to dinner and forget this conversation." His hand brushes my cheek, making me jump. His thumb, warm and smelling like my body wash, presses the bottom of my chin, snapping my gaping mouth closed and lifting my head away from the towel.

Where it's now *very* obvious he likes where I'm looking.

"Look at me."

In all honesty, I prefer my current view. I swear he grows harder, larger while I struggle against Klaus's thumb at my chin, applying gentle pressure.

"Keep staring and he'll want to say hello. He likes hand-shakes but prefers kisses. And he's waited a very, very long time to greet you properly. He might demand a *lot* of kisses. Open-mouthed."

"You're talking 'bout your dick."

"I am."

I grin. "Like he's his own person."

He smirks. That godawful, tempting smirk. "He's big enough to be."

That is *not* a lie.

He's also losing his mind.

"I think all the blood in your brain is rushing to your dick and you're not thinking straight."

"Funny." His hand at my cheek slides to the back of my neck, cupping the back of my head. Fingers tangle in my hair as he leans closer. "I don't think I've ever had a more clear thought in my life."

He kisses me, firmly, sweetly. He kisses me until I melt into him, my hands finally falling to that tight towel.

"I want this, Jilly-Bean, but if you don't, we can forget it ever happened."

There's not a snowball's chance in hell I'm ever forget-ting this moment.

But is what he's saying smart? The best thing? Fear rushes in, slow and angry like the ocean waves before a storm, loud and rumbling in my conscience, screaming at me to slow down. To put a stop to this madness.

And yet still, he's bewitched me. My thoughts still scrambled from the orgasm and his kisses and that hard bull pressing my still wet center and all my fears flee like a popped balloon.

"Okay," I whisper.

Klaus pulls back, shock in his eyes and a sweet, surprised smile on his lips, and I duck my head.

I have no idea if I've just made the best decision of my life... or the worst.

**12**

---

## JILLIAN

To my complete non-surprise, Roman is already at the dinner table when Klaus and I enter, fingers entwined and linked together.

"Are you fucking serious?" he mutters, loud enough for only me to hear.

Funny, because the same question still lingers on my tongue from everything he said upstairs less than an hour ago, and yet I'm not nearly brave enough to ask.

At this point, Roman at my family's less formal dining area, at an empty table because my parents aren't even here yet, doesn't surprise me one bit.

"Going in search of a food truck sounds like a really damn good idea to me right now," Klaus says, making me laugh.

"Don't be silly. Food trucks have horrible vegetarian options."

Not that my parents' menu will be any more palatable for me, but I've long since stopped reminding them I don't eat meat. Whether they don't honestly remember or don't care, my dinners here have me relating to rabbits considering I can only eat a few sides and a salad. No rolls, because carbs are my mother's devil child.

"Dinner with us again?" I ask Roman.

"Your mother insisted."

"Of course she did." I avoid the table and head straight for the bar on the other side. Klaus follows me and pours me a glass of red wine, without asking.

He knows me well... *very* well after earlier. What he's offering is something I've wanted for so long and he's easily handing it to me. So why aren't I more excited?

Possibly because of what he exactly offered. *I don't want to pretend this weekend. I want to live it.*

So what happens when the weekend is done?

"Don't let him get to you," Klaus says quietly as he pours himself a whiskey.

"I can find some tea or water for you."

"Nonsense. Something tells me I'll need this tonight."

"No doubt." I start to turn, but Klaus stops me with his hand at my waist, pulling me back to him and kissing my temple.

"Say the word whenever you want and we can get out of here. It's always an option."

I bring my glass of wine to my lips. Out of the corner of my eyes, Roman is at the table, eyes narrowed at a blank space in front of him, jaw set. I'm beyond caring about rubbing my faux-maybe-real-relationship with Klaus in his face, but seeing him upset makes me grin.

As if he has any reason to be mad at me.

Klaus pulls back and escorts me to the table. As he holds out my seat for me and waits for me to drape my napkin in my lap, my parents enter, Nana immediately behind them.

She looks like smoke is ready to pour out her ears and mother's lips are pressed tight together.

Great. When Nana and Mom get mad at each other, all bets are off on southern politeness and hospitality. Their fights are more reminiscent of a cage match.

Probably why Mom can't stand Nana. Nana brings out the small town, low country girl she used to be and not the refined socialist she turned herself into.

As they go to the bar and get drinks, Nana plops down in the seat next to Roman with a grumpy flourish.

"Everything okay?" I ask, despite the fact it's clearly not.

She shoves her thumb toward Roman. "Ask him."

Nana might have her own sense of comedic flair and a laissez-faire attitude, but she's rarely mean or outright rude.

Before I can do as she commanded, Roman clears his throat. "Your mom says there are details to finalize for the rehearsal celebration tomorrow night."

"And that has anything to do with her, because...?"

I can't finish. Roman leers at me in a way that makes something cold and heavy settle low in my gut. "Because the rehearsal celebration is here. You should really call your mom more often. Do a better job of keeping in touch."

And here's the part of Roman I remember hating before I hated him. His condescension. Thinking he knows what's better for me than I do.

I ignore the dig at me, keeping in touch with my mom. She only calls me when she's requesting my presence back in Charleston. Never, in all the years since I left for college, has she once called to see how her only child is doing. Settling into freshman college life? Didn't hear a peep. Congratulating me on my new job? Not a single text. Being proud of me for being able to afford my home at the age of twenty-five without relying on a trust fund? Nothing.

I'm seething, fingers reach out and dig into Klaus's thigh. I'd apologize for it, but he has to be used to the way I claw him by now. He'll have physical reminders of his hands on me like I do him in one way or another by the time we blow this pop stand.

My mother is at her chair, waiting for my dad to pull hers out in the same gentlemanly way Klaus did for me. "You're hosting the rehearsal dinner? Here? What the hell for?"

They'd said something about it earlier, but it must not have registered they are hosting.

My voice is rising, earning an irritated scowl from my mom.

Placing the napkin on her lap, she smoothes it out. "Really, Jillian. You should watch your language. That's no way a lady speaks."

She takes a sip of her white wine. I begin to think she's going to ignore my entire question but instead, she simply says yes. "He's family and so are Teresa and Norman. We've offered to help them while they're dealing with some things, and we're closer to the church, so it makes sense."

"No. It doesn't. And he's *not* family." Screw politeness. I might not want to marry Roman, but doesn't she have any sense as to why this is not only a good idea, but humiliating her own daughter? "He's the son of a business associate and my ex-fiancé. Can't you see at all how inappropriate and frankly, unkind that is to me?"

Your daughter. Her ability to hurt me with her lack of care or thought of me will never cease to surprise me.

At my side, Klaus covers his hand with mine. Prying my fingers off of his thigh, he rubs my hand between both of us. It's soothing and warming.

Too bad I'm a volcano ready to blow.

I turn back to Roman. "For a long time, I figured you were a selfish jerk who only thought of himself, but this is low. Even for you. Why would you even want to throw this continually in my face?"

"You tell him!" Nana cheers, complete with a fist pumped into the air. "All a'this is nonsense. Utter nonsense." She turns to Mom, whose cheeks are growing redder by the second. "And I raised you better than this, Clarabella. You might think you're something better than me, but when you changed all a'you to become someone new and rich, I'll gosh darn just say you forgot to bring along the best parts of everything I taught ya."

"What? How to be poor?"

"No. How to be kind, Clarabella."

My mother takes the verbal slap with a flinch. With a grip so tight on the stem of her wine glass it's a wonder it doesn't snap in two, she takes a sip, sucks it in between her teeth, leaving not a hint of her pale pink lipstick on the crystal rim and seethes, "My name, mother, is Claire. As I've repeatedly requested. And you never taught me to be kind. You were hardly ever around to teach me anything."

What? My spine snaps straight at the accusation. I've never once heard my mom talk like this about Nana.

"The hell it is. The Good Lord gave me to you and the right to name you and I had those nurses scribble down in that tiny box the name I wanted you to have, which is Clara-bella. You can change it all you want, but I gave you that name and I got the right to call you anything I want. You should be happy all I'm calling you is your birth name 'cuz you might think you're better than where you came from, but you sure ain't actin' like it tonight."

She sits back in a huff, her heavy bosom heaving from her anger with her daughter. I watch both of them like it's the most fascinating pingpong match and when Nana meets my gaze, she winks.

As if winking at me will make things better.

I grin down at my lap as Klaus's hand rubs my shoulder.

"You might think very little of me, Mother, but don't be bitter because I had goals for my life and worked my behind off to accomplish them. I will not apologize for that and I will remind you I did it all with very little support or encouragement from you. However, in this instance, I am being the woman you raised. We're helping out friends." She slides her narrowed, angry glare toward me, and I almost believe there's a hint of regret in it before she faces my nana again. "Business associates, maybe, but they're still family. And Norman is ill. Teresa is taking care of him and wants their house quiet and peaceful. She asked for my help, knowing the situation it puts me in, but I will not say no to the oldest and dearest friends we have here. Now, if you'll excuse me, I believe I've lost my appetite."

"Claire," my dad calls. He's been so silent I forgot he was still here. "Take a moment. Return. I believe this family has a lot to discuss."

"We are not one of your business arrangements, Stetson. I believe we've said all we need to tonight."

She squeezes his shoulder as she passes, kisses his temple, easing the sting of her words. My jaw is still scraping the wood floor when she disappears.

So much for my mother and I not having anything in common. An unsupportive mother? I know what that's like. Wanting to do something right, even when it's hard? I didn't know she was capable of such a thing.

I turn to Roman, the shock of Mom and Nana's fighting still a living, breathing, thing, but my mother's comments becoming clearer. "What's wrong with your dad?"

One of the hardest things about leaving Roman was saying goodbye to Teresa. I often wondered how she could have such a genuine relationship with my mom. Teresa is the complete opposite. She treated me as if I was her own daughter for as long as I can remember. I've known them my entire life, and while Norman is often as gruff as my own dad, he's always shown me much more affection than my own and together, they've always been a light presence. Teresa is kind and gentle with a sweet sense of humor.

Across from me, Roman has paled, lips thinned. "Pancreatic cancer. He has at most three months."

Which means in three months, if he isn't already, Roman will be taking his spot next to my dad as the co-owner of their business. Norman is dying.

"I'm sorry to hear that." My chin quivers and I turn to my dad. He's looking into his whiskey glass, frown marring his typical stoic features. "I'm sorry for you too, Dad."

"He's a good man," he says and takes a large swig of his drink. "And as for your mother, she's done the best she can with you, given how she was raised."

He spears Nana with a contemptuous glare and pushes his chair back from the table. "Excuse me while I go check on my wife."

Once he's gone, it's Nana who speaks next. "Well, that escalated quickly."

Truer words have never been spoken, and all those words have left me questioning everything.

Especially my own relationship with my mom.

I FIND her in the library, sitting in a chair that faces the backyard patio. My father is sitting next to her, hand holding hers. Their heads are bent close while he whispers something in her ear.

It's the most intimate I've ever seen my parents look, and when my mom brushes her finger under her eyes and sniffs, it's almost my undoing.

My mother? Crying? I never knew such a thing is possible.

I clear my throat and step into the room, unapologetic for breaking their moment or for watching them for far too long.

Dad stands and pats her hand and comes toward me, arms loose at his side. "Take it easy on her, kiddo."

He kisses my cheek and saunters out.

It's possible stepping into their home this weekend swept me into an alternate dimension. One where my dad calls me names like *kiddo* and my mom cries and Klaus wants to *live us being in love and not pretending.*

Giving my mom a moment, I walk straight toward the windows. They're floor to ceiling, looking out over the portico and the luscious gardens Mom herself used to tend and grow until she hired gardeners. Working with her, digging in the dirt, and listening to her talk about how she cares for her roses and myriad other shrubs was the highlight of my week when I was a little girl.

Bonus points because it meant I didn't have to be stuffed into frilly, scratchy dresses, and could wear sweats and sloppy boots. It was the one time I didn't get scolded for making messes and dirtying myself up.

It's the one memory I have of *loving* being with my mom. Seeing her not care about manicures and makeup and her next hosted volunteer event or ladies' luncheon.

I think about all of this, hands clasped together in front of me, wringing madly while trying to figure out what to say.

Mom beats me to it.

"For the longest time, when I was a little girl, I grew up

with Nana thinking that love made the world go around. She lived so freely, didn't care about much, and while I know you love that about her, as her daughter, it often meant we didn't have food on the table. She'd be out, having the time of her life with friends and forget to do my laundry and go to the grocery store. Your grandma has always had a personality greater than life but I learned very early on that her personality often overtook her sense of duty and responsibility."

Yeah. Definitely a different dimension. I'd scan for a portal but I'm too stunned by what my mom is saying. I spin and face her, putting my back to the windows and for the first time in my life, I'm struck by the grief and guilt weighing my own mom down as she sits, hunched over on the chair, a fresh glass of wine from the library's small bar area untouched in front of her.

"I didn't want children," she says, staring at the wine. "I didn't know how to care for someone else, and I'd spent so much of life having to take care of me, hiding how bad things were, I wasn't sure I ever wanted that responsibility."

"Mom." I have nothing left to say. Her pain is palpable, and yet, she somehow manages to skewer me at the same time.

"I won't apologize for making something of myself. For changing who I was to have what I wanted. Nana believed college wasn't for people like us. Told me I lived with my head in the clouds and that I was always destined to be just like her, and I fought it. From the moment I could leave her home, I fought those words of hers with every breath I took."

My shoes have frozen themselves to the wood floor. My thoughts have fled. I am staring at Mom, listening to her twist a version of Nana I never saw.

"You never told me."

"She's your grandmother. She loves you. You deserved to have that relationship with her without my interference or my preference." She grabs her wine, glass shaking as she brings it to her lips. "Doesn't mean it's easy for me to be around her."

So much of this makes sense now that I can look back. The irritation Mom always showed when she would take me to Nana's as a little girl, like she was climbing the walls and searching for her escape route the entire time we were there before she eventually refused to take me back there. The home I always assumed was falling apart simply from age, but perhaps it was Nana's neglect. She certainly wasn't the world's best housekeeper by any means.

How much of my growing up had I imagined to be different than reality?

"Why tonight? What happened today that made you blow up and decide to tell me?" Because she wasn't going to. She's acted like Roman living here is copacetic and completely normal when it's anything but.

Her lips thin, and for a while she doesn't say anything, just looks out to her now professionally landscaped gardens with that glass of wine clutched in her manicured fingers like a lifeline.

"She barged into my room earlier, letting me know her thoughts on Roman and the rehearsal dinner. Which isn't any of her business. And frankly, I only invited her to this wedding to be polite, but she's been completely unreasonable ever since her arrival. Harping about every little thing she learns as if it's her right."

"Unreasonable," I mutter. "Because she loves *me* and maybe she's thinking about my feelings in all of this when you aren't?"

She flinches, and that familiar frustration with my mom bubbles like molten lava.

"Why didn't you tell me?" I demand. "Why didn't you bother to give me a heads-up instead of just saying my presence is expected. You couldn't have at least warned me?"

"You left him. I didn't think you cared."

"Because he *cheated* on me... with the woman he's marrying... who was *my* friend! And you didn't think I cared? Or might be embarrassed? But no..." I flip my hand in the air. "You offered to host his freaking rehearsal! Here! In my house!"

"My house," my mother says, calm as a can be. "And what was I supposed to do when Teresa asked for our help?"

My breath leaves me in a rush, limbs still burning with anger and frustration. "I get wanting to help Teresa. Hell, I *feel* for Norman and her, and yes, even Roman. But did you think about me at all in this? Because no offense, Mom, it seems to me that in your determination to end up nothing like your neglectful mother, you sure as hell became exactly like her."

"I gave you a stable home. I made sure you had everything you could possibly want growing up and you throw it in my face?"

"All I wanted was a mother who acted like she gave a damn about me, who supported me, who encouraged me. And strangely enough, you just said yourself those are the exact same reasons why you don't like your own mom. So tell me, how exactly are you two different?"

I'm done. I am absolutely done with this conversation. We can talk in circles for the rest of the night and she'll never see. "As for the rest of what you gave me... that's far down on the list of priorities to knowing your own mother actually likes you."

I leave the library and head straight back to the dining room.

Nana and Klaus are the only two left at the table but the silence is thick as cement and hardening by the moment. I head straight to the bar and pour a glass of wine. The bottle shakes in my hand, wine almost spilling over the rim of the glass as I fill it.

"Shit."

A warm hand covers mine. Klaus's scent envelops me as he presses his chest to my back. "Let me get this for you."

"I... thank you." I rest against him and let my head fall back to his shoulder.

If I could stay here, like this, resting against his strength and warmth for the night, it'd be perfect. Too bad this erupting volcano isn't going anywhere anytime soon.

It's only getting started. I can only hope we're not all burned in the lava's wake by the weekend's end.

"I take it that didn't go well?" He speaks quietly into my ear, only loud enough so I can hear and at her chair, Nana acts like we're not in the room.

"Not great. But it explains some things, I guess."

"We can grab this bottle and go outside, or go get drunk in your room."

Oh, to be able to wash away tonight's revelations with alcohol. What a divine plan.

"I have a better idea. Have you eaten?"

"No. Melinda and Patrice came in and said they're keeping dinner warm and ready when we request it."

"I think I'd rather get out of here and go for a walk. We can find something in the city?"

"Sounds perfect to me." He hands me my glass and kisses my temple. "Let me at least go let them know."

I sip my wine and push off Klaus, facing him as I do. "Thank you. You're the best."

"I think you said I'm your favorite, actually. Not the best." He winks.

The scoundrel.

**13**

---

## KLAUS

It's late and most of the stores are closing, but even though the sun has set, the heat still lingers, keeping us warm as we walk up Meeting Street, dodging other pedestrians on the narrow sidewalks. A couple times, Jillian pauses to watch groups on ghost tours huddled in small groups outside cemeteries, listening to the tour guides.

There's a beauty to Charleston, the age of it and the magnificence I'm always attracted to.

And yet, it seems like such a strange, sheltered place to grow up. It might be a city, but the historic area where Jillian was raised is vastly different than the rest of the city. Yet there is plenty of shopping and restaurants, a college nearby I imagine would be fun as well as the Citadel. All within walking distance to her home and her preschool and high school and everywhere else she would have walked to.

But what it has in charm in spades, it lacks the familiar comforts of suburban living I'm used to with large yards and kids running down neighborhood streets, free from the threat of traffic.

"What was it like growing up here? Not with your

parents, or your home, but the city itself." Although her home is majestic and ancient in its own right, it lacks the warmth of my childhood home. It's been modernized and updated but keeping the original architecture as much as possible, but Jillian's home looks like it could be on the cover of a magazine. No Sharpie markers drawn on walls and kept for sentimental reasons like mine. I'm certain the furniture in the sitting room, a room no one uses, is from the 1800s and for show purposes only.

"I don't know." She shrugs and then frowns. "It was how I grew up. What I knew."

"But did you run and play in parks? Swing sets in back yards?"

She laughs. "I climbed the trees in our yard and helped Mom in the gardens when she still tended them herself, and I think we walked to parks. We had playdates with kids in classes at playgrounds, I guess. Why?"

I tell her what I'm thinking and as I do, she gets a far-off look in her eyes either trying to remember or trying to forget. Perhaps judging her childhood against mine. "Maybe that's why I could never wait to leave. Charleston has grown a lot in the years, gentrified especially on the north edge, and the college keeps young people here at least for a while, but I guess you're right. I mean, I grew up walking on cobblestone streets where slaves were sold centuries ago. I always had the allure and excitement of tourists trailing the sidewalks, enamored with our homes and our narrow streets and overgrown trees. I think to them, it feels beautiful and full of history and while that was ingrained in me, I think I always wanted something normal."

"Less a place of show and more a home of comfort?"

"Something like that. Perhaps trying to give myself something I'd always craved." She shakes her head and then brushes hair off her forehead. "Which is strange considering that's exactly what my own mom said she tried to do... give me everything she didn't have."

"Do you want to talk about it?"

"Not really. I think I'm still processing."

I give her silence, letting her guide us down the streets where during the day, the city market bustles with vendors. She doesn't go in, and instead we walk along the outside, until we come to a restaurant that smells like pasta and garlic with an outdoor deck and twinkling fairy lights illuminating diners scattered across the outdoor deck.

"Want to eat here?" she asks. I thought we were strolling the streets in an effort for Jillian to forget her night, but I suspect she's had this restaurant in mind all along.

Besides me being a carb and meat lover, Italian restaurants are easy for her to find vegetarian options. We both usually end up in a carb coma and well satisfied.

"Looks good. Smells even better."

"Come on." She grabs my hand and tugs me through the front door.

We wait until an outdoor table is open, Jillian claiming she wants the fresh air. After we're seated, bruschetta and wine ordered for Jillian immediately, I lean back in my chair with my ice water.

"The house you grew up in is incredible. What was it like living in it?"

"With my parents? It was formal. Mom always liked us to be fancy. And me, she liked to be quiet."

"Doesn't seem like something that would come easy to you," I tease her, and watch her smile shake. When she reaches to brush hair off her shoulders again, I take her hand in mine, rubbing my thumb along her palm.

Now that I've had the feel of her, I want her more. All the time.

In a way that's stronger than I believed possible before I'd been able to be with her like this.

"No. No, I was never good at being quiet. It drove her crazy. Roman and I used to get in so much trouble, running through the house, slamming doors, sliding down banisters."

I try not to flinch at the mention of Roman, but it's difficult to hide.

"We grew up together," she chides and squeezes my hand. "From the time we were in preschool together. I don't have many memories without him in my life."

"Is that why it's been difficult for you to move on from him?"

In the nine months since they've broken up, she hasn't had a single date, at least not that I'm aware of. And if she was dating, she wouldn't have needed me. Not that I'm complaining.

"Maybe." She shrugs and slides her hand from beneath mine, reaching for her wine as it's delivered. "Thank you," she tells the server, a lean man who introduced himself as Jacques when we were seated. "I mean, it's Roman. I've literally known him my whole life. Even knowing we were growing apart, even knowing we started wanting different things, we always had each other. So yeah, I suppose losing that part of me, the one good part about my childhood I remember, that hurt."

There are so many more things I want to ask her, about Roman, about her family. We've been friends for years and I've heard so many stories about her parents, but seeing it in reality is vastly more eye-opening.

She hasn't had an easy life despite coming from privilege, and yet she's made her own way. It's something she should be proud of.

I tell her this, and she blushes. Jacques returns and we place our order, lasagna for me and a spinach and mushroom gnocchi for her, salads for both of us and a request from Jillian to keep the bread basket filled.

Once he's gone, promising to refresh her glass of wine soon, she waves her hand in the air.

"Enough about me. I'm tired of talking about it and need a break."

Her gaze holds a hint of uncertainty, as if afraid I'll push, but tonight's not the time.

"Tell me about the team. The season."

"We always talk about my team." I grin.

"That's because they're good guys and hot and talented and I like hearing about them."

"Who do you think is hot?"

"Um. All of them?" She rolls her eyes as a fierce stab of jealousy slices my chest. She thinks my teammates are *hot*? How hot? "Calm, Klaus. They're attractive, but I'm not attracted to any of them. Well, except for maybe one or two."

She winks at me and takes a chunk of bread out of the basket.

"Who's the second guy?" I ask.

"Don't you mean the first?"

"No. That's me obviously."

"Please." She snorts and butters her roll. I'd believe her if she wasn't a horrible liar, and if she wasn't blushing. "You're not even top five."

"The hell I'm not."

She throws back her head and laughs, earning glances from other diners, completely uncaring. "Fine. You make the top three. That what you to want to hear?"

"As long as the other two are below me, I'm good with that."

She shrugs and chews her roll. That blush of her burns brighter and she can't keep a straight face.

I know exactly where I fit on that number.

"I'm worried," I admit, and the concern I've been carrying but I haven't said out loud to too many grows.

"Why? Is anyone injured?"

"No. Aging."

"Jason?"

Jason Taylor is the best left winger in the league. But at thirty-three, nearing thirty-four, he's definitely getting up there. His job is tough, his body aching more after every game. Our last two years have been incredible, and he's led us to the top, but that doesn't mean he has many left.

"Him and Maddox. They're getting older. I could see, especially now that they're settling with families, being ready to move on soon, leave while they're on top instead of falling apart."

"This season?"

"After it, depending on how they play, I wouldn't be surprised. Plus, they're also our captains, so if they do step back, that leaves leadership and experience we'll lose. This year alone with trades and bringing up rookies we're looking at least at seven or eight new starters. That's a lot to gel with along with the threat of losing our leaders."

Not that I'm worried about who would take their place. Jason's younger brother Jude is a shoo-in for captain. Along with Sebastian. Sawyer's too damn goofy and wouldn't want the responsibility of it, but there are still others the team would look to.

"Well then you'll have to win them another cup before they go out."

"That is the plan."

We continue talking, me letting her guide the conversation which turns to flowers she's thinking of adding to her garden bed and what her fall travel schedule is like. It's a busy time of year for both of us, and while I know the argument with her mom and Nana is front and center, I let her pretend it's not bothering her.

She has enough to deal with this weekend. I've thrown enough at her in itself.

If she needs the break, I'll be a man of my word and give her anything she needs.

By the time we return to the house, it's dark, only the stairway lit for us.

But Jillian is relaxed, laughing quietly thanks to the few glasses of wine.

She uses the restroom first and while there's nothing more I'd like to do than pull her into my arms and kiss her senseless like I did earlier, tonight's not the night.

Instead, I give her space, use the restroom after her, taking my time, and when I slide into the massive bed behind her, I pull her to me, and kiss her temple.

"Sleep tight, Jilly-Bean. The weekend can only improve from here."

"You're so full of shit."

She falls asleep with the sarcasm and a smile on her lips, telling me I've done my job.

Which means I follow her shortly after, feeling pretty damn proud of myself.

## 14

## JILLIAN

I wake to a throbbing headache, heat from Klaus behind me, and last night's disastrous family dinner lingering in my mind. Klaus and I walked the streets of Charleston, ending up at an Italian restaurant near the market where we ate outdoors, beneath fairy lights. I enjoyed a couple glasses of wine, all the carbs my stomach can handle with the spinach and mushroom gnocchi and bruschetta. After Klaus asked if I wanted to talk about what happened with my mom and I gave a firm no, he let the conversation slide while we switched to talk about his teammates, how his friend Sebastian was doing with his new fiancée, Gigi.

By the time we returned home, the moon was high and the house was quiet. We went straight to my room, took turns in the restroom, and I was already falling asleep when Klaus slipped in behind me, kissed my cheek, and pulled me into his arms.

There will be more tough conversations ahead, I'm certain of it. But last night, Klaus gave me exactly what I needed. Quiet conversation, time to contemplate everything

I learned, and all the lingering disappointment still curdling in my gut.

It appears we didn't move at all in our sleep since his arms are still enclosed around me and while my stress headache is painful, having Klaus here, always here for me, helps calm me some.

"Why are you such a loud thinker?" he mumbles. His thick, heavy voice rumbles against my neck, lips brushing my skin as he speaks.

"I can't help it."

"Every time you worry, your shoulders tighten. Wanna talk about it?"

"No." I pull my hand out from beneath my pillow and trail it down his arm until my hand covers his. As soon as our fingers brush, he flips his hand over, locking our hands together.

"What do you need?"

"Coffee. An incredibly long run, and then to pretend I'm not going to my ex-fiancé's wedding rehearsal celebration tonight where his mom, who I've always loved is dealing with her husband dying soon. Oh, and where my mom still refuses to see how crappy she treats me but has brought a whole new revelation into why she does."

His chuckle warms my neck, travels straight south until I squirm against him.

He groans against me, and presses into me. "Unless you want to wake that beast, I suggest you don't make that sound or do that wiggle again."

Waking the beast, as he so ineloquently puts it, sounds like a great idea. It definitely *feels* like one. It's not a can I'm willing to open, not with so many other flames in the fire.

"Run with me," I say instead, already pulling away from

him. He lets me go slowly, and I lose the contact and his calmness as soon as I'm sitting.

"I can go get you coffee."

"No. I could use a few minutes alone, but you'll run with me?"

I glance back and find Klaus rolling to his back. The sheet falls to his waist and all that's on display is that glorious body, muscled arms he shoves straight to the side, fingers brushing my hip. Oh dear heavens. I'm choosing coffee and a run over throwing myself at half-naked Klaus?

I need to have a serious discussion about my priorities.

"I'll do anything you want," he says, and runs one of his hands over his stomach. His gaze is ravenous as he scans my scantily dressed body, and I doubt it's for the coffee or for the run.

"Jilly-Bean?"

"Yeah?"

"I'll give you three seconds to get out of this bed or you won't need that long run by the time I'm done with you."

I'm out of there in less than two seconds, snagging the robe Melinda hung on the back of the door sometime yesterday on my way to the bathroom, and once again, listening to Klaus's laughter echo behind another closed door.

Greedy, silly man.

Stupid me for not taking him up on his offer.

But while he's still convinced he wants us to live like we're in love, I have too many other battles to blaze before I can consider his offer. What happens when the weekend ends, and we go back to reality? Thirty-six hours, and I'll be back in Charlotte, working in my garden, ensuring Becca hasn't killed half my plants in a record-breaking few days. I'll be back at my job, traveling.

Klaus will dive straight into pre-season where he'll spend the next seven months traveling, more if they make the playoffs again.

No, without more clarity, the risk of what Klaus suggests has too high of a price.

The house is quiet as I make my way down the stairs, through the parlor and the back way toward the kitchen. Not surprising. My father is probably already at work for the day and my mother is probably sleeping in, in preparation for her big night.

Since she's the queen of hosting extravagant parties, I have no doubt the house will soon come alive with decorators and caterers, decking the home up to the nines, but for now I'm thankful for the solitude.

A quiet start to the morning alone with coffee before my run is just what I need.

All hopes of that are dashed as I push through the door to the kitchen.

In front of me is Julianna, wearing a man's striped dress shirt I know too well and what looks like nothing beneath. Her back is to me, but at the sound of the swinging door closing behind me, she turns.

I'm one quick second from ducking back out when the surprise in her eyes changes to something else.

It's the same damn look she gave me in fifth grade when she heard I was running for student council president and threw her hat in the ring. After I won, she didn't speak to me for three weeks. The same look she gave me when she saw the BMW my dad bought for my sixteenth birthday. The same look she gave me when she saw my engagement ring from Roman.

God. It's true.

She's wanted everything I've always had. If she wants it, she can have it.

"I thought you went home last night."

"I came back. Roman called and said he needed me." Her grin turns victorious.

Whatever. If he needed to slake some pent-up aggression or needed comfort after the shitshow that was dinner, so be it.

"So why are you here? Doesn't the carriage house have a coffeemaker?"

"Broken." She shrugs and rests her ass against the counter, crossing her ankles.

Like I need to see how short that shirt is on her, or the length of her legs. She only has the buttons done to close her breasts proving my earlier assumption wrong. She is wearing something beneath the shirt—fire-engine red colored satin panties.

Two can play her fun little game, but mine is done to piss her off and nothing else.

I set a pod into the coffeemaker and once it's gurgling, filling the coffee cup, I glance at her thighs. "That used to be my favorite shirt of Roman's to wear, too."

"It fits me better."

She's two inches taller and her breasts are much larger. She's not wrong. I also don't care.

"So does his life." I grab my coffee and add a dash of sugar.

Her irritation is a pulsing, living thing, wafting off her as I go to the fridge for cream.

"You can't have him back."

My hand stalls on my creamer and I roll my lips together. Is that why she thinks I'm here? Laughable.

I add my cream and put it back into the fridge before turning to her.

I need at least a sip before I deal with this. I'd prefer to not deal with this at all, but here we are.

"I don't want him."

"Why? Not good enough for you? Do you honestly think I don't see through the charade of you and that hockey player you brought home? Like your dad will ever allow that to happen."

The coffee burns my throat as I choke on it. "We're twenty-seven years old, Julianna. I need my father's permission to do anything in life less now than I did when I was twenty-one. It's a shame you've never learned to grow up and live on your own. Maybe you'd actually realize you have more worth than being eye candy or winning frivolous competitions no one else is playing."

Her green eyes narrow and her face turns bright red.

"Julianna."

We both turn as Roman comes through the breezeway separating our house from the carriage home. He's showered, cleaned, and dressed for the day in golf shorts and a polo shirt, casual. Obviously not going to work the day before his big day.

He nods in my direction before going straight to her. "What are you doing in here?"

"Getting coffee. Catching up with Jillian." She holds her coffee mug in front of her like a shield, cupping it with both hands. "Problem with that, honey? After all, once you take your dad's spot, we'll all be practically family."

I can only imagine Roman's expression since he has his back to me. But for me? If I was closer, she'd be wearing my drink. As it is, Roman grabs her bicep and none too politely pulls her toward the door.

"Go shower and get ready. I'll take you home soon."

There's a bite to his tone, easily understood. Julianna's a bigger bitch than I ever gave her credit for. And worse, how in the hell was I friends with her so long? The very idea she'd talk like that about his dad now shows how shallow she truly is, and hell, maybe they are perfect for each other.

"I'm sorry she said that to you," I say, even though it's not for me to apologize for anything. Any decent person would after she practically threw his dad's pending death in his face.

He shoves his hand through his hair, all that perfectly gelled work falls right back into place.

"She's pissed at me. She'll get over it."

It shouldn't make me smile, but I still have difficulty fighting it, so I wrap my lips around the rim of my mug and drink.

I turn to leave, my back to Roman when he says, "I didn't mean for this to happen. I didn't *want* this to happen."

"What exactly?" Curious, I face him. "Me hating you? Me being uncomfortable at your wedding that isn't to me but to a friend? What exactly would you have prevented if you could?"

"Kissing Julianna."

He says it so abruptly, so confidently, I fall back a step. "What?"

"That day. I wouldn't have done that."

"Why, so I wouldn't have caught you?"

"No. Because she isn't you."

Holy freaking shit. A rushing roar reminding me of hurricanes barreling down on coastal shores floods my brain, shooting sensations all the way down to my fingertips. They sizzle and I curl my hands around my coffee.

I ran out of his office so quick that day and hightailed it

back to Charlotte as fast as my car could carry me, I never asked why. How long they'd been together behind my back.

I never asked anything. I got home and blocked his number. I only spoke with him once, when he called from a friend's phone, apologizing, wanting to explain.

"No explanation necessary and no apology wanted," I'd said, right before I hung up on him.

And now? Now he wants to rehash this? The morning before his wedding?

"That's a cruel thing to say about the woman who will be your wife tomorrow."

"I knew you were pulling away. You were changing. And you were so busy and didn't have time for me anymore. I thought... I thought if I could make you jealous, it would show you how much you still loved me."

"Have you lost your damn mind?" I take a step forward and slam my mug on the counter. God, last week he was ruining my donuts and today it's my morning cup of joe... personally, I think Roman has a knack for ruining everything he touches. "You have. You've absolutely lost your mind. You kissed my friend while we were engaged to make me jealous so I'd come *back* to you?"

He cringes and his lips curl. "Yeah. And I knew it wasn't a good idea, but she'd been hitting on me, and I knew you were coming that weekend and you always stopped by to have lunch with your dad, so I thought..."

"You'd use her to get what you wanted. How'd that work out for you?"

"She's not you."

"Stop saying that!" I hiss, teeth clenched together.

Shoving my fingers through my hair, I turn and pace the informal breakfast nook area we never use as a family. This was not the quiet moment I needed. It's so, so much worse.

"You know what?" I spin, flinging my hands out to the side before they slap my thighs. "I don't care. You made your choice and now you have to live with it and don't give me that bullshit song and dance about *me* changing. You were supposed to move to Charlotte with me. That's what we decided on. You chose to stay here. You chose to stay with our family's company. You chose this life and I truly, sure as hell, at least for Julianna, hope you're happy, or can find happiness in the choices you made because none of them have shit to do with me."

"I still love you."

My heart tumbles and twists and I might find some freaking satisfaction for my ego in all of this if I wasn't so damn blown away by his arrogant expression. As if the mere mention of the word love will have me dropping to my knees and begging him to change his mind about the wedding.

As. If.

"I don't think you know what that means." I'm completely sincere. I'm not sure he ever knew what it meant, not when it comes to others, anyway. Roman sure does love himself a whole lot.

"Do you know why Julianna's mad at you this morning and pulled that act she just did in here?"

"I haven't given it a single thought." It's a lie, but I'm too pissed off to care. Julianna can be cranky and selfish and manipulative, but she's got the guy and the wedding and the sparkling diamond, so why be mad at me?

"I called out your name. Last night."

It takes me a second for me to understand why that'd set her off. "Oh my God. Ew. Roman. Seriously! I don't want to hear that. I don't even want to *know* that... what the two of you do *or* what you call her. That's just... I don't even know what that is, or what you think you'd gain from telling me."

"Because I want you to know how much I really do miss you. How much I do love you. I look at her, and I think about you. I sleep next to my fiancée wishing it was you. We can get back what we had."

I'm so stunned, so grossed out and definitely in need of a drink to wash all this disgust out of my throat after his declaration. I don't realize he's moved until he's in front of me with his cool, lean fingers wrapped around my biceps.

"Jillian. Just listen to me for a minute. I didn't want her. I wanted you. That hasn't stopped."

"There is no us." I yank on my arms, but he's gripping me too tight. Not painfully but firm enough I can't escape. "You should have talked with me about that. You should have talked with me when you started changing plans years ago, but you didn't, and you let me believe you'd still move to Charlotte. That's what I wanted... and what I want, or deserve, at the very least, is a man who has a moral compass working enough to be honest."

"I know. And I'm sorry. I really am, but we can still fix this."

"No. You can't." We both freeze at the sound of Klaus's voice, cold as ice, solid as steel. "And I'm going to have to ask you to take your hands off my girlfriend."

In front of me, Roman's gaze narrows, but he's surprised enough his hold loosens. I shake away from him, stepping back, and soon, Klaus is at my back, his hand slipping around me until his palm is at my stomach.

The warmth of his hand and his touch instantly warms me to my toes.

"You okay, honey?" he asks, lips at my ear. His body is pulled tight, readied for battle.

He feels so damn good. So solid, so strong. He's nothing like my ex in front of me, expression still working quick enough I can tell he's plotting something else.

I fall into Klaus's hold and cover his hand at my stomach with my own. "Yeah. I'm good."

"Did he hurt you?"

"No. Roman can't hurt me. I'd have to care about him for that to happen."

In front of me, Roman flinches at my words and my tone. He finally steps back, running a hand down his face.

"I don't know where it all went so wrong."

If what he's saying is true, it went wrong well before he shoved his tongue down Julianna's throat, but the rest of it's not my problem.

"I can't help you with that. I can only tell you that I hope you and Julianna are happy. If you don't love her, don't think you can, you need to walk away from this wedding. It will destroy both of you." I glance up at Klaus. I'm in desperate need of fresh air and the burn in my lungs. "I really, really need to go for that run now."

## 15

## KLAUS

Our feet pound the pavement in tandem as we jog down Bay Street. The water on one side, Rainbow Row and the tree-lined streets of Charleston on the other. We're headed south toward The Battery, and while I know Jillian doesn't have a planned route, I trust she'll make this long enough to hurt. Which is probably exactly what she needs, and everything I've promised to save her from. Except, in opposition to the verbal lashings Roman gave her earlier, this is the kind of pain Jillian likes.

Like last night, I'm taking her lead in letting her take her time to decide how much to tell me. She overthinks, but she's also cautious and wise. Once she's worked out her issues in her head, I know she'll share her thoughts with me, which is only one more thing I like about her. Jillian considers options and feelings and facts into everything she does and how she behaves and treats people. If she didn't, there's no way she'd still be able to find any sort of compassion for Roman or Julianna.

We're barely a quarter mile into our jog, far from done

with our warm-up when she glances at me. "You're not going to ask?"

"What? How far are you planning on going today?" I know what she's really asking, but if she wants to avoid, it's not my job to push. "Six miles?"

"Eight?"

"Ten?"

She smirks at me, puffing out a breath. "How far is it back to Charlotte?"

"We can be there in three hours by car." And frankly, I'm ready to whisk her away. Sticking around for a rehearsal celebration at her house and then the actual wedding seems like a waste of time at this point. Hasn't she been through enough?

"Funny guy. I meant about this morning."

"I know. I don't need to ask."

"Why?"

"Because I heard your voices when I came down the stairs. Heard you two talking so I figured I'd give you a minute."

She laughs through her spaced breathing. "Spying on me?"

I keep my gaze on the uneven, old sidewalks and ahead of me. "Knew you could take care of yourself, figured I'd give him a minute. Took a lot out of me not to shove my fist in his face when I came out though, especially when I saw him holding you."

"As much as I wish I could have avoided all of that, I'm glad I actually had that conversation with him. If there was any doubt in my mind before if I was over him, this morning sealed it."

"He's a dick. Actually, I take that back. He's not a dick because I don't think he has one. The man is spineless and weak. He, and I hope you don't take offense to this, but he reminds me of your mom. Always fighting for something better, not caring who he lays out as he gets there."

"Too bad he's not as refined as my mother. Maybe then he'd have some class while he's shoving people to the side."

"What are you going to do?"

"About what?"

"Julianna and what he said to you."

"What about her?"

"Are you going to tell her Roman's only marrying her because she reminds him of you? Seems something she should at least know, don't you think?"

We reach The Battery and curve the road, following where I know will take us toward the U.S. Coast Guard Station.

Jillian is quiet for a while before she finally says, "You're assuming she doesn't already know the score, Klaus, and that's sweet as well as naive. Hell, he even admitted he called her by my name last night. You think she doesn't know what he's doing?"

"He did what?"

"You said you heard."

"Not that." He's worse than I thought, and I already thought he was nothing more than a chunk of ice on the rink. "I missed most of what he was saying until you started freaking out and started talking loud. Then his voice raised. Tell me what he said."

"Just that. He said he loved me and when I told him he didn't know what that meant he said he called Julianna my name last night. I *assumed* it was during... well, you know." She flips her hand in the air, never breaking her stride. "Personally, I'd like to scrub the memory of that entire conversation out of my brain, so don't make me repeat it."

Thank God we're running off steam. Otherwise, I don't know what I'd do if faced with Roman again. He's absolute scum. "Had I known he said that, I definitely would have punched him."

"Whatever. I could tell Julianna, but she obviously hates me and if I needed to know why before, I definitely know *now*. And the last thing I want to think about is them together like that. But the more I think about it, the more I think Julianna knows exactly what she's getting herself into. Her family doesn't have as much money. By marrying Roman, she gets to think she's reached some high social status, or whatever. She's getting something she wants out of this and she's going to have to live with it. Both of them are. I think that's punishment enough for them, don't you?"

Her breathing is increasing as she rants, telling me it's time to back off.

I don't want her lungs to wear out from talking before the run is over.

"Whatever you say, Jilly-Bean."

Her grin is my reward as we return to our run, talking less, until we find our rhythm and the warm-up is over and our bodies move on autopilot through Charleston, around the Medical Center and Charleston College before dodging pedestrians as the city awakens and we run back to her house.

THERE IS ONLY SO much torture a man can take and I am at my limit.

For well over a year, I've run next to Jillian, been distracted more than once over the bounce of her tits beneath a tank top and sports bra, and sometimes only the bra. I've licked my lips to the sight of her abs and her heavy huffs of breath as we reach mile seven or eight. And I've gone home hard from the sight of her firm ass in her tight running shorts.

Now that I've actually had my hands on her and the freedom to touch her and kiss her whenever I please, I'm ready to punch straight through my shorts as we arrive back at her house.

We fall in through the front door of her parents' house, dripping sweat, faces flushed, and limbs rubbery. All great signs of a perfect run.

She grasps the thick, gleaming railing and drags herself up the stairs. My eyes settle on that ass of hers. So damn perfect.

"This is why treadmills were invented," she moans, pulling herself up the stairs with every slow and painful step.

"We've had harder runs than this around Freedom Park."

She glares back at me, grinning, a thin line of sweat on her upper lip. "Pretty sure I whined and complained then."

Probably. As much as Jillian loves running, she has the habit of good-naturedly complaining all the way through them. "Get upstairs before you collapse. I don't think I can carry you today."

I've had to do it before. When she fell once, blamed a flat stretch of road as the cause afterward. Yet as she said it, she had this glazed look in her eyes—which were focused on my bare chest.

Possibly why I quit wearing a running shirt since then unless necessary.

"Bossy, bossy."

"You haven't seen anything yet." I step up toward her and slap her ass on the way. No man could resist that opening.

She squeals and jumps forward from it, but I race past her.

"I call dibs on the shower."

"The hell you do!" she calls out from behind me, but I know Jillian, she likes a good competition. I half-heartedly race up the stairs letting her catch me and when she does, we elbow and shove each other down the hall and around the corner through the doorway to her bedroom and into her bathroom.

My chest is heaving, and my cheeks hurt from smiling as we both reach the bathroom at the same time. Her wide grin matches mine as she tries to catch her breath.

"Looks like a tie," I say. "What do we do now?"

Jillian reaches for the hem of her tank top and pulls it over her head. Speech flees and my gaze drops.

Her bra has a zippered front. It takes everything in me not to reach for it, give it a good, firm tug so her breasts fall free, right into my waiting palms.

"A gentleman would let the lady go first."

"You're right." I swing my arm out toward the shower. "Ladies first."

"Are you going to give me privacy?"

I settle my hands on my hips. Slowly, she rakes her gaze over my chest. I let her look her fill, happily. "I'm not that much of a gentleman."

She finally meets my eyes, cheeks now flushed for an entirely different reason, right before a flicker of lust flashes in her eyes. "You sure you want me to step out?"

Jillian nibbles her bottom lip, right before her hands lift to the waistband of her shorts. She shoves them down her legs, revealing white underwear, simple, meant for comfort and not sexual appeal but it has that effect on my dick.

I harden as she goes to the zipper at her bra. The zip rings through the room, roaring in my ears. I make a move to close the distance between us as she gives me her back, grinning at me over her shoulder.

"Maybe we can share the shower," she says, "it's big enough for two."

"I can't promise I'll stay on my side."

She pushes off her bra, lets it fall from her arms behind her and steps into the shower. "Who says I want you to?"

I strip out of my own shorts and kick them to the floor right as her white panties get flung over the shower door. The water turns on and I grab my dick, squeezing hard in a futile effort to calm myself down.

Shit. Yes. This. It's what I've wanted for so long and never thought would happen.

Jillian offering herself to me is a thing to behold.

By the time I calm myself down, the glass doors are steamed up. I step in, immediately getting a face full of hot water. Brushing it away, two warm hands settle against my chest, and shove me against the wall.

"Holy shit," I mutter, right before Jillian's wet lips press against mine.

She's taking me by surprise, instigating this and in a heartbeat, I let her take the lead. She was uncertain when I brought up not pretending we're actually dating. If I push this too fast, my shot will vanish, so I wait until her tongue slides against my lips before opening my mouth and allowing her to kiss me.

And it's fucking beautiful. My dick is hard, pressed against her stomach, smashed between the two of us as she grinds against me, pushing her center against my thigh.

"Shit," I groan, sliding my hands down her back to her ass where I apply pressure.

"Klaus."

"Take whatever you need from me, honey."

Her mouth pulls off my mine, sliding to my throat where she sucks my flesh and water from me. My head hits the tile with a heavy thud. Heaven. Jillian putting her hands on me is absolute heaven.

"Klaus," she whimpers my name again, full of need and lust and urgency while she's still grinding on my thigh. There is absolutely no way in hell she's getting off this way.

"Hold on to me," I grunt right before I lift her. Her legs slip and slide on my thighs until she links them behind me and I carry her to the bench near the back of the shower. She wasn't kidding.

This shower can easily fit two with extra room for fun.

Placing her on the bench, I go to my knees. Cold tile with sharp edges dig into my skin, but I'm too focused on spreading and pushing Jillian's thighs open.

"So fucking sexy," I say, looking up at her. Her knees are wide open, her chest heaves, and she's looking down at me with nothing short of need. "You want this."

It's a statement, no room for question and denial, and thank God Jillian doesn't even try.

"Please," she gasps, running a hand through my hair. "I want this. You."

Please, for the love of God, I hope she means *you* in more than just me getting her off, but that's a conversation for another day. Or better moment. Right now, I'm too focused on sliding my finger through her wetness, dancing it around her bundle of nerves that's already swollen. As I enter her with one finger, she braces herself on the bench.

Her hips roll and arch into me, so I give her exactly what she wants.

Shifting my balance, I move higher, take her nipple into my mouth at the same time I add another finger and twist.

"Oh damn!"

"Quiet. Bet you don't want Mom or Nana hearing you getting off in this shower."

"Do not," she gasps, "talk about my mom or Nana right now."

"Yes, ma'am." Command given is a command received. I go back to work, playing with her nipples, tasting the wet skin until they're hardened points and she's clinging to my hair.

It's not long at all before those whimpers turn to bitten down cries and despite the water, she's so fucking soaked and close.

Bending down, I keep my fingers inside, torturing her slowly and take my first taste of her sweet sex, flicking my tongue over her clit again and again until my scalp burns from the way she clutches me, her hips buck with wild abandon and she comes in my mouth and all over my hand, her quieted screams bouncing off the tile.

I taste her through her orgasm, bringing her down slowly. My dick is so damn hard it's painful and when she's done, breathless, she drops to her knees in front of me, pushing me back almost into the water's spray and takes me in her hands.

"Confession," she says, wrapping her long, thin fingers around my thick length and learning the feel of me.

"What?"

"I hate giving blow jobs."

Like I give a shit how she gets me off right now. "What you're doing now is fucking perfect, honey." To prove it, I skate one hand up her arm, to the back of her neck and slam her mouth to mine.

My other hand wraps around hers, and I teach her how I like it. Harder. Long tugs and quick strokes until she reaches down and grabs my balls.

We jack me off together. Tongues tangling, mouths fused, hands connected. Right before I come, I yank my mouth off hers and press our foreheads together.

Together, we watch my dick swell and I come, clenching the back of her neck, grunting like a caveman, spilling my seed all over our hands and the tile at our feet.

"Fucking perfect," I say again and kiss her. "I think you might be my favorite, too."

For that, I get a pinch to my thighs, a wicked gleam in her eye, and a soft kiss I'll be thinking about for days.

Yeah. Jillian's perfect for me.

Now I just have to convince her of that when the weekend is over.

## 16

## JILLIAN

Klaus and I spend the rest of the day lounging in my room, ignoring everyone in my family. A barrage of workers and caterers descend on my parents' home shortly after lunch to decorate for the rehearsal celebration and prepare the dinner which will kick off the night.

For my part, I'm pretty damn languid, boneless from not only the orgasm Klaus gave me in the shower, but from the two he gave me once we got out. One in the bathroom, me watching him use his fingers in the mirror while I gripped the counter's edge and then once again in the bed, when he used his mouth.

I can now say that Klaus was absolutely right.

His dick is huge. Maybe not large enough to be its own person like he claimed, but impressive, in both girth and length, almost scarily so.

"We should probably think about getting out of this bed at some point."

He's propped on his side, one arm bent and resting his head on his palm. He's playing with my hair with his other hand, sliding his fingers through my hair and draping it over my breast. I slid into a tank top and underwear after the last time in case anyone accidentally, or rudely and intentionally, barges in, but Klaus has forgone the same idea. I'm blessed with the display of his chest, his light hair that spreads across his muscles, narrowing at his abs.

"And rejoin reality? No thank you."

Thinking 'bout seeing Teresa tonight makes me sad. And will Norman be here? Looking sickly? It's a shame Roman ended up being such a douche since he had such nice parents.

Plus, there will have to be more conversations with Nana and my mom before we leave.

Klaus ditches my hair and rubs his thumb between my brows. "When you get worried, a line shows here."

I slap his hand away. "Thanks for pointing out my wrinkles."

"It's not a wrinkle. It's a worry line. And you don't have anything to worry about today."

"No. Just hard conversations I'd much rather ignore. Think anyone would notice if we snuck out and went back home?"

He offered during our run and now that I'm not huffing and puffing, I'm seriously considering it.

"Yeah. I think they'd notice."

I flip to my back. Covering my hands with my face, I heave a sigh. And then shiver, as Klaus's warm palm lands on my stomach, pushing up my tank top so his hand rests on my bare flesh.

"What's the thing you're most worried about?"

"Well, Julianna could decide to tell everyone Roman calls my name when they have sex, and trust me, right now it's taking everything in me not to puke at not only the idea of that, but that he had the nerve to tell me."

"With you on that one. You think she'll say something?"

"I think she's a loose cannon, but..." Do I? She has what she wants, and if she's willing to keep him even knowing he's a slimeball that's definitely not my problem. "I don't know if she will, but I'll be subjected to nasty comments and uglier looks for certain. And then there's Teresa."

"You like her."

"Love her. I almost wonder if I would have left Roman years earlier if it hadn't been for her. She was so much more of a mom to me than my own, she was hard to say goodbye to, and Norman... I can't imagine their pain. Plus, Nana."

"Who's probably faking a nap right now in the solarium if you want to go get that one out of the way."

"Stop making sense," I grumble. "I don't even know what to say to her. Last night, she was flat out mean, and I've never seen that from her."

"Yeah, she was mean to your mom, but she was still upset on your behalf. Your grandma loves you, even if you've learned she's not as perfect as you thought she was."

"You're right."

"Ah. The best two words a man can hear. Want to repeat it?"

"No, because now you're being all cocky."

"I'll show you cocky."

He moves quickly, covering me with his body and cages in my legs. I think he's going to kiss me, but then that grin of his I love so much turns salacious.

"Klaus," I whisper.

"What?" he asks, right before his fingers dig into my sides and tickle me.

"Ah! No! Get off!" I buck my hips, digging my fingers into

his wrists, and twist and turn, trying to get him off me. It hurts so good and so awful at the same time. I'm laughing and crying while he tortures me with strong fingers and strong thighs that keep me cemented in place.

"Stop!" I shriek. I buck my hips one more time and somehow manage to loosen his hold just enough until the pressure on his hands yanks him forward.

Right before he falls and hits me, I roll us, flipping us over so I'm on top.

With our positions reversed, I do what I thought he was going to do to me before he attacked, and I kiss him.

His fight leaves him instantly, and he cradles me, holding the back of my head firmly against him. Beneath me is muscles and hardness everywhere.

Glorious. Delightful.

Kissing Klaus is on my top five list of things to do with my spare time.

My hands roam his body, his arms, his shoulders, everywhere I can reach until he takes the kiss deeper, presses against me and groans down my throat.

Pushing off him, I scramble off the bed and to the floor.

"What the hell?" he asks, stunned, hazy-eyed, completely turned-on based on the obvious tenting beneath my sheets. "Get back here," he says, turning to the side to reach for me.

"That's for tickling me."

"I'm not sure the punishment fits the crime." To prove it, he shoves down the sheet and wraps his hand around that long length that makes my mouth wet and other parts soaked.

If I don't get out of here, we're going to spend the rest of the day getting sweaty. Or sweatier. And while we haven't had sex, I'm not ready for that to happen. Not tonight anyway, with our house overtaken with workers and family.

I drag my gaze off his beautiful show and smirk. "I think you've definitely learned a hard lesson today. Next time, remember this."

Hurrying to the closet, I grab a pair of cut-off sweat shorts and a shirt I can throw over my tank top.

"I'm going to go deal with Nana. You take care of... well... that."

"With pleasure," he moans, hips arching. Teasing. God, if he's doing this to impress me, I am sold. Klaus is magnificent. "But remember, while you're in there dealing with Nana, I'll be in here. Hard, horny, and thinking of you."

"You fight dirty." I point a finger at him and scowl.

"Hurry back."

I fly out the door and slam it behind me before I can change my mind. Before I'm saying, "Nana? Who's Nana?"

I FIND her exactly where I thought she'd be, in the solarium, dressed in another bright colored muumuu, but today she's not sleeping. Or pretending to sleep.

Instead, she's pacing, looking like she's been here long enough to wear the shine right off the tiled floor.

Knocking on the door, I get her attention and step inside. Where I'm usually met with cheek kisses and warm hugs, today she stops moving and stays far away, crossing her arms over her chest.

"Wondered how long it'd take you to come yell at me."

I've never once questioned Nana. Always taken her side and believed her ramblings, thinking she was just an eccentric lady who had a rough life and a daughter who turned her back on her, but now I'm seeing things more clear. And I can see it... her flakiness. Her laissez-faire attitude negatively affecting her child who wants compassion and care and doesn't want to have to take care of herself.

I'm not angry with Nana. Not even disappointed. I do plan on having an honest conversation with her.

"I'm not here to yell at you, but I think we should talk, don't you?"

"That boy was never good enough for you, and your mama is in the wrong for bringin' him here and havin' this party."

"I agree." I walk toward her, flinching from the brightness of the sun shining down. "And I let Mom know that last night, too. I also understand where she's coming from, with her perspective about helping Teresa. They're her oldest friends. She wants to help them."

"By putting her own daughter on the back burner?" she scoffs.

A laugh bursts forth at the absurdity. "That's hilarious, Nana. Because last night my mom said the same thing about you. Weren't you out partying, leaving her alone to take care of herself? Didn't you care more about having fun than being a mom?"

"Well. That's just not true." She loosens her arms wrapped around her stomach like a blanket and squeezes her fingers together and begins pacing again. All actions that belie her words. "I loved her."

"I'm sure you did. But maybe you resented her too? That if maybe it wasn't for her, Grandpa wouldn't have left?"

"Please. Good riddance. That man was nothing but trouble since the day I met him."

"But you married him. And you had a baby with him."

"And then he left. He left me. Twenty years old, no

college education, and no job that could handle all of what I was supposed to do."

"And I sympathize, Nana, but don't you think all my mom wanted was her mom to take care of her the best way possible even if she couldn't have everything?"

"I gave her everything she needed."

"Did you?"

"Humph. I did the best I could."

"Did you?"

Her lips curl, clearly irritated I'm pushing her, but maybe I'm not the only one who needs to mend relationships between mother and daughter this weekend. "Why did you come this weekend, Nana? You didn't have to be here."

"We're family." Her gaze slices toward the windows and she shifts back and forth on her feet. "And because I knew it'd be hard for you, so I wanted to be here for you."

"Because you love me."

"Of course I do."

"And because you love my mom? And maybe, because you knew this weekend would be hard for her, too?"

As little credit as I've always given my mom, being more cyborg than compassionate parental figure, so many things are becoming clearer. Her own inability to care for a child because she never had that. In her quest to give me everything she didn't have, she also neglected the most important part.

"Clarabella is my daughter. Of course I love her."

"Then maybe you should tell her. I know I'd like to hear that from my mom every once in a while."

Nana shakes her head and purses her lips. Funny how the two women in my life are certifiably the most stubborn women I've ever met. Not exactly going to look too far into that and inspect my own stubbornness. That's for a different time, and maybe mimosas and donuts with Becca.

Nana sits down on the chair, rests the back of her head against it and closes her eyes. "Wouldn't do but a damn bit of good now, anyhow."

"I don't know." I take the seat next to her. From furious last night to compassionate today, I'm definitely learning a few things about myself. Who knew coming home would be so educational? "I know I'd still like to hear it every once in a while. Maybe have a mom who says, *'great job'* when I get a promotion. When I bought my home, a nice *'I'm proud of you'* would have made me smile for days. I don't think a girl ever stops needing her mom."

"I might not have done a whole lot right by her, but I do know by the time I figured that out, she was already gone," she admits and shakes her head. "Don't think she'd much mind hearing now anything I have to say to her."

"I guess you won't know if it matters unless you try. But you came here when you didn't need to because you knew your daughter would have a hard weekend. Says a lot already about how much you love her. Just might help if she knows it, too."

Silence descends. I'll let Nana stew on this for now. Get back to Klaus. "I need to start getting ready, I think. You going to be there for the party tonight?"

"Yes, child. I'll be there. Give your nana a smooch before you go back to the hottie stashed away in your room."

Nana. She might be realizing things, but she'll always be this Nana to me, even if I have a broader understanding of why she's this way.

"You got it."

I kiss her cheek, expecting that to be the end of it but when I pull back she says, "All those years I had something great living under my roof, a part of me, and I never once loved her for being her, too damn mad she was a part of him, too."

"You should tell her." Lord help her stubborn soul. If I don't keep reminding her, she'll probably head home without fixing anything.

"This weekend isn't about us."

"I'm beginning to think this weekend is about all of us getting second chances and fresh starts, Nana." I kiss her cheek again and stand. Movement at the doorway grabs my attention and I glance, see my mom, face pale, eyes wide. She catches me watching her and ducks out of sight.

"Think about it, okay?" I squeeze her hand, leave her to her thoughts and the sun and her fake nap.

By the time I'm in the hallway, there's no sign of my mom anywhere.

How much has she heard?

And will it change a thing?

**17**

---

**KLAUS**

"And then she just left! Can you believe that?"

I straighten my tie. Behind me in the full-length mirror's reflection in Jillian's room, she's prattling up a storm. Thank God the floors are wood. Carpet fibers would probably set on fire from the heat of her panic. Ever since she came back from her talk with Nana, she's been upset.

Showered, and now with her makeup done, she's told me everything.

The few times I've tried to interject, she's kept talking. Figured not answering her now is the safer alternative.

"Klaus!"

"Yes?"

"I asked if you can believe Mom just walked away like that?"

Oh. So her first non-rhetorical question out of twenty. I smooth down my tie and face her, resting against her dresser. "Your mom doesn't seem like a woman to jump right into confrontation, so yeah, I can believe it."

"But she just walked away! She could have come on in, they could have talked."

"Do you think them talking for five minutes now, before your mom has a busy night ahead of her is going to solve what sounds like fifty years of issues between them?"

She pouts. "I hate it when you make sense." She's still dressed in her robe, hiding all the sexiest parts of her. I already tried distracting her earlier to no avail, so I've pledged to keep my hands to myself.

That doesn't mean I can't comfort her.

"Come here." I hold out my arms and push off the dresser. It takes her a few seconds to decide and then we meet half-way, Jillian falling into my arms. I wrap mine around her and hold her tight. It takes two deep breaths for her shoulders to relax, another two for her to become so close we're almost fused together. She smells like fruit and alluring woman, but now's not the time to have my body run away from my thoughts of how damn good she smells and feels in my arms.

"Do you know what I need right now?"

"Wine?"

"Close. I was thinking mimosas and donuts with Becca."

Ouch. That stings deep considering she's in my arms, burrowing into me, and I've been the one with her all weekend.

"I can get you anything you need or want but that, but if you want to talk to her, I can head downstairs, give you privacy."

The house is empty, outside Nana being somewhere around. Stetson and Claire have left for the rehearsal to be with Teresa. Caterers are still here and from what I've heard, the downstairs main floor looks like roses and gardenias exploded all over the place.

I have no idea how many people are planning on being at the dinner post-rehearsal, but with the amount of activity that's been going on all day, it feels like Claire planned a wedding reception, not the rehearsal dinner portion.

"No." Jillian tugs her arms out from my hold and wraps them around me, holding me loosely. "Stay right here for another minute. You being here is the only good part about this weekend."

"Even better than all the free wine you can drink all night to your heart's content?"

"That's a close second," she murmurs.

My chest vibrates with laughter and Jillian tips her head back. "I didn't mean anything about Becca. Our brunches have always been bitch sessions, mostly about my mom. She's going to freak the hell out when I tell her everything that's gone down this weekend."

"Weekend isn't over. Nana could still puke up her dentures."

She laughs, earning me a smile I haven't seen in days. Wide and gleaming, her blue eyes look more like the ocean than the storm I've seen in them the last few days.

"Let's go crack open the wine before your parents get back. That'll really piss off your mom."

She rolls to her toes and slides her mouth over mine. "That sounds like the best plan. Just let me get dressed."

"What a wonderful idea," I murmur. My hands go to work at the loosely knotted belt at her waist. I push open her robe and step back as it slides off her shoulders.

She's naked in front of me, spiking interest down my spine and straight to my dick.

Standing nude for everything but her beautiful smile in front of me, there isn't a hint of embarrassment. She doesn't attempt to cover up. Her confidence in most things she does might be the sexiest about her.

"Did you want to help me get dressed?" she asks wryly.

"Nope. Just wanted to see you naked again."

"You're a dork."

"Yup." A dork who's in love with her. I'm not sure she's still quite figured that out yet, even if she's let me have her in so many of the ways I've imagined for years.

She has enough drama now without me making it clear though. I will when we get back home. We have time.

Jillian shamelessly struts toward the closet. Firm, tight ass sways with her exaggerated movements and I grip the edges of the dresser so I don't chase after her. My current plan is to get her tipsy enough and happy enough before everyone comes back from the church that she won't even care she's attending the rehearsal dinner for Roman or that she and her mom have unsettled issues. Or that Nana isn't the woman she believed her to be.

My patience is rewarded when she returns a few minutes later, dressed to fucking cause grown men to die of a heart attack at the sight of her. Skintight black dress that hugs every curve of her body like it was poured over her. It flares slightly past the knees, creating a mermaid-like fit and as she walks to me, taller now, thanks to whatever heels she's wearing, she looks like she's gliding along the floor.

It's a simple dress, but beautiful. A modest cleavage cut at her breasts and only held between two of the thinnest dress straps I've seen in my life. And as she turns... holy shit.

*Thunk.* My jaw hits the wood floor.

"Holy shit. Where's the rest of your dress?"

It's missing the back. Cut so damn deeply down her lower back, I can imagine everything she *isn't* wearing. Like a bra. Or underwear.

Heaven help me.

"You like?" My temptress holds out her arms to the side and does a slow spin, grinning evilly at me the entire time.

"Is this punishment for tickling you again?"

"Nope." Still grinning.

"For jerking off while you were leaving earlier?"

She comes toward me and tugs on my tie. With a fierceness in her eyes, she says, "You made me wet and horny before I had to go talk to my nana. Evil."

"So this is you getting back at me?"

"Partly." Her smile gleams and she steps back and winks. "Also because I know it will really, really piss Julianna off and that sounds like fun tonight."

Awesome. More fights and drama. Just what we need.

"I'm going to have to work hard at not murdering Roman or any of the groomsmen with the way they're going to be drooling over you. You know that right?"

"Yes, but if you behave, I'll give you a very nice, very sexy present later."

"You might be the most evil temptress I've ever met."

"Also the nicest."

"Sexiest."

"Loyal and hilarious, too."

"Incredible sweet tasting." A blush hits her cheeks. "Let's go, vixen. Get me drunk so I can blame the alcohol when I give the best man or future groom a black eye."

"See? Already this night sounds like fun!"

I have no idea what's gotten into her, but I'm here for it.

And Jillian.

For as long as she'll have me, bloody knuckled if necessary.

∼

Guests return to the house, Claire and Stetson first among them, leading them inside. Jillian is on her second glass of wine and is sporting a shimmering pink hue to her cheeks showing the wine is taking effect exactly as I hoped.

She's tipsy enough that when Nana makes her entrance, Jillian heads straight to the bar and grabs a glass of wine for her, acting as if their earlier conversation never happened.

It's Stetson who comes to my side and nods at the ice water in my hands.

"Not drinking tonight?"

"I try not to much during pre-season." As it is, even with the run, I've been slacking on the workouts. I'll need to work extra hard tomorrow before the wedding to make up for only getting in the run today.

"You're dedicated."

It sounds like approval. Surely I'm reading him wrong, but when I face him, he's got his sights set on Jillian, a far-off look in his eyes.

"From the time she was little, Jillian was never who Claire hoped she'd be."

My jaw tightens. If he thinks that's a *good* thing, that Claire had expectations already instilled in a daughter before she was born, he's sadly mistaken.

"I think maybe with all of that, we forgot to appreciate who she was becoming, instead Claire kept wondering why they had nothing in common."

"I'm not sure why you're telling me this." Nor do I like the sounds of it.

"Claire didn't have an easy beginning to life as it is. I'm sure you've now heard. For the longest time, she didn't want kids. Was afraid she wouldn't know how to love them and then she thought she'd raise her daughter to have all the things she never did and that'd be enough." He sips his drink, whiskey I'm guessing. Probably expensive. "Suppose we still didn't get it right."

"For as long as I've known Jillian, all she's ever talked about wanting was parents who loved her and were proud of her." I shrug as if it's that simple, but something tells me showing affection doesn't come easy to Stetson either.

"You're a good man, Klaus. Glad she's got someone like you."

He steps to head away, but I stop him with his name. "It's not too late."

He raises his glass. "Enjoy your night."

I stay rooted to the floor, beautiful people all around me still filtering in from the church, stunned to my very core. For all of Jillian's claims over the years, her parents didn't like her, I'm shocked to learn that maybe they just didn't know how.

Freaking bizarre.

Ahead of me, a robust woman with Roman's dark coloring pulls Jillian into a hug, shaking her back and forth. Jillian lifts her hand out to the side to protect her wine glass.

Teresa. Roman's mother, I can only suspect.

I head that way, rescuing Jillian if she needs it, comforting her if she needs that and when I'm close, in a booming, Italian voice, way too loud for what she's saying to be overheard but seemingly uncaring she says, "I tell you what, we just don't know what that boy of ours is thinking."

Yeah... she and me both.

## 18

## JILLIAN

It's painful and beautiful to see Teresa, dark-rimmed eyes showing her exhaustion and pale skin showing her stress, standing in front of me. But her hug is comforting, reminding me of all the years she's showered me with affection I so desperately craved growing up.

"I tell you what," she says, and she hasn't even said hello to me. "We just don't know what our boy is thinking."

She pulls back from our hug and then I'm touched again, right before the scent of Klaus hits me and his hand slides to my stomach. I'd imagine it's because he likes touching me. A part of me is sure it's so he can hide the missing back of my dress from prying eyes.

Possessive he is, in a way I hadn't anticipated and really, freaking love.

"Oh." Teresa's eyes light up. "I heard you brought a date, but this... well, you are handsome," she says to Klaus.

I roll my eyes. I've been getting that a lot this weekend. Mostly from older women. If Klaus objects to being objectified, he doesn't show it.

I tilt my head and am rewarded with his panty-melting

smile. "Thank you. Klaus Newman, Jillian's boyfriend. You must be Teresa."

"I am. Nice to meet you, too. How long have you been together because until your mom said something earlier, I wasn't aware you were dating."

She lets that linger, almost disappointed, like she'd hoped I'd come back for Roman and set her world to rights. I won't go on with how offensive I find her son.

"Not long," I say, at the exact same time Klaus says, "Awhile."

"Oh?"

"What Klaus means is that we've been friends for a few years now but just got together recently."

"I got tired of pretending I wasn't in love with her when I think I started the first time we met."

Heart. Stop. My entire body freezes at his quiet but bold declaration. He said the same thing to Nana before, but now? In front of Teresa. It almost pains me to let the lie settle between us.

But oh, if it were true....

I shake it off and take a sip from my glass, forcing my jaw to relax.

"Oh, well that's lovely, dear. I am truly happy for you if you're happy."

"Thanks, Teresa. And I'm sorry to hear about Norman. Is he here?"

"We had someone take him home. Getting him out, well, it takes a lot out of him."

Tears burn my eyes and I force them down. "I'm truly sorry. He's a good man."

"Well, he's a fighter too, so we're hoping, but, well, we'll make the best of what we're given. It's all we can do, right?"

"And speaking of, I truly do hope Roman and Julianna are happy together."

"Please. That girl probably has the shovel with her to start digging for all our hidden treasures."

Behind me, Klaus barks out a laugh and my own bursts free. "Teresa!"

"It's true. She'll get that ring and my son and she won't stop wanting for the rest of her days. I only hope Roman loves her enough to tell her no every once in a while." She shakes her head, for as much of a smartass as she can be, her frustration is clear as is the lack of love for her daughter-in-law.

"Perhaps Chloe will choose more wisely. How is she?"

Roman's little sister is only twenty-one and last I heard, she fled Charleston for New York to be a fashion designer. Like me, she never fit in with her family which meant even when we were younger, we bonded.

"That girl does my head in. Living life up in New York, going to school, I think at least sometimes, and flying through her trust fund so fast she's going to be broke by the time she graduates. She's here, or will be soon. The wedding party is getting pictures done. At the rehearsal." She rolls her eyes and scoffs. "Don't know how Julianna's parents are affording all this insanity, but I sure am glad I'm not footing her bill. Word on the street is her dress costs more than my first car. Probably tacky as that car, too."

"Teresa," I scold her, but inside, my heart is doing a little happy dance.

"I'll let you go, sugar, and we'll keep that old bitty gossip between us, won't we?"

"Absolutely. We'll talk soon."

"Do." She kisses my cheek. "And don't be a stranger. I know this weekend will be busy, but Norman doesn't have many left, so make sure you come back and see us. We won't even have to let Roman know."

"I will. And I'll make sure I spend time with him before I leave, too. Love you, Teresa."

"Always, my beautiful stubborn girl."

She leans in, says goodbye to Klaus and when she's gone, he bends down to my ear. "Beautiful *and* stubborn? She has you pegged, doesn't she?"

"Hmm?"

He laughs in my ear. "I'm beginning to think I don't know who's crazier, Teresa or Nana, but I'm pretty sure I can guarantee the fun of tonight is just getting started."

"Yeah. Fun. Like a root canal. Come on. I need more wine before the wedding party shows."

"How many of these people do you know?" Klaus asks.

We've moved to the outdoor garden area that's fancily decorated with fairy lights and fresh gardenias potted every-where. Vines drape from the portico. My parents' house looks more like it's been prepped and decorated for a wedding, not the rehearsal. The familiar bubble of irritation is alive and well, rumbling in my gut.

"Most. Except for Julianna's sister's friends. Victoria is three years younger than us so while Julianna and I were close, Victoria was more a nuisance than anything."

Victoria, along with the rest of the wedding party, skipped in an hour ago. The entire wedding party is now outside, drinking at the open bar. The girls are dressed in matching mint green dresses and the men in light gray suits.

Of course Julianna has to have her wedding party match for the rehearsal. After seeing the extravagance of this night,

I can only imagine how overblown her wedding tomorrow will be, despite trying not to think about it.

"And the men?"

"All Roman's friends. One cousin. Some are from when he went to graduate school, but I was busy finding a job in Charlotte, so I didn't spend too much time with him on campus there."

Two of them have been not so inconspicuously shooting glances at Klaus, turning back to their friends, talking with heads close together, and then repeating it all over again. One is Kurt, Roman's graduate school roommate. The other escapes me, but I believe he was one of Roman's fraternity brothers at Charleston College where he did his undergrad.

"It's weird, isn't it, that we were together for so long and yet weren't a part of each other's lives?" It's moments like this when that reality hits me. We dated for six years. Through college, graduate school, finding my first apartment after getting hired at my current job. And yet, we never really entwined our lives together.

Almost as if we were never actually meant to be. Always too different. Funny, how I'm just now realizing that maybe the only reason I stayed with Roman, or even went out with him, was because our families expected it. Hell, not that it was ever mentioned, but I wouldn't now be surprised if my father said he wanted us running their company together.

And I put up with all of it for the sake of family approval.

"It looks like you have fans," I murmur around the rim of my wine glass.

"Hard not to notice. They're not exactly hiding."

"Are you going to go talk to them?"

"Nope. If they want to meet me, they can come to me."

"Playing hard to get?" I nudge him with my hip and

when I pull back, he drops his arm behind my back, holding on to my hip and pressing me against him.

"No. But I'm right where I want to be and I have no intention of leaving you, until you ask me to."

I flush from his praise, from the compliment, and from the warm brush of his breath skimming my cheeks. His lips press against mine and linger. "Have I told you tonight how absolutely ravishing you look? And how badly I want to strip you out of that dress?"

A shiver, having nothing to do with the weather outside rolls down my spine and spreads outward, making my fingertips and toes tingle.

"You haven't mentioned that yet," I say, once the sensations coursing through me give me time to think. "But I do vividly remember the way your jaw dropped when you saw me earlier and that's enough."

"Later," he says, pulling back and giving me a look that sears me straight down to my toes. "It will be your jaw dropping, while you try to not scream my name."

He's right. My jaw's already falling open in shock. My heart is tumbling without thought, head over heels in love with this guy and how much he wants me.

"Excuse me?"

We both turn toward the newcomer. Kurt. Or Karl. One of the guys from the bar is next to him. Their eyes are glassy, pupils dilated. The color on their cheeks and the slight sway of their bodies show how drunk they are.

"Are you Klaus Newman from the Ice Kings?"

"I am."

"Dude," they both drawl, as if they've practiced the synchronization of it. "You freaking rock, and your team is amazing. Do you think we can get your picture taken with us?"

"Do you mind?" he asks me, and slowly trails his hand over my lower back, stepping away from me.

"Go on, superstar. Go be awesome."

He shakes his head, chuckling, and then gets swallowed up in the small throng of people while I look on.

My pretend boyfriend is a famous hockey player and for some reason, after years of our friendship, I realize that it means this... interruptions, fans, public spotlight, and potential photos of us on hockey wives and girlfriends website so female fans can tear into us—me, most likely—with their criticism.

All things I managed to avoid as his friend and running partner.

The question is, does it matter?

I stay on the peripheral while he takes photos with the *dude* bros and then is accosted by other members of the wedding party. I glance around, finding Julianna, hands wrapped around Roman's forearm, holding him tightly, but her gaze is on me.

Fiery. Irate.

Probably at having the attention stolen from her on her own night of glory.

I try to summon the energy to be pleased about this, and right as I go to tip my glass in her direction and rub it in, I stop. Being catty isn't me, nor is it who I want to be. Once Roman and Julianna get married, they'll both continue to be in my life in some way. There's no way to avoid it. I will have a lifetime ahead of me of seeing them at holidays or when I come back to visit.

And truly, I'm so damn happy this isn't going to be my life, I don't have the energy to be mad at Julianna anymore, either.

I go to her, weave through tall tables and wedding party

guests, most I know or recognize but I don't stop until I'm at Julianna's side, her face pinched with irritation as Klaus steals her glory.

"You look beautiful tonight," I tell her. She always does.

"I know."

"Are you nervous at all about tomorrow?"

"Why would I be?"

I sigh. Of course she isn't going to make this easy. "I don't know, Julianna, maybe because you're getting married. Committing to someone for the rest of your life. I just... we were friends once, I think." As much as we could be with the competition between us I hadn't ever been aware of. "I was hoping we could put all of this behind us. Once you two are married, like it or not, you'll be connected to my family forever, to me. Wouldn't it be nice if we could see each other and not hate each other?"

She sips her drink, and for a moment, I swear I see her eyes soften to the girl I used to remember but it's gone in a flash as she faces me. "I'm fully aware of the commitment I'm making tomorrow, Jillian. I get Roman and everything that comes with him. We might not have what you two had, but what we have works."

"I hope so. I really do. I really do hope you two are happy."

"Please." She scoffs, as if happiness and marriage is a foreign concept. "As long as he gives me children, I don't really care whose name he calls while he's with me. He'll give me exactly what I want and in return, he knows he'll have a wife who will always be with him. It's easy and we both walk away winners."

I cringe at her words. At the memory I'm trying so hard to scrub from my brain and how quickly she can use it like a whip. But I can see the honesty in her eyes. Perhaps they're right.

Maybe they're not marrying for love like Roman admitted earlier, but they're both getting something from this. And truly, it's not my place to care or judge.

"I wish you both the best of luck, then. And I mean that." I figure they'll need it. "Enjoy the rest of your evening."

I walk away before she can toss any more verbal assaults my way. So much for trying to be the bigger person here. After refreshing my drink, I head toward Klaus, to his side, because bloggers and online photos be damned... I'm thrilled to be with him, in any way.

Only, I hope we can figure out what that is soon, before my heart falls to its doom and splatters to the cement.

## 19

## JILLIAN

Klaus's mouth trailing down my throat pulls me from slumber. For a moment, while his hand skims my stomach, sliding against my flesh and beneath my tank top, I believe I'm still dreaming. After all, it's not the first time I've dreamed of this happening.

But no, this is real, with the evidence of his own arousal hard against my hip.

"You like that spot," I murmur, voice thick from sleep and dry from too much alcohol last night. I've discovered he really loves kissing me behind my ear. Not that I'm complaining. Sensations spark to life whenever he touches me there.

"I like the way it makes you shiver and the cute little sounds you make when I kiss you here."

To prove his point, he kisses me again, finding that spot perfectly that I'm certain has a direct line to my sex. My body warms and ignites, and my hips roll on their own accord, seeking further contact. I whisper his name and turn to him, shoving my face in the crook of his shoulder. My lips find his skin and I close my eyes as I taste him.

It also spurns him on, his hand at my stomach slides farther up to my breasts. He cups one, feels the weight of me before tracing my nipple with his thumb. His hands, calloused and rough from his hard work on the ice scrape my flesh, creating the most delicious friction against my skin.

"Oh God," I whisper a groan into his throat and turn to him. I throw one of my legs over his hips and his erection presses right to my core.

I'm already panting, rolling my hips against him while he kisses my throat and shoulder and his fingers do a dance of their own on my nipple, tugging and scraping with a pinch that shoves my hips forward into him.

"Oh God."

I'm already so close and he's barely touched me. "Klaus."

"I love the way you light up for me, Jilly-Bean."

I huff a laugh. That stupid nickname at a time like this. And then I'm shoved to my back, Klaus's legs falling to either side of me, caging me in while his body hovers over me. He stares down at me and licks his lips.

"Tell me you want this."

If by this he's meaning him inside me, I'm all for it. The entire weekend has led up to this moment. Days of foreplay primed me for this.

In answer, I lift my hips, brushing my center over the tip of him. Both of us are still clothed, at least I am. Klaus is in nothing but boxer briefs that don't hide his need for me and my top is shoved up above my breasts. Breasts that are heaving from everything he's done to me already and anticipating everything still to come.

"Jillian—"

I don't answer with words. Instead, I curl my hand around the back of his head and pull him to me, fusing our mouths together. I ache to increase the speed, the depth, and the intensity but Klaus keeps it a slow, languid kiss where he learns my mouth and lips. Where our tongues battle for dominance and my body craves him more than it already did.

"Please," I groan against his mouth, and he shakes his head. "Slow."

"Now."

He chuckles against my mouth. "Not the time for our wordplay games."

He pulls back and brushes his thumb over my cheekbone, circles my lips. I attempt to bite his tongue, suck him into my mouth to turn him on but he pulls his thumb away, eyes flashing a stormy blue, flecks of gold I rarely see edge around his dilated pupils.

"I want you." And it feels like he means it. For more than this moment right now.

Before I can let fear send me running, I press my hand to his cheek and lift my head, meeting him halfway.

He kisses me, slides his tongue into my mouth and settles his weight between my legs.

"Then take me," I whisper against his mouth, before kissing him again.

He promised slow and he delivers. He teases me with whisper-light brushes of his hands and his lips all over my body until there's an inferno boiling inside me.

I lift my arms, letting him shove off my tank top. His eyes turn molten, heated with desire and then his mouth descends, sucking a nipple in his mouth as his hands work at my boy shorts, yanking them down.

As he drives me crazy, forcing my fingers to claw at the sheets to maintain some kind of control and bite my lip so I don't cry out, he shoves off his own boxers.

He kneels up in front of me in all his full, God-given glory, stroking himself. My gaze is riveted to his hand. The bunch of his muscles on his arms. The tightness of his abs, but most importantly, the impressive size of his erection, long and thick, and hard—for me.

"Oh my," I sigh, licking my lips.

He slides back and I reach for him, grabbing his thighs before he can scoot off the bed. "Where are you going?"

"To get a condom," he says, giving me the most adorable look. So I'm not doing a good job of hiding how much I want him.

But at this point, why would I?

"I'm on the pill. I haven't been with anyone since..." I don't say Roman's name. As I speak, Klaus's jaw slackens and he inhales a heavy breath.

"I get tested for the team. But..."

"I trust you."

He closes his eyes for a moment, tense shoulders and another large exhale. "I'm not going to lie. I would really like to be inside you without anything separating us, but if you want to wait..."

"No." This weekend might be the only time I have to enjoy him, and I want to enjoy *all* of him.

"Please, Klaus. It's okay. I promise."

Decision made, he stalks back to me and pushes my legs apart as he retakes his position between my legs, spreading me wide open for his languid perusal. And peruse he does, like he has all day and years to take his time with me.

"I'm a bit nervous," he says, as he trails his fingers through my center, pushing them into me. I slide up the bed from the force and groan.

"Oh God. That's... that's good."

"It's been years since I haven't worn a condom. I might not last from how good I know you'll feel."

"Keep doing what you're doing and I won't last long at all."

"Good." He bends down and the last thing I see is the wicked gleam in his eyes before he settles his mouth at my center.

I come almost immediately. Grabbing the sheets. His hair, his shoulder. The faint tinge of metallic hits my tongue. I've bitten myself to stop from screaming out.

"Shit, shit," I chant, my body feeling like it's exploding from the inside out, and right as I come down, he settles himself at my center and slides forward.

One orgasm rolls straight into a second, or the world's longest orgasm on record but I can't stop. He feels *incredible*, filling me, almost painfully so as my body stretches to accommodate him.

"Klaus." I reach for him, and as if he knows how much I need his touch, he falls forward, clasping his hands into mine on the pillow.

He sears his mouth to mine, hips moving hard, slow, rolling and threatening to ignite my very core.

"Oh shit. You feel so damn good, honey." He shoves his mouth against my throat, and I roll my hips to meet his powerful thrusts.

This is Klaus. In all his beautiful glory and he's giving it all to me.

Soon, it's the sounds of our pleasure, the scent of our joining finding all my senses. And as I get close, digging my nails into his back when he pulls back, inches from me, our eyes meet. His jaw is tight. His expression says everything he needs to.

This isn't *just* sex or getting off. It feels like so much more in the weight of his gaze, the heat of his body and the fire sparking at my core and spreading. It's almost too much.

I come again, before I can warn him, mouth falling open in a silent scream while our eyes stay locked on each other.

And then he comes. Heavy, fast, and hard thrusts hitting the end of me but finding my soul at the same time.

"WILL it ruin your smile if I say how amazed I am you're doing so well today?"

Nothing can wipe the smile off my face today, thanks to the orgasm Klaus gave me this morning. I'm still thinking about it. He went to shower, leaving me with a smile on my face, limbs loose and limber, and my head in the clouds. I'm still floating, hours later, able to ignore the reality of what's about to occur.

Or it's possible I simply don't care.

Not after last night's revelations of both who Roman is, and who Julianna wants to be. Talking to her last night was eye-opening.

I sink into Klaus's side and squeeze his hand. "I'm actually doing okay. I want to get through this ceremony, and head to the reception, get drunk, and then put this weekend in our rearview."

Klaus's hand in mine tenses. "All of it?"

"Yes." My family, this ridiculous affair. Sure, I now understand why they're hosting the reception at their house, and why they've allowed Roman to move in. I feel horrible for what his mom is going through. Teresa is the only decent Vitrianni I know, but that doesn't mean I want to linger in Charleston any more than necessary or give any of what's happened here, outside my orgasm a second thought.

It occurs to me that's what Klaus meant, and I turn to him to apologize.

His blue eyes have turned glacial, jaw hardened, and I swear there's sadness in his eyes.

"Klaus," I say, at the exact same time the wedding march begins and everyone stands.

"Don't worry about it. I understand."

But I don't think he does, and now it'll have to wait until later. Do I want what he's offering when I don't exactly know the offer on the table? Fear keeps holding me back. What we have now works for me, even if it's not everything, but that doesn't mean I'm willing to risk the greatness of our friendship for nothing.

I need time to figure that out.

He stands behind me, one hand settled politely at my hip, his fingers almost exactly where they were this morning, and my face burns as I fight down a pleasurable shiver. In front of us, bridesmaids, girls I went to school with who I haven't spoken to since, and two of Julianna's cousins make their entrance, flowing beautifully down the aisle in shimmery champagne-colored gowns that probably cost more than my mortgage each. There are eight of them and I still haven't looked up to the church's altar to see Roman standing there waiting for his bride, because I don't want to see the look on his face when he gets that first glimpse of her. The music changes, and two beautiful heavy wood doors at the back of the church open.

Julianna takes that first step forward, dressed in the most elegant gown I've ever seen. It's so beautiful, I almost forget I hate her and turn green with envy but then I see the smile on her face. It's stretched tight across her face, a victorious and thrilling grin that shows everything she said last night is true.

It's then I glance at Roman. As my head turns, Klaus's hand on my hip tenses. When I see him, I blink.

He's not focused on Julianna at all. His dark brown eyes are on me, guilty and remorseful in a way it makes me want to cry.

Not for him.

Not for me.

Certainly not for what we had.

But for Julianna, who's marrying a man who doesn't love her and most likely never will, but will give her a lifestyle she desires. She's getting exactly what she wants and for whatever reasons he has, Roman is going along with it. It's not my issue to figure out or a problem to solve. It's their choice, and one they've both agreed to.

I turn back as she nears our pew, only to find her gaze exactly where Roman's is—on me. I shake my head, apologizing for nothing, but understanding what she's feeling, and why. Yet it's her own choices that have brought her to this moment when she suddenly pales and stops.

The flowers in her hand tremble and Klaus, behind me, mutters, "Oh shit."

It's the curse of the church's ghost, the story we all know well. Legend has it a woman was once poisoned on her wedding day and dropped dead in the aisle, right where Julianna has paused. She shivers again and takes another step, slower, as if trying to resist the urge to go forward but then whatever happened is gone. Julianna passes us with her face pale, her expression knowing what she's signing her life away to, and she's doing it despite everything.

And there goes my sadness for Julianna.

She's been warned up until the last possible moment, by ghosts and mortals and old friends and even her fiancé.

This is the bed she's made. Time for her to lie in it.

Once she's passed us, we all sit, the sound of suits and silks and satin dresses shuffling among the wooden pews and I can't help but grin at Klaus when his lips brush against my ear.

"I'm not going to lie. I was hoping that would happen ever since you told me this is where they're getting married."

I press my lips together to stave off a laugh. "It's poetic and just."

I send up a simple, quiet prayer and thank you to the ghost of Harriett before facing the front and grinning up at the bride and groom. *'Til death do they part.*

## 20

## JILLIAN

I take a sip of my wine, scanning the reception of hundreds at the Fox Lounge. Klaus has left me for the bar, and while I'd love nothing more than to sit at the table where we ate dinner with my parents and Nana, with barely any of us talking, but where it allows me to avoid everyone else, I take my leave and walk the perimeter of the room.

The table centerpieces are alight with candles and three-foot-high vases holding Calla Lilies and blush-colored roses. White drapery drips from the ceiling in elegant waves tucked around exposed and arched reclaimed wood beams. Crystal chandeliers are centered between the drapery, sending the prisms sparkling and dancing across the ceiling like it's a star-filled sky. The Fox Lounge is one of the most luxurious places to host events.

All of it is so elaborate, so undeniably beautiful, but also incredibly showy, I can't wait to leave. There are few people in this room I care to spend much time with, including my own family.

And one of them, Adrianna, meets my gaze from where

she's standing at a circular table, manicured hand pressed to the shoulder of a schoolmate we both know and despise. Daniel Johanssen. Her grin is fake but as she lets go of him, he clasps her hand, making her already fake grin smash into a thin line. Any manner of pretense evaporates when Daniel says something to her and then he lets her go, dismissing her as he refocuses his attention on the other couples at the table, now all sharing uncomfortable looks.

Daniel Johanssen is a slimeball.

So what is Adrianna Marquess, one of the few people I actually keep in contact with, doing with him? She greets me with a soft and seemingly sincere smile before giving me a kiss on the cheek.

"Your parents," she murmurs as she pulls back. "I just heard about the rehearsal dinner last night. It's sad about Norman, don't get me wrong, but what in the hell were they thinking?"

"Roman's the son my father never had and always wanted. He'll do anything for him."

Amazingly enough, I'm able to swallow that reality without gagging. Look at me, growing and maturing in only forty-eight hours.

"They're cracked. Did you see Julianna shiver in the aisle? Thought she was going to pass out."

"Be nice," I chide while chuckling with her. I haven't spoken to Adrianna in months, even though she's called many times. She and Julianna are friends as well so I wasn't sure if she was calling for honest intentions. Seeing her genuine smile sends a sliver of guilt through me.

"Hey, I'm sorry, about these last couple of months."

"Try almost a year, but whatever, I get it." She flips her hand in the air. I go to apologize again when she takes a sip of her champagne, but I stop as she says, "I was calling for advice though. Some guidance."

"You want guidance from me?"

"Yeah. I mean, you're the only one of us to escape. How'd you do it so easily?"

She makes it sound like we're all in a prison and maybe it is. With history and expectations and duties all lined up for us before many of us reach primary school, the old brick walls and moss dripping trees can definitely feel like a cage.

"I went to college, Adrianna. Not the moon."

"Yeah, but your parents let you. Mine didn't. I was forced to go to the College of Charleston with everyone else like we're in some sort of historical cult."

I snort at her description. "Preservation of history is the only thing keeping it from disappearing." It's a phrase we heard all too often, particularly when in cotillion or the DAR.

"My parents and Daniel's are discussing an engagement soon," she says, lowering her voice.

My heart beats faster. For her. "You and Daniel are together?"

"Yeah." Her look is as unhappy as mine when I'm served anything with meat. Grossed out and ready to vomit. "We've been dating for a year. I thought if I went along with it for a while they'd let me break up with him, but every time I try, they shove us back together."

Daniel is an arrogant jerk, far worse than Roman because he doesn't even try to sell the lie of goodness that doesn't reside in his soul. He cheats on every woman he's with, throws it in their face, and because his dad's the mayor and his daddy's dad was the mayor and his daddy's dad's dad was the mayor and so forth... he thinks it gives him a ticket to do whatever he pleases. None of it is kind or respectful. He's the king of gaslighting and frequently crosses the line of emotional abuse.

"Adrianna—"

"I think Dad's in some kind of trouble." She says it quietly and quickly as if speaking her fears out loud will doom her forever.

This is silly. It's the twenty-first century and we're in a city of hundreds of thousands. There shouldn't be a need, but we both know the truth. Old money talks and those with it rule.

"Marrying Daniel will keep him safe, I think."

"Don't do it." My hand holding my wine glass trembles and I hold it out to the nearest waiter who whisks it away. "Seriously, Adrianna, just leave. Say no. They can't *force* you to do anything."

As I say it, her green eyes darken and widen. She licks her lips, glancing all over the reception hall as if there are hidden cameras and microphones.

Jesus. My father deals in shipping and hers in finance. It's not like we're in the mafia. We're just rich.

Something dark flashes in her green eyes that makes my heart double-time its natural beat. There were whispers in high school of how Daniel had raped a couple underclassmen, all quietly swept under the rug. I grab her arm, ensuring I have her attention. "Adrianna, please tell me Daniel didn't—"

"Once," she whispers as her chin trembles. "Just once, but God, Jillian..." Her voice rattles again and I yank her into a hug, holding her tight. "If I have to marry him—"

"It's okay and it's not your fault, but please. Promise me, just leave. Stay with me if you need to or find someone else, but don't do this to yourself. Don't marry someone you don't love. Look what almost happened to Julianna for crying out loud."

At the reminder of her shivering in the exact spot of the aisle where Harriett's ghost is said to have collapsed and died, Adrianna chuckles into my shoulder.

"That was funny." She sniffs and pulls back, patting her undereye with her fingertips before she reaches for a new fresh glasses of champagne, and I take a glass of red wine, delivered by waiters who seem to appear out of thin air. "So, now that we have all of that out of the way, you *have* to tell me about this sexy new man who's been hanging on you all day. Who is he?" She leans in and winks conspiratorially. "And is he rich and does he have a twin?"

"No twin," I say.

But rich? Yeah. Klaus is rich in all the ways that matter and all the ways that don't.

"He's just a friend," I admit. The lies are getting to me and she's been so open and honest. It hurts to even attempt lying to her. "A really good friend. He's just playing it up so no one would think I cared about Roman and Julianna."

"Please. If that guy's pretending to be anything more than friends with you, I'll go ahead and marry Daniel."

"Ugh. What a horrid thing to say. And you're wrong."

"He wasn't able to take his eyes off you the entire ceremony and even now he's looking at you like he wants to throw you over his shoulder and whisk you away. And I should know. I was two rows right behind you."

*I don't want to pretend. I want to live it.*

*I want you.*

Is it truly possible Klaus feels things as heavily and deeply as I do?

"You're seeing things."

"Only the truth. Look." She nods in the direction of where the bar is located.

Without trying to look like I'm seeking him out, I shift my footing so he's in my peripheral view. Lifting my head, I take a peek, but it's not necessary.

I can feel the way he's looking at me. Predatory. Needy. Full of hunger and want. As our eyes meet across the room, an electric spark hits my core and sizzles outward until I can't fight the shiver.

"Oh yeah," Adrianna murmurs. "That's hot. So what are you going to do about it?"

I take a sip of wine. It does nothing to cool the sudden heat coursing through me.

"I don't know. He's one of my closest friends I've made in Charlotte. Without him... I don't know if it's worth the risk. For now, his friendship is what I need."

"Yeah but if it comes with a hot dose of that man meat in bed with you, what's the harm?"

"Losing him." I shake off the lingering effects of her words and Klaus's seeing expression. "Don't marry Daniel. You'll regret it for the rest of your life."

She shrugs sadly. "Not all of us have options. Not like I can do a whole lot with the women's studies degree I got."

"You can do it. And if you ever need a place to stay, my home is open to you."

"Thanks, honey." She kisses my cheek and pulls back. "I need to go play the part for now, though. In the future, stop ignoring my calls, would you?"

"Only if you promise me to do what's best for you and not your family."

She swigs back the rest of her champagne and grimaces. "Easier said than done."

She tips her glass in my direction and flounces off, once

again playing the part she's expected to and I now know hates, leaving me frowning and wanting to whisk her away with me.

But we all have to make our own choices in life, much like Julianna has done, despite the costs.

Ironic, since I'm not willing to do the same.

IT FEELS like it's been hours by the time Klaus and I find each other again. Much like last night, he's been surrounded by men. I've walked by overhearing them talk of stats and playoff potential this year, if it's possible they'll make another run for the Stanley Cup.

Klaus seems pretty confident they will. For my part, I'm thrumming with the excitement for the season to start. Seeing Klaus fly across the ice in full gear and ripping off his helmet after every victory game is practically orgasmic.

Women have tried to drag him to the dance floor, but he's played the part of doting boyfriend perfectly. The only one he managed to allow to dance with him was Nana. And within minutes, they were leading a conga line through the dance floor and weaving in and out of tables, much to my mother's chagrin.

Although, admittedly, my dad and I joined in near the end when we were standing close to each other and Adrianna happened to snag both of our hands.

"Having fun?" Klaus asks me, handing me a fresh glass of wine.

Perspiration dots his hairline, and he's long since ditched his suit coat like so many of the other men.

My cheeks are warm in a way I know it has nothing to do with all the dancing I've done myself.

"Some. The party doesn't suck if I forget what we're celebrating."

"I get that. Come on." He takes my hand and pulls me toward the dance floor without giving me the chance to decline.

Not that I would.

Being wrapped in Klaus's arms is becoming one of my favorite things. He leads me into the throng on the dance floor right as a slow song hits. The band has been playing instrumental classics all night and thankfully, my mother never forced me to take music lessons like so many other girls in my class, so while I can appreciate the flow of the music, I have no idea what famous composer I'm dancing to.

Klaus, on the other hand, has seemed to master the waltz and takes my hands, steadies our frames, and glides me across the dance floor like he's getting ready to compete in a dancing show on national television. I shouldn't be surprised.

"You even dance well," I mutter, almost unhappy about all the ways in which he excels.

He laughs, grinning down at me. "I can step on your toes once or twice if it'll make you happy."

I stick my tongue out at him like the mature adult I am. "Not necessary."

"Come here." He pulls me to him closer, dropping the formal waltz and instead, we're swaying together where it's so easy to rest my cheek on his shoulder and feel the beat of his heart.

"This is better," he says, kissing the top of my head.

We sway like this, seamlessly moving together as if we were built as one and at the mere thought, tears beckon. I should tell him. Now is the perfect time to tell Klaus everything I want, everything I feel for him.

It's *Klaus,* for crying out loud. My friend. Even if he truly doesn't feel the same there's no way he'd hurt me, no way we won't recover.

I open my mouth to do that as the song winds to its conclusion when suddenly, Klaus begins laughing. His shoulders and chest shake first, and as I glance up at him, all my emotion and feelings for him having to be so evident in my gaze, I find his not on me at all... but on my nana.

She's swaying back and forth with a broomstick in her hand she's managed to find somewhere, raised in the air.

"You might still have issues to work through with your nana, but I swear she's one of my favorite people in the world."

"Yeah." I choke down all my words, everything I want to express because Klaus is already pulling back, guiding me to the edge of the dance floor where my mom is, hand clutching her chest. He's completely oblivious to everything I've just been feeling and maybe it's for the best.

Tonight must not be the right time.

"It's limbo time!" Nana shouts. Everyone under the age of thirty, outside Klaus and I, cheer.

"Oh dear heavens," my mom mutters, clutching her hand to her chest.

"You ladies going to join in?" Klaus asks, already heading toward the line. Leave it to him to be as nutty as Nana.

"In a minute," I tell him and wave him off. With a smile stretching his face, he blows me a kiss, full of sass and playfulness before getting in line.

My mom and I watch the crowd gather in a line, bridal party first in line with Victoria, Julianna's sister, and her younger friends jumping in. At the head table, Julianna appears bored and alone. I only now realize I haven't even seen Roman in hours. And Julianna hasn't once left her chair.

I turn back to my mom, ready to enjoy myself and stop thinking about them. "It's okay to have fun, too, you know?"

"She is something else, isn't she? She used to make me do this in the living room with her."

"She did? And you liked it?"

"I was probably seven. Maybe younger." A far-off smile curls at the edges of her lips. "I used to be pretty good."

I bump my hip into hers. "Maybe you should go join her. See if you've still got it."

It's foreign, teasing my mom, her smiling at me, us both looking at Nana like she's batshit crazy but in a good way instead of the disdainful looks Mom usually gives.

For a moment, it seems like she will, but then she scans the crowd and shakes her head. As if she can't be seen acting so improperly around her friends.

"I think I'll pass. But you should go." She winks and shows me a full-fledged smile. It catches me by surprise. "See if good limbo genes run in the family."

"I will. And Mom?" I ask, stepping away and looking back at her. "You're even more beautiful when you smile like that."

Her smile slips and then if possible, widens even more so.

By the time I reach the dance floor, lining up with the rest of the fools willing to embarrass themselves in front of hundreds, my smile stretches from ear to ear, cheeks aching from it.

"Hey." I grab Klaus and pull him to the back of the line with me.

"I was wondering how long it'd take you to get out here. Good talk with your mom?"

"You know? Possibly the best we've ever had. Now" —I wave him on ahead of me— "show me how helpful all those years of yoga have improved that flexibility of yours."

"I believe I showed you that this morning."

Boy, did he.

## 21

## KLAUS

I intend to play a round or two of limbo with Jillian, but as it gets close to our turns, I change my mind. There are too many cameras filming, many of them aimed at me. The last thing I want is to be on stranger's Instagram feeds, them soaking up fifteen minutes of viral fame while using me to get it. As Jillian dips down to go first, I butt out. By the time she goes under the broom pole, to polite claps, smiling wide and searching for me, she immediately scowls.

"You faker!" she shouts.

I lift my hands out to my sides and shrug. It's too loud for me to yell back at her, and as I attempt to make my way toward her, already cheering on the other fools, a feminine hand wraps around my elbow.

I tense immediately. I can imagine Julianna has some thoughts about the attention stolen from her tonight due to yours truly but when I turn, I see someone else.

An attractive blonde with light green eyes almost the color of mint and a red dress that matches her nail polish on her fingers is gripping my elbow.

"I've been waiting all night to talk to you."

"Excuse me?" I saw her earlier talking to Jillian. They seemed friendly and their conversation had Jillian genuinely smiling, but I've been here long enough to know there are vipers in our midst.

"I'm Adrianna. Come have a drink with me?"

"Why would I do that?" I rock back on my heels and slide my hands into my pockets.

"Because you and I both love Jillian, so I figure we should get to know one another. Come on. I'm harmless. Promise."

"I doubt that."

Her grin is a mile wide and her laugh is carefree.

"Easy there, hockey superstar. I don't want anything from you except conversation. Cross my heart." She makes the sign with her index finger over her chest, but I keep my gaze on her eyes.

She has me curious, though. "I'm not drinking, but I'm happy to keep you company."

"Of course you are. I'm awesome."

This girl. She has a personality as large as Jillian's. Up until now, I wasn't sure that it was possible, but it does explain why, if they're friends, they connect.

We reach the end of the bar. Cheers from the limbo contest ring loud in the background, more muted conversations and tinkling laughter echo around us.

"I have to admit, Jillian and I have been friends for years and not to be rude, but I don't believe she's ever mentioned you. Care to explain why?"

"Who knows? Maybe she didn't want you to run down here and sweep me off my feet. She probably wants you all to herself."

"Hm." There's a gleam in this girl's eyes. I can't decide if it's playfulness or vindictiveness.

"You're not buying it?" She takes a sip from her glass and sets it on the bar. "No. Probably not. And your rudeness aside, I'm not offended. Jillian and I have been friends since we were kids. We keep in touch, not weekly or even monthly, but I would venture to guess she's one of the most genuine people you'll ever meet, certainly one of the best women I've ever known."

Adrianna's tone softens enough I believe she's being honest. "So what do you want with me?"

"To see if you love her as much as it looks like you do, or if you two really are just friends like she claims." She shrugs.

My insides turn cold. *Just friends*? After this morning? That's what Jillian still thinks of us? Granted, my approach this weekend hasn't been nearly as direct as I could have been, but if there'd been a question about what I wanted before this morning, I thought I'd erased anything when I made love to her.

And that's what it was. Not sex. Not fucking. Not even friends with benefits. No two people connect in bed like we did unless there are serious emotions involved.

She was able to pull that off because we're *friends?*

What in the hell have I been doing?

"She said that to you?"

I glance at the bar. A drink has never sounded so good. Something to wash away the burn in my gut.

Friends.

I've never hated a singular word before now.

"Yeah, but gosh, you two look like you belong together when I've seen you together today. You're really just friends?"

"Um. Yeah." I choke it out. No point in throwing myself on this sword. Not to someone I barely know. "We're friends."

"Just friends?" She leans in, an impish grin curling her lips up. "Are you sure?"

"Yeah. Of course. What else would we be?"

"Hmph." She takes another sip. "That's so disappointing."

"Why's that?"

"Because usually my radar for people meant to be together is more spot on." She shrugs as if it means nothing, completely unaware she's just punched me straight into the chest harder than any slam I've had into the boards. "Oh well. I suppose that means I don't have to interrogate you regarding your intentions for my friend then. Enjoy your night."

She raises her glass in a toasting gesture and glides off, like she hasn't just rocked my entire world.

I wait at the bar until I get a glass of whiskey and face the crowd, searching for Jillian. I can't see her anywhere. The limbo game is winding down and slow music plays. I push and slide through the dance floor, certain she'll be out here living it up but still can't find her.

I do, however, find her dad. "Hey, Mr. Stearns. Have you seen Jillian?"

"Sure. I saw her headed toward the restroom a few minutes ago."

"Thank you, sir."

"Please, Klaus. Call me Stetson."

He slaps my shoulder as I pass him, like we're old friends. Earlier, that might have been the oddest part of the night but then there were conga lines and limbo competitions and Adrianna rocking my world. Stetson acting like we've known each other forever is a mere speck compared to how bizarre this night has turned.

The hallways outside the restrooms are empty so I settle

myself against the wall, drink in hand, foot braced to the wall.

What in the hell am I even doing here? Trying to convince Jillian we're something else?

Has she really not *felt* anything more for me this weekend?

I've screwed this up, somehow. I wasn't clear enough with what I wanted, what I thought she agreed to. On the flip side, it's entirely possible she was very much aware. She just doesn't want the same thing as me. I swallow that thought with another swig of my drink.

*Friends.*

"Hell."

My glass is half-emptied by the time the door opens and Jillian comes out, dressed to kill in the baby blue dress she's wearing that flares at her knees, belts at her waist, and is loose on top. She looks regal and beautiful... and like she's been crying.

"What's wrong?" I push off the wall.

She's so busy wiping beneath her eyes, she jumps.

"You scared me," she says, placing her hand on her chest. "What are you doing here?"

"What happened?" My hand cups her cheek and she flinches when I touch her. What the hell? "Jilly-Bean?"

"Nothing. I think I'm just tired. It's been a long day." She gently pulls my hand off her and doesn't hold my hand like we've always done. At least lately.

That punch to the gut from Adrianna burns deep. "You're okay?"

"Yeah." Her gaze skates all over the hallway, ignoring me. She never avoids me. "Just tired and probably had too much to drink. Do you mind if we head out? Go back to my parents'? I think I need some sleep."

Liar. She doesn't get sleepy drunk on wine. She gets energetic and giggly and loud and rambunctious, especially with Becca, but she's never looked like this. Like someone's ripped out her heart and stomped all over it, which is odd, considering that's how I feel right now.

Still, I've promised to give her whatever she needs. "Sure, honey. Let's get you to bed."

I'll give her the night to rest. To sober up. Tomorrow, when we're back in Charlotte, I'll make sure we take the time to figure things out. Either move forward, or figure out how to get us back to where we used to without ruining what we already have.

**22**

---

**JILLIAN**

I'm awake well before the sun rises. The sky is still dark, the city quiet outside my windows. The only thing I hear is Klaus's gentle breaths as he sleeps next to me, far on the other side of the bed.

*We're only friends.*

It pounds my brain, giving me a hangover-sized headache even though I didn't drink too much last night. No, hearing him say the words I feared he would, hurt more than anything.

It took me hours to fall asleep and then I slept horribly, tossing and turning all night. Now that I'm awake before the sun, there's no way I'll go back to sleep, so I climb out of the bed, careful not to wake Klaus and get dressed in running clothes.

I have no intention of running this morning, but I need to clear my head. Thankfully the kitchen is dark and quiet so I can enjoy a quick cup of coffee in peace. This weekend trip was supposed to be a silly weekend where Klaus and I have fun, pretend I'm not bothered by Roman's wedding, and survive being under the same roof with my parents.

Instead, it's turned into more drama than I ever saw coming, and Roman and Julianna are the least of it.

Between all the things I'm learning about my own parents, and Nana....

"Oh shit." *Norman.* I promised Teresa I'd go see him before I left town, and yesterday I didn't get to talk to him. I barely saw him, in fact.

It might still be before six in the morning, but I don't doubt he's awake. Sickly and tired or not, the man has always been an early riser, often already on the phone with my dad, on speakerphone and talking about work before my dad has his first cup of coffee. For Norman, six o'clock is probably sleeping in.

Decision made, I pour my coffee mug into a travel cup and lace up my sneakers. They only live a mile away, close enough I can walk. I sneak out the front door, careful of closing it too loudly behind me, and head down the walkway to the street.

Less than twenty minutes later, I'm knocking quietly on their front door, shuffling back and forth on my feet.

Hearing about Norman and seeing Teresa and how frail he looked yesterday is more added pain to a weekend that's been full of it. I knock again, louder this time, in case I'm wrong and they're still sleeping but if I don't see Norman now, I don't know when I'll be able to.

Fortunately, their front door opens and the man I came to see is in the doorway. Dressed in flannel plaid pants and a gray T-shirt, as I take him in, tears beckon and fill my eyes.

"Norman." My breath hitches.

He's frail. Skinnier than I believed he was yesterday and his thick head of hair is now thin and gray. His skin has that sickly hue to it and my knees threaten to collapse.

"Jillian. Don't cry." He steps back and lets me in, but it's too late for me to obey his quiet order because I already am.

And then I'm wrapped in his frail, cool arms despite the early heat and humidity outside.

"Come in. Come in. Teresa hoped you'd stopped by before you left."

"I told her I would."

"And a promise made is a promise kept." He chuckles and pulls back. I don't know if a month went by growing up he didn't say the same thing. Always. Be a man of your word. A man of honor. Keep your promises and let your yes mean yes and your no mean no.

"That's right," I say, grinning up at him through my tears. I swipe them away.

"Do you need more coffee? I was just getting settled on the patio out back with my paper if you'd care to join me."

"I'd love to."

I follow Norman through their house, into the kitchen. The walls of the home hold so many memories for me. I grew up in this house as much as I did my own and the familiar scents of Teresa's floral perfume as well as a lilac potpourri she always refreshed on their kitchen counter assault me almost as much as the strong scent of the brewed coffee. After refilling my travel mug, I follow Norman to the back patio.

"Took me a minute to realize there was a knock at the door and longer to get to it." He eases himself slowly into the chair, as if bending ligaments and muscles requires great effort. "I'm not the spry man I used to be, I'm afraid."

"I know, Teresa told me. I'm so sorry to hear you're sick."

He brings his coffee mug to his mouth and blows gently. "The only two things we can be certain of in this life are death and taxes. I've definitely paid my fair share of the latter and the former, well... I've lived a good life. I'm not afraid."

"Can you fight it?"

"Until my dying breath, I'll try."

I want to pummel him with questions. I know nothing about pancreatic cancer except that he has cancer and it's scary and according to Teresa, terminal, but I already know they'll do everything they can.

"Tell me about you. Teresa mentioned this man... Klaus? I believe?"

"He's a good man."

"Plays hockey."

"For Charlotte Ice Kings, yes. He's quite good."

"I've seen him." Unlike my own dad, who thinks athletes are barbarians and far beneath him, Norman has a healthy obsession with all things sports-related, including football and hockey. There's almost always a game on in his house on the weekends and late nights. "And he treats you well? Better than my own son did, I hope?"

"He does." As well as any best friend can treat a girl. "But as for Roman, I think we realized much too late we wanted different things. I'm not angry with him, you know. Not anymore anyway."

"Well, I can only hope he's made the right choice then."

"Too late for second-guessing, isn't it?"

"Considering they've boarded the plane for their honeymoon, I'd say so."

"And I'd pray it'd crash if it meant Roman wouldn't go down with it." Teresa's voice comes from behind, startling me with her volume and her words.

"Teresa," I scold her, but she's grinning.

"We make the decisions we make and we learn to live with them. It's a good thing I chose so wisely, isn't it dear?"

She bends down and kisses Norman's cheek, settling her hand on his other one while he leans into her.

"Good morning, dear," he murmurs. "We have a beautiful visitor."

"Quite. You're here early," she says to me and kisses the top of my head. "But it's lovely to see you."

Teresa is dressed in cozy gray lounge pants probably cashmere and soft and silky along with a matching top. Her dark hair is pulled back with a clip and even without makeup, she's still beautiful.

"Difficult weekend and I was up early. We head back today, so I figured I'd enjoy breakfast with you instead of the insanity at my house."

"Ah. Your mother mentioned fireworks with Iris this weekend. Are they still sparking?"

"I think once the flames end, there may be some difficult conversations ahead. But good ones, I hope."

"Your parents do love you."

"I think I'm finally beginning to understand that." I sip my coffee and turn to Norman.

We chat about nothing. The weather. My job and my house. We avoid the talk of Norman's cancer and further discussion of Roman or his wedding, but it's an enjoyable morning all the same and when my coffee is emptied, I know, despite not wanting to face what's waiting for me, I have hidden long enough.

"I should head back," I say regretfully. "I need to pack and see Nana before she leaves. It was so good to see you." I cover Norman's hand with mine and he holds me tightly.

"You are a beautiful young woman with a bright future ahead of you. Never forget that and never settle for less than everything you've earned and deserve."

"I won't." My chin wobbles and I fight back tears. With a shaky smile, I say, "I promise."

He gives me a solemn look, one of sadness but acceptance. "Try not to stay away so long again, okay?"

"I won't." Not now that I know he's sick without much time. I make a silent vow to return again while I still can and turn to Teresa who's already standing from her chair.

"I'll walk you out."

I kiss Norman's cheek, lingering there and tell him I love him before I allow Teresa to guide me back through the house. Once she sees I didn't drive, but walked over, she asks, "Do you want to borrow our car so you can drive back?"

"No. The walk will do me good."

"You seem to have a lot on your mind."

"It's been a long few days. Hard ones."

"Well, seems to me that you've got a man at your side with shoulders strong enough to carry it if you let him."

It's too bad Klaus is the cause of most of the weight she's referring to. I open my mouth to tell Teresa the truth but stop. There's no point, and it's better for her to believe what she thinks she sees than the truth.

I kiss her cheek and hug her tightly before saying my goodbyes and head down their stone path.

It's too bad the walk isn't long enough to solve anything, because when I return, Klaus is on the front steps of my parents' house, arms crossed, broad stance, looking pretty damn angry, and I'm pretty certain my morning has gone from bad to worse.

## 23

## KLAUS

"Where were you?" I can't hide the irritation I'm feeling, so I don't bother. After avoiding me all night last night, for her to be gone when I woke up this morning ticked me off.

And then when she wasn't in the house at all—and trust me, I looked. That irritation turned to anger. And then worry when I realized she'd left her cell phone.

She took nothing with her when she disappeared, and I had no idea where she went or how long she'd been gone.

As it is, everyone is awake, bustling for the day, and Nana is packing and talking about heading out.

In front of me, Jillian trudges up the steps with a metal coffee cup in one hand and red eyes from what looks like crying.

"What's wrong?"

She shakes her head, barely glancing at me. "I went and saw Norman. Said I'd see him before I left."

Oh. Well don't I feel like a jackass. Although a note would have been nice. Maybe a kiss and a whisper but that's probably asking too much after the wall she threw up last night when we left the reception.

"How is he?" My shoulders slump, tension draining now that I know she's okay—relatively—and back home.

"Dying," she says and blinks several times. She brushes past me up the stairs, barely giving me the time of day and while I'm glad she's home and safe, the fact she's still avoiding me hurts.

"Jillian?" I call to her. She hardly pauses in her race to get away from me. At least that's what it feels like.

"Yeah?"

"Nana was looking for you before she leaves."

"Right." She heads inside, and I'm left out here, glaring at the rising sun and the bright blue sky.

Seriously. What in the hell went so sideways, and why is she taking it out on me?

I let loose a growl of frustration and head back inside. I'm already packed, my bags in Jillian's room, and I find her there, grabbing clothes and heading into the shower.

"Is there anything you want to do today before we head back?"

Like, talk to me?

"No. I think I just want to head home. Make sure Becca hasn't killed my plants."

Despite the distance I can feel her putting between us like cement blocks, one by one, thick with mortar between them, I still laugh.

It quickly evaporates along with the click of the bathroom door closing behind her and the sound of the water turning on.

She's locked the door for the first time all weekend.

Locked me out.

What in the fuck happened?

"Get my daughter home safe."

I shake Stetson's offered hand. My, how quickly things can change. "I will. Thanks for everything this weekend."

"Perhaps we'll have more of them."

I'm not sure I believe that.

After she showered and dressed, she went and said goodbye to Nana, again without me, leaving me to hunt her down.

Some day I might find the humor in this, but today isn't that day. I have no idea what she's so upset about or what I've done, but the last thing I want to do is start an argument when we have a three-hour drive ahead of us.

Lucky me, it appears I'll be spending it with a thick block of awkward tension between us instead. My already cramped Ferrari might not be able to handle any more weight.

Claire has her hands clasped gently together in front of her, but she's smiling at Jillian. An improvement in seventy-two hours I didn't think I'd witness. But oh, things are changing.

"After you get home, you can check your calendar and let me know when you have a free weekend. Perhaps your father and I can come up and visit? See your gardens you've told me about for so long?"

Jillian's face registers complete shock from her raised brows and slack jaw. "Yeah, sure, Mom. I'd like that."

She presses her lips together to stave off emotion. I know her too damn well. Any other time I'd step in, place a hand on her back, offer her support. Today I doubt that's welcome. I stand close, waiting for my time to say goodbye and after Claire is polite to me, and Jillian is settled in the car, I put it in reverse to back out of their narrow driveway.

"That was nice, what your mom said."

Her gaze is out her window, eyes on her parents still standing on their front porch stairs, watching us leave. "It was."

"Maybe things will be better with them from now on."

"Maybe."

And that's the last word she speaks for three, long, torturous hours, until I pull up to her house and she jumps out of my car before I've placed it in park.

She grabs her suitcases from the trunk and says goodbye and it's the most final sounding word I've ever word.

There's more to her silence and her avoiding me then it has to do with her family. If only she'd open up, I could fix it.

But perhaps this weekend has been long and hard enough for her.

I'll give her time.

Then I'll tell her how I feel. I don't want the weekend, the drama with her family or her sadness about Norman making her doubt me. Hell, when I add up all the emotional rollercoasters she took this weekend, I don't even want to broach anything now. That'd make me a dick, and I only want what's best for her.

"Jillian," I call to her as she struggles with her luggage on the narrow walkway, not accepting my help. "If you need me, I'm always here."

"Have a good week. And thanks... for everything this weekend."

She turns and heads toward her front door. Watching her walk away from me is the most dreaded feeling.

Worse than a playoff game loss.

I fear I've spent the weekend trying to get my best friend to fall in love with me, like I am with her, and I lost.

Big time.

## 24

## JILLIAN

My doorbell rings, the dulcet tones echoing through my house into the back yard where I've been digging in dirt since I got back from my pre-sunrise morning run. It's all I can do to keep the thoughts of last weekend away and even then it's pointless.

*We're friends. Of course we are. What else would we be?*

I'd almost been right behind Klaus when I heard him talking to Adrianna. The girl is a wild one and once I saw her dragging him to the bar, I figured I should save him. She'd probably have him doing body shots within a blink.

Shame on me.

*We're just friends.*

It explains everything and nothing. None of it makes sense. The weekend. His bullshit "let's not pretend but live it" claim. The way he made love to me that very morning. What was this? Him trying to start a friends-with-benefits arrangement with me without telling me first?

I've played the weekend over and over in my head all week long and worse, after he texted me Monday and Tuesday, I haven't heard from him since.

Not that I want to.

I'm not sure we have anything left to say to one another.

I stupidly and naively thought he wanted more than friendship with me. I've hidden the fact I've been in love with Klaus for long enough and to finally see the opportunity we could have together, I blindly dove into it. And here I thought the only thing I was afraid of was it not working out. Not him playing me like a fiddle.

Who the hell knows. Maybe all the emotion I thought was involved wasn't there at all.

Thank God I didn't open my mouth on the dance floor when I finally found my courage to let him know the truth. I would have made a complete fool of myself.

"Get your ass out of the dirt and into the shower, because girl, you have some explaining to do!"

At the first shout, I jump, but as I see Becca in the doorway to my kitchen, champagne bottle in one hand and box of cheap donuts in her other, I groan.

"Go away. I thought I told you I didn't want to do brunch today."

"Yes. And that means you're dying, so as your best friend, it's my responsibility to come check on you."

I toss the weeds I've pulled into my compost bucket and brush dirt off my hands. "I would like my day back to what I said before."

"No, you don't. You just want to be alone and to keep ignoring me. Two very different things."

"And yet you're here."

"Because I love you and you haven't told me anything that happened last weekend. Was it that bad?"

"Worse." I pluck the champagne bottle from her hand and tear off the foil.

Her green eyes are filled with worry, as is the twist in her lips.

"It was a shitshow of all weekends and one I would very much like to forget ever happened. Is that possible?"

"Not with all the champagne in the world, honey. Talk to me."

She won't leave. I don't want her to. I've spent a week alone, throwing myself into work, running more miles in a week than I usually do in three. I've worn out my body and brain and none of it's helping.

"I'll talk, but only if you bought my favorite cream-filled twists."

"Oh honey." She grins and opens the box so I can see today's haul. "I bought out the entire section."

"Then let's eat." She turns and heads into the kitchen. I follow her, setting down the champagne on the counter. "I'll go take your advice and shower. Don't even think of starting without me."

As I say it, Becca reaches for the champagne and pops the cork. "No promises. That depends on how long you take."

It takes me fifteen minutes to shower and get dressed. I come back downstairs, wrapping my hair into a bun at the top of my head until it dries and find Becca seated at one of the barstools, two glasses of champagne poured and donuts spread out on a platter.

Apparently we're forgoing the orange juice component of the mimosa.

"You actually waited?"

"I figured with the mood you've been in this week, I didn't want to get my head ripped off by not listening."

"Funny." I shove her shoulder and take a seat next to her.

"So this shitshow…"

"Can't a girl at least get a donut in her own home you broke into before being interrogated?"

"Nope. Whatever it is that happened while you and Klaus were gone has made you look like you haven't slept in a week and worse than I felt when my dad accidentally ran over my puppy."

The donut I've just grabbed freezes at my mouth. "Your dad did what?"

She flips her hand in the air dismissively. "I was seven. Eventually recovered after years of therapy. Don't change the subject."

"Have you always been this crazy?"

She grins, manic and wide, and she laughs a bit like a lunatic. "Of course. That's why you love me."

"Not today," I mutter, but she's right. It's Saturday, and I've already broken my cardinal rule of no running on Saturdays.

Klaus wants to be friends.

I have no idea how to move on from this.

Becca, mimosas, and donuts are a great way to start trying.

"I'm not even sure where to begin. Let's see, there was Roman and Julianna, Roman telling me he called my name during sex with her two nights before his wedding—"

"You're kidding."

"Would I joke about that? I don't even want to remember he told me."

"Gross." Her face scrunches up and she gags.

"Exactly. Then there was the epic fight between my mom and Nana at dinner one night that completely blew my mind and might have actually improved not only their relationship, but mine with my mom."

"Holy shit." She sips her champagne, wide-eyed and in awe.

"Exactly." I take a much larger, and very unladylike gulp from my glass and cringe as the bubbles slide down my throat. "And then there's Klaus."

"The reason you look like a sad puppy."

I take another drink, trying to fortify myself. Useless. "We had sex," I admit and my tears are already burning my eyes. "And then he bailed."

"What? No way. No fucking way would Klaus do that to you."

"He did. Gave me this whole spiel all weekend about he didn't want us to pretend to be in love, wanted us to live it. I had some of the best sex of my life, even with all the non-sex work up to the sex stuff—"

"No..."

"Yes." My chin trembles and my body heats. It has nothing to do with the alcohol slipping through my veins. This is all, one hundred percent embarrassment and shame, memories of Klaus's body, the way he touched me, the things he said to me. All of it a lie. Or something I read into *way* too deeply and incorrectly. "And then, I... we made love the morning of the wedding and it wasn't sex, it was... it was incredible. Passionate."

I stop, shake my head and wipe away tears.

"What happened?"

"I heard him talking to my friend Adrianna."

"I remember her. Gorgeous blonde and slightly unhinged?"

"That's her." I chuckle despite myself. Becca has visited Charleston with me many times over the years. "Anyway, I saw them at the bar talking so I went to go join them, save

Klaus from her if he needed it and instead, I heard him tell her we were just friends."

"Oh honey." She pulls me over and hugs me. It's warm and firm, and she smells like things I can count on and believe in. Something, up until last weekend I would have felt with Klaus, too. "I'm so sorry. Is it possible he didn't mean it?"

"She asked him. Said it looked like he was in love with me and he denied it. I don't know why he'd lie to her."

I sniff against her shoulder and pull back, and what the hell. Why be sober today? I drain the rest of my glass and pour another.

"To be honest, I've always thought the same as Adrianna. I mean, the way he looks at you when you're not paying attention. I was sure he would have made his move."

"He did. Apparently, though, he loves me like a friend and just wanted me to get off. It's so unlike him. It doesn't make sense and the more I think about it the more my head hurts."

"Jillian, that boy wouldn't hurt you and he wouldn't use you. Not like that. I can't believe it for a second which means there has to be another explanation. Maybe your dad said something to him? Scared him away?"

"I doubt it. I think Dad actually likes him. And honestly, I don't want to rehash it. The whole weekend was miserable and he hasn't texted since Tuesday anyway."

"Did you respond?"

"No. I have nothing to say to him. Not right now."

"You two need to talk."

"Why? So I can get hurt all over again? No thanks."

I am really going to town on this champagne. If I was in a better mood, I'd probably stop. Like the last time Becca and I got together for brunch, my taste in donuts is waning.

Screw men for making me dislike donuts. I grab one and take a large bite, swiping at the cream-filled center left on my lips.

"So... Nana and your mom?"

I'm so thankful for the change in topic. Anything to take thoughts of Klaus away and the mess we've brought home with us.

"Get this." I slap my palms to the counter and tell her everything. The dinner with Nana and my mom. The after-effects. We even get around to talking about the conversation with Roman and Julianna that shall never now be mentioned again. I tell her about mom's parting words about coming up to visit and how she actually teased me when it came to the limbo contest. We laugh about the rest of it, drinking our way through the three champagne bottles she brought with her and when we pass out on the couches in my living room later, claiming we need a nap, I wake up several hours later to an empty house, a note from Becca saying she headed out earlier after she woke up (and left me a donut), and a hole in my heart that still hurts whenever I think of Klaus.

25

## KLAUS

"What is it with you? You've been a man on a mission for the last week and a half."

I shrug off Jude's question with a shrug. As our team's first-line right winger, he and I are frequently in competition for that role... usually me, competing for his line spot and except for when he was injured a couple years ago, I've never been there. Not that I don't like my line. Our entire team is close, and the line mates tend to be closer. Sebastian especially is like a brother to me but regardless of my friendship with Jude, there's always a simmering, underlying tension. At any moment, we could change roles. He'll do anything to be able to stay on the line with his brother and I'll do anything to be the guy hitting the ice first.

"Nothing, really."

Jude laughs. "Please. You think you can fool me?"

"I think you're all sorts of a fool, Taylor."

"Yeah, but come on. What is it?"

Around us, the team parties at Taylor's mansion south of the city. He and his wife Kate have been married for two years now and host team events frequently during the off-season. Now the pre-season is only a week away, we're having one last fun get together.

Where the women are clustered by the pool, on floats or sitting at the edge, dipping their toes in the water. The guys are nearby. Mikah and his wife, Paisley, are taking turns chasing their one-year-old boy Angelo over the patio so he doesn't waddle into the deep end and Gigi, Sebastian's fiancée, is doing her own waddling with her growing belly, due to give birth in a couple of months from what he says.

And me? I'm here alone and dateless, without Jillian, and still trying to figure out what in the hell went wrong that last day in Charleston and why she hasn't returned any of the texts I've sent.

It's driving me crazy, and it's unlike her. We had always talked daily. Always have, but she made it pretty damn clear before we even left her parents' house that she was done with anything related to me.

Because we had sex?

Who the hell knows, but it's making me crazy which means Jude isn't entirely wrong.

I've been at team skates in the morning, busting my ass, skating like I need to earn my spot on the team, like a rookie in danger of being sent back down to the minors instead of secure in my spot.

It's all sorts of fucked up.

Jude won't give up and behind him, Sebastian is headed toward us. He's been giving me odd looks for the last week and a half. Based on the intensity of his expression, if he reaches me, he's going to do more than just ask like Jude is doing. He'll dig in and pry and won't let anything lie until I spill my guts.

And considering I have no desire to do that at a family team meeting, I set down my water bottle.

"You know what? I'm outta here." I slap his shoulder playfully.

"Seriously? You won't talk?"

"Nope." Not until I have something to talk about. Shooting my shot and ending up the loser isn't a situation I'm familiar with, but I didn't get to where I am by being a quitter either.

I'll give Jillian until the weekend, try one more time, to text, and then she has forty-eight hours to respond before we figure this out.

Because losing the woman I love is killing me.

But losing one of my best friends?

That might just hurt worse.

Hey. Work going okay? We still on for our Sunday run? Lunch after?

It's the exact same text I'd send her every week. If she wants us to be friends, I'll start there.

Unfortunately, it's been twenty-four hours and like the creep I am, I did a drive-by of her home last night, lights on, car in the driveway, which means she's not out of town for work and didn't bother letting me know.

Nope. She's ignoring me.

But I've promised forty-eight hours to give her time to come around so I do nothing when I see her home and head back to my own place where I run another four miles on the treadmill to burn off the sinking sensation in my gut.

Lacing up my skates for another round of conditioning in a locker room full of guys is the last place I want to be, especially after punking out last night at the party. Half of my team looks green, probably enjoying the night far more than they should have. My recent kamikaze skating is going to look even more insane if all their asses are running on fumes and yesterday's alcohol.

"Hey." Sebastian drops down next to me, laced up, dressed, and ready to go. "What's going on? You've been quiet all week."

"You know that thing we do where we tease each other about acting crazy and it all comes out it's because of a woman who's got us twisted up?"

"Yeah?"

"I don't really want to do that with you or anyone right now."

"Ah. So the weekend with Jillian didn't go so great."

"Nope." It went perfectly. I'd thought we were on the same page. Outside her family drama and the bullshit with Roman that at this point is laughable—the man's on his honeymoon for Christ's sake, probably thinking of a woman he still loves and can't have.

A woman I also love who doesn't want to be anything more than friends with me.

I finish lacing my skates and stand, grabbing my helmet from my locker. "Remember when I said I didn't want to talk about it?"

"Yeah, but I don't really listen all that well. Drives Gigi fucking crazy."

"I imagine."

"So Jillian?" He stands, helmet already in his hands. Like it or not, I guess we're heading to the ice together. It's too bad you can't run fast in skates and full gear.

I seriously do not want to sit around, mulling this over with guys and drinks, acting like I didn't spend the weekend making a fool out of myself.

And if only I could pinpoint where it all went wrong.

What happened?

What changed?

"We had a great weekend. It ended shitty. We came home. That's it."

Because it was a great weekend. All up until the wedding reception. Hell, she'd been smiling with her mom, laughing with Nana. She was having so much fun, until....

The bathroom.

I pull to an abrupt stop.

"What?"

I ignore Sebastian.

The bathroom. Her red eyes from crying. Something—or someone—hurt her, or pissed her off or made her cry—and if it was anyone else who said or did something to piss her off or make her cry, she'd come to me. She'd tell me. She wouldn't brush me off and run without me and say nothing for three hours. Hell, Jillian's never been silent for more than ten minutes around me.

The girl's a talker.

And my best friend.

She'd tell me.

Which means the person who hurt her is me.

"Oh fuck," I groan. "She fucking heard."

And it hurt her.

Which means she doesn't want to be friends any more than I do.

Fucking hell. How stupid are we?

## 26

## JILLIAN

I t takes me almost two full days to respond to Klaus's text message. Two days where I debate, where I cry some more, and where I get really, really pissed off.

I've run through so many emotions over the last week and a half it feels as if I'm stuck on a rollercoaster, no off switch in sight.

But still, I think back to what Becca has said to me, what I've ignored all week, and what I felt with Klaus.

Something has to change, so I finally reply to his text he sent me Thursday.

**A run sounds good. Tomorrow, 8am, Freedom Park?**

Now, all I have to do is get through another brunch with Becca where we talk about nothing else. I'm mentally prepping myself for this, psyching myself up and dressed to kill the lazy Saturday ahead of me in a messy bun, unwashed hair. No makeup on and I'm barely dressed in something better than pajamas, my cut-off sweat shorts and a pink tank top that says: RISE AND SHINE, IT'S MIMOSA TIME. It used to be a sparkling silver print, but it's now faded due to the years and millions of washes.

I look a hot mess and am more than ready to start drinking the orange juice and champagne I've already mixed when my doorbell rings.

"It's open!" I shout from where I'm at in the kitchen. Becca usually barges on in, last Saturday's surprise visit not the first time she's helped herself to her key of mine. While I'm expecting her, I also expect her cheery voice as the door opens. I'm anticipating her immediately launching into something about Klaus so with my back to the room, I begin loading the dishwasher from last night's mess I haven't cleaned up yet and say, "If you're going to rag on me all day again about Klaus, we're ending this conversation now. He's on our do not speak of list of conversations today."

"Oh? And why is that exactly?"

I freeze, bent over the dishwasher, loading a blue dinner plate.

*Oh freaking shit.*

That is *not* Becca.

The plate clatters into the dishwasher and I stand, drying my hands on a towel. Klaus is on the other side of my island, running shorts and a white athletic shirt that clings to muscles I've now run my fingers and mouth all over.

His arms are crossed over his chest, sunglasses perched on top of his side-swept hair, and those oceanic blue, stormy eyes of his I love so much hold a wicked gleam.

"What are you doing here?"

"Couldn't wait until tomorrow. Thought we could talk."

"Becca—"

"Isn't coming. I texted her."

"What?"

He shrugs and unfolds his arms, bracing his palms on my counter. Straightening out those strong, muscled arms of his where veins draw maps along his flesh before disappearing into sleeves that are stretched so tight over ridiculous sexy biceps.

His head dips, and one corner of his lips kick up. Oh God. I'm growing flushed with heat from scoping out his body and he's letting me.

"You don't think we have anything to talk about?"

I close the dishwasher and rest my backside against it. "Why would we?"

"If we didn't, why would you tell Becca I was on your list of things not to discuss today?"

Oh. Well, sure. He has a point there.

Klaus, confident and slightly arrogant as always, reaches for the pitcher of mimosas and helps himself to a glass.

"What are you doing?"

"Having a drink. Want one?"

Oh yeah. I think I'm going to need several.

I push off the counter and take the champagne flute he slides across the island to me. We're separated by three and a half feet of granite and yet my body is buzzing like we're pressed together. Warm and tingly all over.

He's caught me off guard and his expression hides everything. He might be here because we have to talk, but there's not a chance in hell I'm starting the conversation. I have absolutely no desire to hear the *last weekend shouldn't have happened, let's go back to being just friends* speech I'm certain he has in mind.

I take a drink, quickly setting the glass down when I realize my hand is trembling, shaking the contents.

"So, how's your week been?" Klaus asks. Nonchalance rings in his tone, but the tightness around his eyes hides nothing.

He's pissed. *At me?* What in the hell have I done? A question I'm not asking.

Following his lead of pretending we didn't just blow up into an epic mess, I shrug. "Fine."

"Because you look like crap, like you haven't slept in a week."

Ten days, but who's counting.

"Geez. Thanks, Klaus. If you're done insulting me now and hijacking my Saturday, you can show yourself to the door."

"What happened at the reception that made you cry?"

"What?" His change in topic gives me whiplash.

"At the reception, when I found you leaving the restroom. You were crying."

Tears of heartbreaking sadness. Hearing him confirm what I'd been terrified of, why I never made my move, and why I never let on how much I cared for him, was a stake to my heart.

"I was tired. I told you that."

"And then you didn't speak a word to me the rest of the night, barely three words the next day and you've been avoiding me ever since. So I want to know what happened. What made you cry?"

*You.* The word burns the tip of my tongue. He's backing me into a corner without having moved a single muscle. I can *feel* the weight of him, of this moment, threatening to force me to show all my vulnerabilities while he hides his.

No freaking thank you.

"It was an emotional day. I was drinking. That's all. Why are you asking?"

"Why won't you answer me honestly?"

"Why do you keep asking me the same question without telling me why you want to know?"

His lips press together and he exhales a slow breath, making his shoulders rise and his chest heave with the force of it. "Has it occurred to you it's because I know something made you mad that night and what it was has made you avoid me, and because I *care* about you, I want to help you? To be there for you and fix it if I can."

*We're friends. Of course we are. What else would we be?*

Nothing. Because even now he's only concerned because he cares about me... as a friend. Why did I let myself forget this?

Shaking my head, I take another drink. "It was nothing, Klaus. Really. As far as avoiding you, I haven't been. We signed new players last week and I've been busy prepping new upcoming signings in New York and Wisconsin."

"I think you're forgetting right now how long we've been friends, how long we've known each other. If you think I believe any of what you're saying, then maybe you're also forgetting how well I know you... and that I know you're a really crappy liar."

He pushes off the counter and strolls around the island like he has all the time in the world. With every step he takes toward me, my pulse kicks up a notch.

"Do you know what I think?"

I shake my head, mouth suddenly going bone dry. No amount of mimosas or water could hydrate me right now.

"I think," he continues, stopping when he's within touching distance, close enough I can smell his cologne. Close enough I can see the pulse beat at the base of his throat and if I wanted—which I most definitely do not— close enough I can reach out and touch it. Touch him. Pull him to me and kiss him. "I think you got mad when I was talking to Adrianna. I think you overheard me saying something that hurt you, and I think that's why you were crying. The only thing I want to know is, why would me telling Adrianna we're just friends—which you also said, according to her—hurt you so much to send you running to the restroom with tears in your eyes?"

"We are friends."

He nods, a slow curl of his lips lift. "I know. And we'll always be friends, but what happened between us Saturday morning or in the days leading up to wasn't just friends, was it?"

Of course it wasn't. Definitely not to me. To me, it was a dream come true. Years of hoping and wishing came to fruition and for one glorious moment, was a reality I didn't want to end.

"Klaus—"

He lifts his hand and holds it against my cheek. Without thought, I lean into him and close my eyes. I've missed his warmth and his strength. "I thought we were more than friends. I thought you understood what I wanted from you. But then I was talking to Adrianna and she said you had told her we were just friends and it *hurt*, Jilly-Bean. After all that we shared, after we made love Saturday morning, it hurt me to hear that's how you thought of us still. I only said it to her because of that. I wasn't telling a friend of yours I'd just met that I cared about you a whole lot more than that."

"But—"

"And I know that's why you took off. I know you overheard, at probably the absolute wrong time, and I'm pretty confident that's why you were crying. All you have to do is admit it and I can make this right, honey. I swear it."

Oh God. *Made love?* He said it. We were on the same page after all. He's telling me what I wanted to hear for so long.

All I have to do is tell him. Tell him I love him. It should be so easy. He's opened the door, given me the perfect opportunity. I take him in, his pleading expression and those eyes rimmed with golden lashes I love so much and open my mouth to tell him, and stop.

Fear rushes through me, choking me, fear of this getting even worse between us than it was in the last week.

What happens next time? What happens when it doesn't work?

I've barely been able to crawl out of bed and go to work this week.

What happens if I give him everything and we *still* fail?

"I... I like us as friends." I choke it out.

His brows jump on his forehead and his mouth falls open. "What?"

There's pain in his voice, mixed with surprise. I want to claw at my words and yank them back out of thin air, but it's too late.

Klaus drops his hand from me and steps back. Rolling his lips together, he then pushes them out and nods. "I see. Wow."

"Klaus."

I reach for him but he takes another step, looking over my shoulder, jaw hardening. "I didn't expect that."

"Let me explain."

"No need." He lifts his hands and puts more space between us. "Wow. Shit. I mean, I really read that wrong, then. Probably all in my head." He rubs his chest like it aches.

My God. I've done this to him.

"Friends."

"Klaus."

"No. Friends is good. Right. We'll just... go back to that, I guess, right?"

He can't even look at me. Hell, I don't even want to be around me right now. Who can blame Klaus for still stepping backward, unable to meet my gaze and see my own pain probably radiating all over me and from me.

"So tomorrow. We'll run?" He grins at me, fake as hell.

A run? Tomorrow? I don't know how in the hell I'll ever be able to face him again.

"Jillian? A run tomorrow?"

"Sure." Sandpaper must be lodged in my throat. It hurts to answer and I flinch from the pain both internally and externally that I'm causing. "We'll go for that run."

"Good." He finally glances at me, quick and his eyes dart away as fast as they meet mine and then he's in front of me, kissing my forehead like he's always done and backing away. "I'll text Becca. Tell her you two can have your Saturday after all. And I'll see you tomorrow... right?"

"Yeah." I clear my throat.

Why? Why have I done this and why can't I stop it?

He puts his back to me and walks out of my kitchen, taking half my heart with him and leaving me broken all over again.

But this time, it's my own damn fault because I'm too big of a coward.

My front door closes and along with the thud of it shutting, I fall forward and drop my head to the granite counter with a resounding *thump*.

## 27

# KLAUS

"**C**ongratulations on your first win!"

"Thanks, George."

"Team is looking good this year. You feeling good about it?"

We've just had our first pre-season home game. The starters don't get much playing time, pre-season mostly meant to see what the newly drafted players can do and to get a closer look at the guys from the minor leagues we've pulled up. This year, we have several new players, the youngest only twenty-one, and a few older players who have bounced around the minors for several years, sometimes being called up, sometimes drafted, almost always being sent back down eventually.

Our team is still looking solid, though, and I'll get my time on the ice when it gets closer to regular season starting.

I take my beer from the bartender and father to Sebastian's fiancée, Gigi. She's in the process of taking over the bar our team loves to hang out. While George is ready to retire and has given the bar he's run for thirty years to his daughter, he also doesn't appear to be in any big hurry to actually leave.

Especially not with Gigi looking more pregnant by the day.

"And here's the glass of wine for Jillian."

He pours my beer and reaches for one of the new sections in the bar—the wine fridge. One of the few additions and changes Gigi has insisted on.

I tip him well, and in the brief moment before I have to see Jillian and plaster on the friendship-fake smile I've worn around her for the last month, force myself to relax.

A month ago, I stood in front of her, trying to tell her exactly how I felt about her, what I wanted. But as soon as I mentioned the words *made love*, I couldn't deny the look of panic I saw flash in her eyes and steel her features.

She is terrified at the idea of falling in love with me.

Not that she isn't... or doesn't want to love me—but that it scares her.

And as shocking as it was that day, as hurtful as it was, I've spent the last month trying to be exactly what she wanted me to be—

Her friend.

It fucking sucks. Not only do I still love her, I now know the sounds she makes when she's close to coming. I know how she *feels*. I hear her cry my name in ecstasy when I get myself off. I'm unable to do a damn thing about it until Jillian finally wakes up and realizes that what she needs, and who she loves, is right here in front of her—not going anywhere—not running or fleeing, or throwing it away.

I'll continue to be that guy for her, as much as it kills me, for as long as it takes or until she stops looking at me like she really does love me.

I drop off her glass of wine at the table where she's sitting with Paisley and Hannah.

"Thanks, Klaus."

"No problem." I nod to the other women and head to where I've been with Sebastian, Gigi when she takes a break, and Duke and his wife, Regan. Most of the team is here tonight, taking over George's bar like we typically do after home game wins.

That this is pre-season doesn't change our rituals. Hockey players are bound by our superstitions and traditions.

Tonight, it's the last place I want to be considering the number of looks both Jillian and I have had tossed in our directions. It's not unusual for her to hang out with the team since so many of them know her and we've been friends for so long. What is unusual is for us to avoid each other. In truth, when I gave her season tickets like I did last year, I didn't really expect her to use them. But like so much of her behavior lately, she did the completely unexpected move and showed up tonight, sitting where I can see her from the bench, and she showed alone. Usually she brings Becca with her to the games. Occasionally she brings a coworker. She's never come alone and stupid me hoped that tonight it meant she'd end it differently.

Nope. So much for that. She's still just as scared to move forward. She refuses to give up what we have.

It slices deep in my chest that after knowing me for so long she can be so uncertain of me, how I'd treat her, how well I'd love her.

We're both miserable, dancing to two different songs and ending up nowhere.

Which means I have a choice to make.

I can either force myself to get over her and truly stay her friend.

Or I'm going to have to let her go completely.

Because one thing is for certain, this is not a dance I'm willing to continue.

Which leaves only one thing to do—an ultimatum. Where I risk the worst-case scenario. At this point, I'm not sure there's anything left to try to save but my sanity.

## 28

## JILLIAN

I've never felt more out of place.

For the first time since I met Klaus, hanging out with his teammates and their wives and girlfriends is almost unbearable. I'm the outsider of my own making and as time goes on, I want more than anything to suck back my words that day in the kitchen.

Unfortunately, it seems like he doesn't mind. Outside the initial shock he had when I said I wanted us to be friends. For him, everything seems to have gone back to normal. He showed up at our meeting place at Freedom Park the very next day and acted exactly how he always did. My best friend. We ran in tense silence for a mile or two, but by the end of our first run together, he'd somehow managed to sweep any awkwardness away.

He was my friend, acting like nothing happened between us, exactly what I asked him to do and he's done it every day since then when we've seen each other, which isn't often now that the season is starting.

But it all shows me one thing.

Whatever happened between us in Charleston is a memory to him, possibly a fond one, but definitely not a life-changing one.

Klaus sets down my wine glass and I thank him, surreptitiously watching him as he heads to the table where he's sitting with Sebastian and Duke.

"Okay. What is going on with you two?" Paisley, Mikah's fiancée, asks. Their wedding is coming up in a few months during a break in their schedule, delaying their honeymoon until after the season. She's been talking about it all night, and I don't blame her. Originally they were going to wait until she was done with grad school. They were going to push it up, but Paisley said she really wanted to do it right, so they pushed it back again so she can focus on it. Now, with only student teaching for her last semester of school to do, they're moving full steam ahead with the wedding planning and she's so damn giddy about it, it's a little bit difficult not to seethe with jealousy.

"What?" I slide my wine glass closer. Had Klaus put it any farther from me, it would have slid right off the table.

"You and Klaus. It looks like you're fighting, but you're still friendly. It's weird." Hannah's face scrunches up. She's hilarious. Wife to the head goalie and with two kids of her own, Hannah's known to spout off anything and everything she thinks.

"We're not fighting. And we are friends."

"Friends with a whole lot of crazy, twisted, sexual tension flying around whenever you're near each other."

"Not even close."

"Well, it's something," Paisley says and glances at him. His back is to us so I don't know what she's expecting to see unless she can read his mind.

Which would be nice.

I've spent a month regretting what I did and rethinking and wishing I would have been smarter that day a month ago. At least braver. But every time I even think of bringing it up with Klaus, letting him know I might have made a mistake, he gives me that friendly smile, keeps his hands to himself, and acts like everything is copacetic, so I don't.

At this point, I think I need to move on and find a way to get over him. Otherwise, continuing to be his friend is going to be torture.

"I really thought you two would get together by now. It's not like either of you are dating anyone. Why don't you get together?" Paisley asks. "Because I agree with Hannah. The tension between you two is thick."

"Probably about as thick as—"

"Don't." Paisley slaps her hand over Hannah's mouth. "Don't even finish that thought."

"What? I was talking about Byron."

"Sure you weren't."

I laugh. These girls are nutty. And their friends. That they're clueless at least means Klaus hasn't spilled our business all over the team and I've been around all of them long enough to know how difficult it is to keep everyone out of your business.

"Honest?" I ask them.

"Yes."

"Of course."

"I think I want us to be together... but I screwed up. Royally. And now I'm not sure I can fix it."

"Sure you can," Paisley says. Always sweet and optimistic I'm not surprised when her next words are, "Just talk to him. Tell him. You and Klaus have known each other way too long to not be able to figure things out, right?"

"I think you should just jump him. While you're naked. I bet that'd work."

"Hannah," Paisley groans and rolls her eyes.

"Unfortunately, I think getting naked is what screwed it all up to begin with." That and my cowardice.

Paisley's advice is logical, but that means risking everything. Hannah's advice is well... exactly something Hannah would say and not the route I'll ever choose.

"In all seriousness," Hannah says.

"You can be serious?" Paisley quips. "Huh. Who woulda thought?" She winks at me and nudges Hannah so hard she almost flies off her stool.

Gripping the table and flashing a quick glare at Paisley, Hannah turns to me, hair flying all over the place. "I've known Klaus since he was traded, which granted, isn't that long, but Byron and I are like the old people on the team. They're all like my younger brothers, and I know Klaus is a great guy. I also know he won't risk losing you for anything. *Talk* to him, Jillian. It's the only way."

They're right. I know it.

It's too damn bad I don't have a trip to Oz planned in my future where I can find some of that missing courage.

"Hey." I settle my hand on Klaus's shoulder where he's still sitting with Sebastian. Outside of him stopping by the table and dropping off two glasses of wine when he refilled his own, we've barely spoken all evening. "I'm going to take off. It's getting late."

He looks up at me with a furrowed brow. "You okay to drive?"

"I'm good. Only had a couple glasses."

"All right." He pushes back his chair and I say goodbye to the rest of the guys and congratulate them on their win.

"Thanks Jillian," Sebastian says. "We'll see more of you this season, right?"

"Sure." I'm not hopeful. Based on the look Klaus gives Sebastian, he's as doubtful as me.

"I'll walk you out."

"Oh. That's okay."

"Come on." He gives me a smile, bordering on sadness in his expression. Before I can tell him it's not necessary, he's already guiding me through the bar where I say goodnight to Gigi and George and two of his friends who are here almost every time we are.

Outside, I already have my keys in my hand, beeping the locks on my Camry when we get close. Klaus walks me to the door, asking, "Did you have fun tonight?"

"Hard not to with Hannah around. Did you?"

He huffs a laugh and as I'm about to open my door, he stops me by putting his hand at the top, forcing me to turn and face him.

"I didn't really have fun," he says, and there's such a serious look to his expression, jaw tight, eyes rimmed with lines I can make out from the parking lot lights, it stalls my breath.

"Why not?" I ask, although I'm sure I don't want to know why.

His lips pull to one side and then with a heaving breath, he exhales. "I don't know if I can keep doing this, Jilly-Bean."

His nickname for me, for the first time, doesn't make me smile.

"Klaus—"

"I've tried doing the friends thing with you, just like you wanted, but I don't think I can keep it up."

Oh God. My eyes burn at his words and my chin trembles. I can't believe he's doing this, after this last month when it seemed so easy for him. "I thought... I thought you were okay with it. You seemed to be."

"I'm tired of acting and I can't keep doing it. It's not good for me, or you, or us." He leans forward, caging me in against the car. I'm so stunned, I have nothing to say but when I open my mouth to speak, to plead, to do *something*, he continues. "I've loved you for much longer than our weekend away, Jillian. I waited until I knew you were over Roman, and I tried to wait until I saw my opportunity, but after the weekend we spent together, I can't go back. It's too hard."

"You... what?"

"You know how I feel. Even if I didn't say the words, I wasn't that inept at showing you. If you think back, I think you'll know that. But you either love me back, or you don't, either way, it will take me a while to get back to what we used to have. And I need you to give that time to me."

Tears stream down my cheeks. "I don't want to lose you."

He brushes away my tears and gives me a sad smile. "And I want to give you everything, but I can't only give half of me. It's not fair." He leans forward, and I gasp as his mouth touches mine. He steals my breath, pressing his lips firmly to mine. He kisses me intensely, passionately, as if it may be his last kiss and then pulls back.

"Take the time you need to decide and be certain. Get home safe, honey."

He steps away from me, shoves his hands into the

pockets of his pants and turns and walks back into the bar before I can form a thought, much less a sentence.

I fall into my driver's seat and cry, wiping my tears as fast as they fall.

He loves me.

And he still walked away from me.

## 29

## JILLIAN

This is a sight I never thought I'd see in my life. The morning sun is rising in my back yard, leaves from the gardens and trees glistening with the morning dew.

And my mom, dressed in jeans and a short-sleeve T-shirt, gardening gloves on her hands, and my cheap sandals I leave at the back door on her feet, bent over one of the beds, weeding it.

I almost want to grab my camera and snap a picture, but I fear by the time I turn back to the windows, the scene in front of me will be gone. Better to take it in and remember it.

"She's been looking forward to this." My dad comes and stands next to me, coffee mug in hand, and takes a sip.

I glance at him, the mug, and bite down a smile. The sight of him, dressed in business slacks and a golf shirt, holding a hot pink mug that says GIRL BOSS in gold metallic, is quite a thing to behold.

"If she loves this stuff so much, why'd she stop?"

"Priorities shifted. Perhaps she's realizing, like me, they didn't exactly shift for the better. And perhaps, with everything going on with Norman, we're learning there are amends to make, priorities to reshift before it's too late."

I'm speechless and take a drink of my coffee. My father barely flinched when he saw me in my cut-off sweat shorts and ripped and worn short-sleeve shirt. His eyes *did* widen as he read the words: SIZE MATTERS. NO ONE WANTS A SMALL GLASS OF WINE.

I have to give them credit. For the last month, since I saw them, they've made an effort. Our relationships are still strained, but improving, and surprisingly enough, I know from Nana, Mom has called her every week "just to chat."

I never imagined going to Charleston would forever alter my relationship with my parents for the better.

And alter my relationship with Klaus for the worst.

His words from a week ago reverberate in my brain, like they've been doing incessantly.

*Take the time you need.*

He said it right before he walked away.

I wanted to jump out of my car, race after him and scream to the dark night sky how much I loved him. Fear held me back.

This time, not in fear of losing him, but fear he wouldn't believe me in the heat of the moment. True to his word, he hasn't texted all week. I have no idea where his head is at, but I know where mine is.

I have to fix things with him. And I have to do it quickly before I lose him forever.

Unfortunately, they've been on the road all week, and on his one night back in town, I had an overnight trip to Wisconsin, so I haven't been able to see him or talk to him.

What I have to say has to be done face-to-face.

Which I plan on doing as soon as possible.

"Will we see Klaus after the game tonight?"

Right. The game. Where I have tickets and in another shocking move, my dad and mom want to go see him.

"I'm not sure."

"I'm surprised we haven't seen him this weekend."

"Things aren't... well, I messed them up," I admit and feel that familiar sting in my eyes. The heaviness to my shoulders.

I've messed everything up by being afraid. By thinking that if I love Klaus and admit it, it will ruin us. Like with Roman. Or wanting my parents' love for so long and not getting it. And yet it's Klaus.

I've always been able to trust him and I should have trusted him before, in my kitchen. In Charleston when he said he wanted to live it. I should have known him enough to know everything he showed me was exactly what I've been hoping for so long to see.

"Seems to me with how much he cares about you, you couldn't have messed up too big."

"I didn't trust him when I should have." I shrug like that answers everything.

"Do you know what I loved about your mom when we met?"

"No." A grin breaks on my face, that sting in my eyes different this time. Sweeter. My parents *never* talk about love, or how they met. Things, they are a-changing. "What was it?"

I face him, and yet his gaze is on my mom, smiling softly at her as he watches her work in a way I don't know if I ever saw before that night in the library.

Or I never noticed.

"Her coldness toward me."

"What?"

He turned his grin on me then. "When we met, I thought she was the most beautiful woman I'd ever seen. Love at first sight? Lightning striking? Thunder rolling? I felt all of that the first time I saw your mom walk across the quad at school and when I tried to talk to her, she basically told me to shove off."

"No." I drawl it out, overdramatic.

My dad chuckles and his gaze softens. Like he's remembering that very moment and it's too special to mention. "She was hard. I think now you might know why a little bit but back then, well, she was an ice queen toward everyone. I think she was trying so hard to be so different from how she grew up, from Iris, that she didn't give anyone the time of day."

Ah. It makes sense now. "And as a guy who grew up with everything, who probably had girls falling all over you for your money and your status in Charleston, that probably ticked you off."

He shrugs, as if that's completely how it was. "She made me work for her. Earn her. It took *months* of chasing after her, proving myself to her that she wasn't some game. And for that, her fire and her determination, well, it all made me love her more."

Outside, my mom stands and pulls off her gloves. She places her hands at her lower back and stretches, catching us gawking at her from the window. Her eyes widen in surprise and then she nods, a small, barely-there grin on her face at being caught working in my gardens.

"She's not an easy woman to love. Never has been, and

yet I also know that once she opens that door, it's a gentle, quiet, steadfast love she provides. She gives stability and loyalty and in an era when everyone bases love on feelings and commitment, and well, she's a special woman once you get to that part of her."

I think I understand her now more than I ever did and yet that pain is still there. "I wish I would have known all this before. It would have been helpful instead of growing up thinking I was a nuisance."

He settles his arm across my back, hand at my shoulder. His grip is warm but timid. Probably because he *never* does this. "And that is our mistake we will continue to work to rectify, but I do want you to know I'm proud of you, of this life you built. You can do anything you set your mind to, Jillian, even fix whatever you messed up with Klaus." He gives me a soft kiss on my temple and then walks away, opens the door for my mom, and as she kicks off my sandals and brushes hair off her face, he does the same to her, asking her if he can get her coffee.

It's beautiful and sweet and quiet and I allow the love my parents have for each other and so rarely shown to warm me to my soul along with Dad's words.

I have their approval.

And once I do what my dad says and fix things, I'll have Klaus.

I'll have everything I've always wanted.

"I THOUGHT it'd be cooler in here," my mom says. She's still wearing thin gloves, rubbing her hands together as we take our seats. "What with all the ice and all."

She goes down the aisle first, my dad following and me bringing up the rear. The tagboard sign I'm holding shakes in my hands and has nothing to do with how wobbly it is.

I can't believe I'm doing this.

I'm going to make a complete spectacle of myself. And yet, if I don't go all in and show Klaus how much I truly love him, I'm afraid he might not believe me.

"Nervous?" my dad asks, brushing wrinkles off his pants as he sits. "I can go get you a drink."

Funny, how this was actually his idea. At least part of it.

And I never imagined my mom would sip Prosecco with me, coloring in block letters with glitter pens in my kitchen.

That's exactly what happened this morning after we finished breakfast.

I'm working on trusting what I'm learning about her, and in doing so, a light has dawned.

She's always been quiet and steadfast, exactly what my dad said. As a little girl and teenager, I took it to mean she didn't care.

She does, but in her own way. She might not be outgoing in her love, and she might not be the most expressive woman with her emotions, but that doesn't mean she doesn't have them.

She shows them quietly. And today, she did the same, when I nervously brought up my idea to fix things with Klaus.

She even came with me to the craft store where I bought supplies.

Then we came home and she spread everything out on the kitchen island. My dad went to the living room, whiskey on ice in his hand and remote in his other to turn on a golf tournament, leaving us to our drinks and glitter.

It continues to surprise me how much fun I've had with them this weekend.

How quickly things are changing. I'm under no illusions we'll be the perfect family, but we've come a long way in a short amount of time.

It's enough of a reason to celebrate, but now I want it all.

Seated, my knee bounces wildly and inside my own thin gloves, my hands grow clammy.

My dad's hand lands on my leg, settling me.

"Calm. You'll be fine."

I can't help it. I'm about to make a major fool of myself. Fortunately, the arena is mostly empty. We're here early in part to the parking spot I have along with my tickets so I don't have to wait in the long row of cars stuck in traffic for general parking. Also because I planned it this way.

I might be ready to act a fool, but I'm not going to do it with a stadium filled with approximately twenty-thousand strangers watching.

I wait, anticipating the moment the Ice Kings will take the ice for their pre-game warm-up skate. They always come out in the same way, by line, which means as soon as I see Jason Taylor, team captain, appear in the doorway that leads from the ice and their bench to their locker room, I stand on trembling legs and shaking ankles and hurry down to the ice level seats. Thank goodness the section where I'm sitting is still empty. It gives me space, and a meager amount of privacy.

As the guys hit the ice to the quiet cheers and claps of fans already seated, thousands getting their pregame drinks and snacks, my heart races like a herd of wild horses, thundering along the beaches of the Outer Banks.

*This is it.*

Oh God, I might puke.

Jason leads the team in one giant, slow lap around the ice and as he reaches my side of the rink, his eyes flash and then he grins. I'm never down here, always in my seats, so I know I've surprised him.

But then I see Klaus, taking to the ice on the far side, and the cheers of the crowd all fall away to the pounding in my heart.

This is it. I keep my gaze on Klaus, trying to get his attention. I see the exact moment he glances up to my seats he probably expects to be empty and his mouth opens in surprise. If I were to turn around, I'd see my parents, probably sitting stoically, perhaps lifting a hand, but Klaus's gaze darts down the line and then straight to me as he reaches the corner of the ice nearest me.

And I lift my sign.

My stupid, girly, and basic tagboard sign that reads in blue and teal lettering like their jerseys.

*I'm really sorry.*

*I love you.*

Ice sprays from the sudden stop of his skates. He halts directly in front of me, hand going to his chin guard strap, and he tears it away, ripping off his helmet faster than I've seen him do when he gets in fights during games.

Behind him, Duke makes a quick adjustment so he doesn't run smack into him and Klaus comes my way.

Right to the boards. Directly across the glass from me.

He bangs on the glass with his stick, like I haven't already been staring at him, waiting for his reaction.

"You love me?" I can barely hear him shouting.

I nod, knowing he can't hear it back but like the fool he is, grinning like a maniac, he holds his hand to his ear and shouts, "What?"

"Yes! Yes, I love you."

Tears fall down my cheeks. His smile is infectious, better than anything I've seen in months. Maybe years.

Klaus's lips press together, firm and so sexy I wish there wasn't a thick wall of shatterproof plexiglass between us.

Instead, he places his hand on the glass.

I do the same.

"We'll talk. After the game."

For a moment, my bravery falters, but then he licks his lips. Dropping his gloves and his stick to the ice, he points to himself and mouths the word I. Makes a heart with his hands and says love and then points to me.

And I swear the point is filled with burning hot flames that shoot straight to my own heart. "*You,*" he mouths and my world erupts at the same time it finally comes together.

"I'm sorry," I mouth.

"Later," he says. "Hallway?"

He gestures to where the locker rooms are. I know what he means. If I have the right pass, I can get back to the hall where the players will exit. I don't have that pass, but I'll trust Klaus to take care of it.

The time for me to be afraid, to fear him is gone. I've always been able to trust him. It's just taken me too long to know it.

"I love you," he mouths again.

"I love you too," I say it slowly so he can see it and then his smile is almost as blinding as the sun. He gathers his gear he chucked to the ice and skates away.

"That looks like it went well," my mom says politely, hands folded in her lap.

She'll never be the emotional woman or overly affectionate mom I always dreamed of. But now I think that's okay. Seems to me I got enough crazy in us for the both of us.

"It did." I take my seat next to my dad and am surprised as hell when he reaches over and squeezes my hand.

"Proud of you, for putting yourself out there like that. And I like him. Good job."

I squeeze his hand back and fight down my own tears. "Thanks, Dad."

## 30

## KLAUS

We win the game easily.

Before I'm stripping out of my gear, I already know I've won more.

Jillian loves me. And not only has she finally admitted it to my face, she did it in a ridiculously cheesy way sure to bring her and me attention. It's a stupid little sign, that says nothing, not when there's so much for us to talk about, but it also says all it needs to.

She loves me.

We'll work the rest out.

"You heading to George's tonight?" Jude asks, passing me in the locker room. "Bunch of us are headed there."

"Nope. Not tonight."

"I have a feeling he has his own one-on-one celebration planned."

I shove Sebastian's shoulder so hard he falls to the bench.

"Easy, old man."

"I'm the same age as you."

"Oh. Then why are you slow out there?"

He punches my thigh playfully from his spot on the bench. "Asshole."

"Maybe." I don't care what they think of me right now. Our team has won. We're off to a great start and a few of the new players are playing as well as we hoped, if not better, especially Owen Bennard. From Michigan, he's spent three years working his way through the minors and spent last season at Carolina Ice Kings affiliate team in Missouri. So far, he's doing so well as the center on my line, giving me confidence we'll be kicking some serious ass this season. Not that I had much doubt with our already existing talent, but a new season and a new crop of players always brings uncertainty.

Now, all the uncertainty I've had for the last month has vanished into a plume of shredded ice.

*She loves me.*

"So what was that with Jillian earlier?" Sebastian gives me a cocky ass smile. Like he hasn't already figured it out.

"Remember that thing we do when we get worked up about our women and don't know what to do?"

"Yeah. Vaguely."

Because he royally screwed things up with Gigi. Pushed her away when he didn't want to because he was scared to love her.

"Well I'm smarter than that. And I took care of it on my own."

He laughs and shakes his head. "You're a conceited dick."

"Maybe. But I think I just got the girl, so I'm also a smart dick."

I finish shredding out of my gear, take the world's fastest shower known to man and after a talk from our coach, mostly telling us how much work we still have to do, I head out to the hall where families and girlfriends gather.

I find her immediately. All her brown hair pulled up into a knot that's sticking out of the top of her Ice Kings knitted cap. She's nibbling her bottom lip, standing off to the side near Sawyer's wife, Debbie, and their son, Samson.

I'm vaguely aware of Debbie's existence. Or the fact Jillian's parents aren't with her.

I don't care.

I go to her.

She jolts as I reach her, already placing my hands at her cheeks. "Klaus—"

"You love me?"

Eyes wide, fear trickles in, perhaps because I've startled her.

"Yes," she says, and it's one word. Three letters.

The best word.

I smash my mouth to hers and lift her off her feet, wrapping one arm around her lower back until I'm bent nearly in half.

Hoots and hollers from my teammates echo in the background, but I keep kissing Jillian like my life depends on it until she pulls back, cheeks flaming hot pink, lips swollen, and eyes shimmering with happiness.

No more fear.

"I love you, too, you know."

"I know. You've shown me all along, I think. I'm sorry—"

I kiss her again. "No apologies. Let me take you home and we'll talk, okay?"

Setting her on her feet, I playfully tug on her beanie. "I was really glad to see you at the game. Sign or no sign."

"You played well and I think my dad got into it."

"Speaking of... where are they?"

"They went home, well, back to my place. But my mom said she'd see me in the morning, so if you want—"

"You're coming home with me then."

"And maybe you'll let me finish a sentence?"

"Perhaps." I let my gaze show her everything I'm feeling. "Unless we get distracted by other, better activities that don't involve a lot of talking at all."

Jillian laughs and it's beautifully perfect. "That all sounds too good to be true."

"It's true." I lean in and kiss her temple, because she loves me, and now I don't think I'll ever be able to stop kissing her. "And it will be good. *Very* good."

She shivers in my arms, letting me know she feels the exact same way. For once, we're on the same page.

And it's perfect.

WE ENTER my house through the laundry room, a room I never use outside dumping my shoes and hockey gear in which means there are piles everywhere and a small pathway to maneuver. Despite the mess, I kick off my shoes and drop my bag and wait impatiently for Jillian to remove her hat, refluff her hair and hang her coat on the door handle. Taking her hand, I pull her to the kitchen where I go to the wine rack on my kitchen counter. It's always stocked with her favorites.

Without looking, I dig through the drawer, searching for my wine opener. "Drink?"

"Water."

"I'm sorry?" I look at her over my shoulder and I must look aghast because Jillian laughs.

She shrugs. "I'd rather make sure we're both sober for tonight."

What a fantastic idea. "Have some plans for us, do you?"

"Hoping."

"There's no need. I am a man at your disposal. Come on. Let's go sit." I head toward her and take her hand when she turns on the stool and we make our way to the living room. My couches are enormous, could probably fit most of my team, all spread out, but tonight I don't give her that option.

I sit in the corner of the couch, and pull her so she's curled next to me, legs draped over my lap so I can settle my hand on her thighs. My other arm lands on the back of the couch where I can run my fingers through her curled and messy hair.

Now that I have free rein to touch her when I want, I'm not sure I'll ever stop.

"So," I start. "You want to tell me what happened at the wedding reception?"

"I heard what you said to Adrianna. And it hurt more than I expected it would."

I already figured all this. Not that she confirmed it the day I hijacked her mimosa morning and confronted her.

She runs her tongue along her bottom lip, wetting it and inhales so deeply her breasts push out, snagging my attention for a moment before I refocus.

Boobs later. Talking now. As much as I want her, I won't have her until I know we're on the same page.

"I think," she says and pauses. "I think I've been in love with you for a long time. Maybe even it started when I was still with Roman and then we broke up, and you were still dating all those girls."

"Two," I correct. There were two girls. Bailey and I went on two dates with Bianca. Bailey was the only one who was significant, and that's only because she thought she was. "And that was months ago."

"I know, you said. But after Roman and I had been broken up a while, you still never treated me differently. Never shown interest and so I figured you really just did think we were friends. And then the wedding weekend happened, and I was dealing with so much, with Roman and Julianna, my family, and you were there, giving me all I ever wanted from you. I only told Adrianna we were friends because I was scared to hope for more until we could talk. Then, I heard you say that and it was my worst fear come true."

"Jilly..." I stop, not certain what else to say besides reassuring her how much I do care, how long I've wanted her, but she stops me and presses her finger to my lips.

"It's okay. I get it, I get why you told her, and I wish I would have been brave enough when you asked me about it that day, but there was still so much swirling in my brain, I panicked."

"I get it." I kiss the pad of her fingertip, making her grin.

"I think I grew up not really knowing what love is, or at least not experiencing it the way I wanted to. And then there was Roman..." She flips her hand in the air and brushes it away. We've discussed Roman enough so I don't push. "But everything that weekend was too much to handle and you... well, I *need* you. I need you in my life and I guess I knew, in some way, even if I pushed you away that morning, you'd still be there. But I couldn't risk losing you completely. Not then."

"You won't ever have to. And I'm sorry I gave you that ultimatum last week. It killed me to hurt you, to walk away when I knew I made you cry again."

"I know." Tears swell in her eyes again. More freaking tears, but this time I can do something about it.

Cupping her cheek, I wipe away a tear off her cheekbone and whisper her name. "I shouldn't have pushed. I should have given you the time I knew you needed, but I was impatient. I've wanted you for so long and yeah, after Roman and you broke up, I knew you needed space, but I thought the same way about you. You'd never given me any indication you wanted me like this."

"I know. I'm sorry. Because I did."

"Still do?"

"Now more than ever."

My hand at her cheek slides to the back of her neck and head where I cradle her and bring her to me. "Good. Because I've loved you for a long time and now that I have you, you should know I'll probably never let you go."

"I don't need to be anywhere else."

I keep bringing her closer until her lips are brushing mine and then I seal our promises with a kiss that makes her shiver in my arms. My body is already ready for her. The results of her being so sweet, so beautiful, and pressed against me, and for wanting her for so long. It takes effort, but I keep our kiss slow, sensual. I show her with action and not words how much I want her, how much I love her.

And when she's breathless, making those cute, needy little sounds that shows me how turned-on she is, I stand with her in my arms, carry her up the stairs, and spend the rest of the night showing her exactly how perfect we are together.

# EPILOGUE

Klaus
Three Months Later

"The truck is gone."

"Now we just have to unpack."

Next to me, Jillian gives me her weight, settling her head on my shoulder. As her body relaxes, I swoop her up.

"Klaus!" she squeals as I grab her behind her knees and at her back.

"Aren't I supposed to carry you over the threshold?"

"I think that's after you get married."

"I'll do it then, too." Her eyes widen at my statement. If she's surprised, she shouldn't be. We just bought a house with six bedrooms for crying out loud. "But first homes together should be celebrated."

She grins, it's blindingly bright even in the crisp December air. Like always when she looks at me like I've hung the moon, I kiss her and carry her through the entryway of our new home.

One we bought together.

It took a week for us to realize we didn't want to live apart. With our crazy schedules, one of us was always exhausted by the time we got to the other's house. It took another week to realize neither house would work enough to combine our homes together. Her home was too small and didn't give me the exercise space I need or room to grow. Mine didn't have the back yard she wanted with room to garden or a kitchen large enough to hold everything she owned.

We immediately went to work, scouring listings, finding our dream home. One with lots of bedrooms so we can fill it —my idea which made Jillian jump me in the living room, on her plush rug, which delayed our search or a few hours.

Fortunately, we hired the best realtor ever who within days, heard of a home going on the market in the neighborhood we wanted, with the land space we wanted. It has an old-world charm to it, because I know Jillian loves the history and architecture of older homes and not the cookie-cutter style new ones. It has three floors, a walkout basement and a private balcony outside our master bedroom on the top level so she can have her morning coffee or late-night glass of wine overlooking the pool and her gardens in raised beds surrounding it.

It has everything and more that we need, a movie room downstairs with an extra-large exercise room. Folding glass doors off the family room on the main level that open to our covered porch and then the pool and another half-acre of land beyond. It's the perfect home for us to come together in, to truly start our lives together.

She laughs as I swing her through the massive two-story

entryway, spin her around the curved banister and stairway railings. I dance with her and kiss her until we're in the kitchen and set her down on the massive island that can sit at least eight adults and probably more.

"Welcome to your new home." I kiss her and step in between her knees, reaching behind her for the box I'd brought with me in my truck. Inside the cooler is a bottle of champagne and two glasses.

"Our new home." She kisses me back and looks to where I'm digging into the box behind her. "What do you have there?"

"Celebration supplies," I say, pulling out the bottle of champagne.

"Huh." She frowns. "I had something else in mind for celebration supplies."

"What's that?" She crosses her arms in front of her and grabs the hem of her faded pink shirt. She rips it off and over her head making the messy knot on top of her head bob and fall. I only notice it for one little bounce before my gaze falls to her breasts, nipples already hard and peeking through her white lace bra.

"I thought our celebration would include nothing at all, really."

Best idea ever.

I grab the edges of her leggings and begin pulling them down. She lifts her hips and shimmies while I tug them down and by the time I have them ripped off her legs, she's torn away her bra, leaving her absolutely bare, skin flushed, holding the bottle of champagne, and looking sexier than ever.

Taking the bottle from Jillian, I unwrap the foil. She shoves down my athletic pants past my hips and uses her feet to help push them to the floor. While I pop the cork, she slides her hands into my boxers, wrapping her cool hand around my heavy and hot arousal.

I take a swig of the bottle and hand it to her which she greedily takes, still sliding her hand up and down my length.

As she drinks, I throw off my shirt. She hands the bottle back to me, and I place my hand at her chest, applying pressure until she's splayed out on the counter, all her chocolatey brown hair and tan skin in direct contrast to the white countertop.

"Goddamn, you are beautiful," I murmur, earning a laugh from Jillian. Her abs contract and her breasts shake from her laughter. "Although I think I'm still thirsty."

I hold the champagne over her breasts.

"What are you—Oh!" she squeals as the first cold drops of champagne fall onto her pebbled nipples. It runs down her sides, between the deviation of her abs and I drizzle more on her skin, watching the bubbles ripple and fall, heading toward her belly button and below it.

"You better clean that up," she says, panting.

Already I can see her slick center between her legs.

"Oh no. I think we'll be getting a lot dirtier." I bend down and lick a drop of champagne and go lower, tasting her mixed with the bubbly champagne on my tongue as she squirms beneath me.

"Klaus."

Her hands slap the counter. She has nowhere to go, no way to steady herself as I begin my assault on her. I alternate between tastes of champagne and tastes of her until I've cleaned up her flesh by kissing and licking every inch of her. I drive her crazy with my mouth at her breasts while my fingers push her to the edge deep inside of her.

And as she screams my name, it bounces off the walls

and echoes through our massive home and I love every damn second of it.

And when she's done, listless, well-used and flushed and anything but pure and clean, I slam my dick inside of her and make her scream my name over and over again until my own orgasm hits and our shouts are mixed together.

"We need a shower," Jillian pants, running her now hot hands down the sweat on my shoulders and back. "And I hope you bought more than one bottle of champagne because we're going to need that, too. You didn't let me play."

"You'll have all the time in the world to play with me," I tell her.

"Yeah." Her smile is sweet. Knowing. Content and confident. "I guess I will, won't I."

Damn straight.

I gather our clothes so we can shower before getting to work unpacking when my phone rings.

I check it, the team knows we're moving today so no one should be calling.

"Hello?"

"It's Sebastian. Gigi's at the hospital. You and Jillian need to get here."

"Is everything okay?" I ask.

"Yeah. Yeah. I'm just... I'm going to be a dad today, so get your ass down here, would you?"

I grin at Jillian. "We'll be there. Go take care of your girl and boy."

I hang up and Jillian heads to me. "Everything okay?"

"Sebastian. Gigi's at the hospital having their baby. He wants us to get there."

"Oh my gosh, that's so exciting!" she screams and grabs

her clothes, hauls off toward the stairs. "I have to shower and we have to get cleaned up! Come on! Come on, let's go!"

I chase after her, laughing. The girl is loud and with nothing set up in the house her excited voice bounces off every arched ceiling and exposed beam and corner.

"I think we have time."

"How do you know?"

I have no idea. "Don't babies take a while or something?"

"How the hell would I know?"

This woman. "Come on." I shove her toward the bathroom with a hand at her lower back, reach around her to the walk-in behemoth shower large enough to hold a rave party and flip on the water.

"I'm just saying we can take our time. He didn't make it sound like it was immediate."

"Fine." She shoves her finger into my chest. "But no more sexy shenanigans. I don't want to show up at the hospital and see a new baby smelling like sex or anything."

"No shenanigans," I promise. "Until we get home."

THE BIRTHING CENTER'S waiting room is packed with teammates by the time we arrive. George, Gigi's dad, and his friend Steve are on the far wall, staring out the windows that overlook Charlotte. I find Mikah first, sitting close to Paisley who's holding Angelo by the fingertips as he stands in front of her on wobbling knees and legs and happily drooling as he dances in place. Next to them are Hannah and Byron whose two kids are sitting at a small child-size table nearby and fighting over crayons.

"How's everything going? How's Gigi?"

"Last update from the nurse is that Gigi's had her epidural and she's six centimeters dilated."

Like I understand any of that. "What the hell does that even mean?"

Hannah rolls her eyes and mutters *men* at Byron before shaking her head at me. "It means she's doing great. Not in pain, and she's moving along quickly and smoothly. As long as things keep moving, it could still be a few hours."

"Has anyone talked to Sebastian?"

"He came out and grabbed George. Gigi wanted to see him, but that was a while ago."

From Sebastian, I know Gigi's mom died several years ago, leaving George to practically raise her. He's done a damn good job because Gigi kicks ass. As for Sebastian, I also know he once learned he wasn't able to have children. Even though this pregnancy came at a time when he was just starting to fall in love with Gigi while also getting over his ex-wife leaving him, Sebastian calls this boy his miracle baby. Doctors told Sebastian he might never be able to have a biological child, to say he's been nervous and overprotective of Gigi the entire pregnancy is putting it lightly.

Jillian kisses my cheek and points toward where Katie and Debbie are sitting in the corner. Debbie's cradling a sleeping Abram, the boy she and Sawyer had in May. "I'm going to go snuggle Abram."

"I'm going to pace and freak out. I mean, we still have hours to go yet?"

"I guess we could have unpacked a little bit first, huh?" She's teasing and I scowl at her.

"Unpack at a time like this?"

"It's not like the world's ending, it's a baby being born. Women do it every day."

Yeah, but it's not every day it's one of my best friends

who's had a really shitty few years of stress and heartache, so I might want this to go more smoothly and perfectly than Sebastian himself wants it.

He's a good guy. He deserves it.

Time moves as slow as molasses.

Jude eventually orders lunch for everyone, and since half the team is here and he received a text saying Sebastian's parents are on their way from the airport from Minnesota, he calls Chipotle and orders catering, probably magically greasing hands and pleading and promising an appearance or something in order for them to get it here as fast as they do. We have so much food, some of the nurses swing by and fill up plates on their breaks.

I've aged a decade and paced so much up and down the hallway between the two birthing wings, I won't need to do cardio for weeks.

It's Jillian who comes to me as I'm preparing to turn and pace another lap and settles her hand at my back, one at my chest. "Hey. Calm down. Everything's fine."

A nurse came out thirty minutes ago and said Gigi was about ready to push. What is taking so long?

"Something could go wrong."

"Nothing's going to go wrong."

"But it could."

It's not my baby. But Sebastian's family.

"Come here." Jillian pulls me in for a hug and I go reluctantly but as soon as I get a whiff of her perfume and feel her arms wrapped around me, the world rights and centers again. I press my lips to the side of her head and squeeze her tight.

"Thank you," I murmur. "I needed this. Need you."

"You have me for always and always," she whispers back.

Then she grins up at me and rolls to her toes, giving me a quick kiss.

I kiss her back, calmed by her presence, her steadfast love for me when the doors behind her open, squealing from their weight.

Sebastian steps through them, looking worn-out and exhilarated at the same time. His hair is a mess. His face is red. His smile is so big I can count all his teeth from here.

I go to him immediately, pulling Jillian with me as she laughs at me.

"He's here. He's healthy. Nine pounds which doctor says is big for a woman as small as Gigi but she did it." His face turns even more red, tears swell in his eyes.

I throw my arms around him and hold him tight. "Congratulations. So damn happy for you."

"Me too, man. Holy shit. I'm a dad."

I pull back and smirk. "That poor, poor child."

"Fuck off." Sebastian shoves me playfully and then he's embraced by women and men, all giving him their congratulations.

"How's Gigi?" Hannah asks.

"Incredible. Amazing. Beautiful," he says. I think all the women sigh at Sebastian.

I pull Jillian closer to me as Sebastian tells us she's tired, but both she and Samson are healthy and doing well before he goes to George and receives a hug from his future father-in-law.

"I'm going to take George back," Sebastian tells us, "and check with Gigi, but I know she'd like visitors so stick around if you want to. And thank you, thank you guys for everything." Emotions grab him and more than one man feel the same sting in their eyes as I do. "Thank you for being brothers, for being there for me and us."

"Oh shit. I need tissues," Jillian says, tears streaming down her cheeks. She glances around the room. She's not the only one. "I think we all do."

"I'll get them." After we pass around kisses and clean our faces, I pull Jillian back into my arms.

"Someday," I whisper in her ear, "this is going to be us, and this family, this family we build together will be here for us. And hopefully, the families we were given at birth will be too."

She grins at me, tears in her eyes and a wobble to her smile.

She and her family are still working on their issues, but things are moving in the right direction for Jillian. She talks to her mom and Claire has sounded excited about getting ready to help Jillian put in gardens and redo flower beds in the spring. They'll be here for Christmas to celebrate it in our first home together. As for Norman, he continues to decline slowly so unless things change, we're headed to Charleston on my first break after Christmas to see him.

"I'm ready to start whenever you are," she says, surprising the hell out of me. After shocking her with my demand for a large home for kids, she'd been so surprised we haven't talked about that anymore.

I chalked it up to us rushing forward, moving in so quickly. The future can wait.

But hell.

Why should it?

We've already waited long enough.

It's a damn good thing I already have the ring, wrapped up and hidden away for Christmas.

"Anything you want, Jilly-Bean. I'll give you anything you want, whenever you want it."

She kisses me and pulls back, smiling. "You already do."

THANK you for reading Fighting Dirty! If you enjoyed it, please leave an honest review on the retailer where this book was purchased.

I hope you've enjoyed falling in love with the Ice Kings. If so, keep reading to check out the first chapter in my book, This Time Around. If you loved the Ice Kings, you'll love the men in America's Heartland.

WANT to stay up to date on all my future releases and sales? Join my newsletter! As a thank you, you'll receive a FREE EBOOK.

# THE TIME AROUND


**Rebecca**

"Come on Max, you can't be serious about this."

"I think it'll be good for him, Rebecca. And you could use the help."

Boy, could I. With my cell phone in one hand, my other curled around the kitchen countertop. Outside my small kitchen window, cows roamed in the pasture and goats ate their hay. I was behind on everything—the cattle, the other animals, the house, *and* the bills.

Knowing a defeat when I sensed one through the silence coming through the phone line, I asked, "What's his name again?"

My uncle chuckled good-naturedly. "Cooper Hawke, and you're probably the only female I know who doesn't know who he is."

"Well, who has time to watch TV these days?"

"Movies, Rebecca. He does movies."

Whatever. That was worse. I had less time for those. I blew out a breath, flipping wisps of my black hair out of my face where they'd escaped my falling apart ponytail. "When will he be here?"

"I have to run it by him first, but I'm hoping by Saturday."

Great. I had four days to prepare for Hollywood's heart-throb to step foot on my ranch. I didn't like the idea of any of this, but Uncle Max was the only family I had left besides my brother Jordan. Even though he lived out in Los Angeles, we'd always been close. He wouldn't be asking for my help if he didn't desperately need it.

And because I loved Max so much, I found myself finally putting a voice to the largest fear I had since he called. "There hasn't been a man here, Max, not since...."

"I know, darling. I know." His voice went soft, that caring tone being almost enough to burst through the dam I barely held together on the best of days. Today was not one of them. "But Joseph is gone, and you need the help. Cooper needs this. He needs to get out of town, blow off the paparazzi following him. It's been months and it's driving him insane. I need him focused before he starts filming in a few months. Put him to work and distract him. He can use it right now, and I promise you he's a good man."

I trusted Max implicitly. He wouldn't set me loose around a jerk.

Although, I also had Jordan to watch my back if I needed it. I rarely got messed with when people find out my brother was Jordan Marx, former MLB Pitcher for the Colorado Rockies. He lived here in town now and ran the Carlton Golf Resort and Spa. He designed and opened it after he walked away from his professional baseball career.

I was excited to have my family back together, finally, after years of wanting nothing more than for us all to be together again, but just like everything else in life, a curveball came my way.

First it was our parents.

Then it was Joseph.

And since then, I'd been treading water. If I didn't get some serious help, it wouldn't be long until I drowned completely.

"I trust you, Max, and you know I'll do anything I can for you, but—"

"I know, sweetheart, and I appreciate this. It'll be good. I promise. I'll call you back once I meet with Cooper and we've finalized everything."

"Are you sure he'll even want to come?" My thumb found its way between my teeth and I nibbled. It was possible this might not even happen.

I despised the idea of another man working on my ranch. It was stubborn pride and lingering grief mixed with a barrel of anger, but I wanted to be enough to do everything like I'd always dreamed of.

"He'll come," Max said. "He'll do what I say because he knows the risk if he doesn't."

My uncle was an agent. The best one in L.A. from what he said, and even though I rarely watched television, I didn't doubt him. He wasn't only charismatic, he was also intelligent and powerful. He started and ruined more careers than anyone else in Hollywood in the last twenty years. I figured Cooper Hawke knew this.

If he wanted to stay popular in the business, he had to listen to Max.

"Okay, I need to get to work. Call me when you know more."

"Will do, sweetheart. Make sure you get some rest."

"Right."

*Right. Because working a ranch allowed for spa days and naps.*

We said our goodbyes, and by the time I was back in the horse barn feeding the horses, I'd compiled a mental list of everything to be done before Cooper arrived.

We had a guesthouse, a small, two-bedroom house one hundred yards from the main house. It hadn't been used since the last time we had company, during my parents' funeral.

I'd need to spend the nights when I was done with the farm work getting it ready, dusting and vacuuming and cleaning and changing sheets.

"Yeah, definitely no spa days for me," I muttered to Gray, one of my favorite Arabian horses. He was the horse I learned to ride on. Now that he was getting old, I couldn't ride him much to do work, but he was my favorite.

He neighed against my palm as I handed him an extra apple, gave him a good rubdown, and then I headed back outside.

By the time night fell and I climbed into bed exhausted, barely managing to find the energy to pull on one of Joseph's old college shirts from Iowa State University, I'd completely forgotten all about Max's phone call or the impending visit from Cooper Hawke.

I never should have Googled Cooper Hawke. After spending hours preparing the guesthouse for him, looking him up online had to be one of the largest mistakes I'd ever made in my life.

He was everything masculine that single girls dreamed about at night when they didn't have a man to help them take care of their needs. A few hours spent reading the gossip surrounding his recent estrangement from his wife—a Brazilian supermodel—and I could understand the attraction.

Not that I'd dreamed of him taking care of my needs. That part of me died the day Joseph did—the same night we'd had a horrific fight, our worst ever, and he'd lost control of his truck on icy roads.

The day Joseph died, my world darkened. He left me with a pile of anger and questions that would never be answered.

But I was still a female, one who could understand why Cooper, a ridiculously famous actor, could drive women crazy with a wink from his light green and intoxicating eyes. As I spent my time searching through photos and articles of him, I could also see the friendly and teasing grin he used on red carpet appearances and when talking about his upcoming movies on late night talk shows had darkened over the last few months.

His wife, Camilla Rinaldi, was claiming she came home and found Cooper in a compromising position with their housekeeper. More than once, he'd denied the accusations.

Considering her expression hadn't changed in the recent months and her voice was the loudest, I figured she was the guilty party. In my experience, the most deafening voice tried to blare out the truth with volume. A part of me admired Cooper for not going for her throat in what had become an evil and contestable pending divorce settlement.

It wasn't only the financial arguments that made me feel for Cooper. It was the lost look in his eyes. The haze of grief and sadness told me he was mourning the loss of something—someone—dear to him. I recognized that same haze in my own expression.

I didn't want anything to bind Cooper and I together. He was coming here to get some space from the gossip in Hollywood. He was coming to be put to work on a ranch.

We'd work long hours together. I'd teach him everything I knew, and I hoped like hell he wasn't too good, too arrogant or too *preppy* to get his hands and boots a bit dirty while he was here.

I'd help him. Give him some peace and quiet.

And then I'd send him back to California where he could return to his life.

Then, I'd be left alone with mine.


Find out what happens when Cooper Hawke steps foot in Kansas, and right onto Rebecca's farm!

Download today!

# ACKNOWLEDGMENTS

HUGE thank you to Hilary and all of Social Butterfly PR for throwing your full enthusiasm and support behind each and every book I write. I have loved working with all of you and can't wait to see what's ahead! Hilary, I miss you most of all. ;-)

Ellie and Virginia, as always, thanks for putting up with my mess and spit-shining each manuscript until it sparkles. Thank you especially during this crazy time in our world for your flexibility and your extra hard work.

Shannon, you're the best. Always. Forever. Your talent is astounding and I'm thankful I can call you a friend.

Special, enormous thank you to my family who is always here, cheering me on and being so patient when I'm in my office. Your support is everything to me and I love you all with all of my heart.

To my Sweeties! I love you ladies and your excitement for my books! Special thanks to you this time for coming up with Brenna's name for me. It fits her perfectly.

To all the bloggers who devote their time and passion into reading books, book tours, release events, leaving reviews, promoting and pimping – you are all rockstars! Thank you for all the love over the years.

My family— I love you all to the moon and back. I don't know what I would do without you in my corner, cheering me on every step of the way.

And last but definitely not least – to you the reader. I'm blown away with every release how much you adore my books. You have made my dream a reality and I hope I can cheer you on with yours.

# ABOUT THE AUTHOR

Stacey Lynn likes her coffee with a dash of sugar, her heroes with a side of bossy, and her wine a deep shade of red.

The author of over thirty romance novels, many of which have been best-selling titles on Amazon, AppleBooks, and Barnes & Noble, she loves being able to turn her vivid imagination into a career that brings entertainment and joy to her readers. Focused on sports romance and emotional, small-town romance, she also loves stretching herself in different genres.

Born in Texas and raised in the Midwest, she now makes her home in North Carolina and loves all things Southern. Together with her ultimate tall, dark, and handsome hero, she has four children. Her life is a chaotic mess that fights with her Type-A, list-making, neurotically organized preferences and she wouldn't have it any other way.

Subscribe to her newsletter so you can stay up to date on all her new releases. www.staceylynnbooks.com

# OTHER BOOKS BY STACEY LYNN

### <u>Ice Kings Series</u>
<u>Playing With Fire – Prequel Novella</u>

Playing To Win

Scoring Off The Ice

Hooked On Her

Hard Checked

### <u>The Rough Riders Series</u>

Dirty Player

Filthy Player

Wicked Player

Cocky Player

### <u>Love In The Heartland</u>

Captivated By You

This Time Around

Long Road Home

Before We Fell

### <u>Crazy Love Series</u>

Fake Wife

Knocked Up

28 Dates

Weekend Fling

**The Fireside Series**

His to Love

His to Protect

His to Cherish

His to Seduce

**Just One Series**

Just One Song

Just One Week

Just One Regret

Just One Moment

**Tangled Love Series**

Entice

Embrace

Enflame

**The Luminous Series**

Dominate Me

Crave Me

Long For Me

**The Nordic Lords Series**

Point of Return

Point of Redemption

Point of Freedom

Point of Surrender

**Standalones**

Remembering Us

Don't Lie To Me

Try Me – A Don't Lie To Me Novella